PROBABILITY OF DETECTION

MICHAEL MANLEY

Harmon House
Copyright © 2014 Kenneth M. Sheldon
All rights reserved.
ISBN: 0990939405
ISBN-13: 978-0-9909394-0-5

To the memory of Stan Miastkowski
and to the dedicated, selfless canine search and rescue
community that was so important to him.

Prologue

The missionary had been to the farm before, a cluster of decrepit buildings on the outskirts of the village, where an elderly man named Ishmael had recited his daily prayers, cared for his orphaned grandson and tended a few sheep. She had brought medicine, drunk tea, and purchased vegetables she did not need, simply to supplement the old man's meager income.

But all that was before the grandson had grown and gone off to join the militia, before the old man had passed away. After that, the farm had fallen into ruin, the surrounding fields overgrown with weeds, the barns and outbuildings leaning like old men themselves.

She had been brought back to the farm, she and the other four, bound and blindfolded. But even blindfolded, she had been there often enough to recognize the smells, the sounds of other farms in the distance. Then she recognized the grandson's voice. Later, she became sure it was him, despite the traditional keffiyeh covering his face, the gun belt, and the swagger.

Why had they been kidnapped? Probably because they

were easy targets. Their captors were not professional criminals, they were barely more than boys, who only a few years before had been chasing a soccer ball around a dirt playground. The fact that she and the others were missionaries was probably of no real importance to them, though the hard-core among them doubtless used that fact to justify the abduction.

She had lived in the valley long enough to feel certain the kidnappers did not intend to harm them. She and the others were merely pawns, chess pieces in the complex battleground that Lebanon had become. That did not guarantee they would come to no harm, of course. But if both sides were patient, if no one did anything foolish, she believed they would be OK.

She lay back on the cot, watching a sliver of moonlight that shone in through the single window, repeating the words of a Psalm that had been her theme ever since coming to the valley, words that had become her lifeline in the past weeks.

Blessed are those whose strength is in you,
whose hearts are set on pilgrimage.
As they pass through the Valley of Baka,
they make it a place of springs.

Early Aramaic versions of the scriptures translated the last line as "the valley of tears" or "weeping," a translation that made sense given the parallel image of springs. It also spoke to her own experience.

"Blessed are those whose strength is in you," she whispered. "Blessed are those whose strength is in you."

From beyond the outbuildings came gunshots, and then shouting. An explosion of gunfire followed, and more shouting. Doors slammed in the house, cries of pain and anger. In the midst of the chaos, she heard a sound that confused, then dismayed her.

Some of the shouting was in English.

1

The conditions for finding a missing person were bad and getting worse. The day had dawned humid, the sun filtering through layers of mountain haze. The forecast called for temperatures in the 90s, unseasonably hot for spring in Vermont. The air was a sponge and thunderstorms were likely.

Darcy Cameron's hiking boot came down on a dew-soaked rock and slipped. The next moment, she was down, draped over a fallen tree, a broken branch sticking up like a dagger inches away. If she had fallen on it, the branch would have impaled her.

She picked herself up and whistled softly. Pepper, a four-year-old black Lab wearing an orange search vest, leaped a fallen tree and bounded to her side.

"I'm OK, girl," Darcy said. She squirted her water bottle into the dog's open mouth and took a drink herself. "OK, let's go."

The dog moved off, zigzagging through an area that looked like the aftermath of an apocalyptic battle. Recently logged, it was covered with gnarled trees, stubs and broken branches, the leftover rubble of the timber harvest. Last winter's ice storms had added to the devastation, bringing down countless branches and smaller trees. The forest floor was thick with wild blueberries, bittersweet and honeysuckle, pioneer species that always appeared after logging.

The ground began to slope uphill, and the tangle of wood became even denser, a larger-than-life game of pick-up-sticks. Several hundred feet further, they came to a level area and Pepper's behavior changed. She stopped and put her nose high into the air, her whole body tense. Ahead of her lay a massive pile of fallen trees and branches, thrown together by the elements. Roughly round and at least a hundred feet in diameter, it looked like a primeval fortress.

Pepper's behavior became more frantic now. She darted around the pile, looking for a way in. She spotted a narrow opening, climbed up, and crawled into the mass of debris, disappearing from sight.

Darcy headed for the spot where Pepper had entered the pile, hindered by the slash and branches. Before she got there, Pepper crawled out, leaped to the forest floor and ran to her, barking furiously. There was no mistaking this behavior. She had made a find.

"Show me, girl. Show me."

Pepper ran back to the pile and crawled in. Darcy grabbed her radio. "Base, this is Unit 14. I have K-9 alert and find behavior. Going is difficult. It'll take me a couple minutes to work to the site. Stand by."

She studied the massive heap before her. She would never be able to get into the tiny space through which Pepper had crawled. She circled the pile in search of another entry point, still struggling over the debris, till she found a space that looked big enough for a human to squeeze through.

A low rumbling in the distance had resolved into sharper booms and cracks. It was getting dark fast. The storm was close. She mumbled a short prayer that it wouldn't track directly over their location.

Working her way through the opening took several

minutes. She wished she'd brought her leather gloves. Broken branches scratched her hands, and she didn't even want to think about what kind of wildlife might be lurking in the pile.

She inched forward carefully, not wanting to dislodge anything that might bring the whole structure down on her head. A moment later she emerged into an open space and realized that the pile was actually a huge donut-shaped structure, like an open-air theater. Inside was a large flat area, surprisingly clear of forest rubble. In the middle sat Pepper, her tail wagging wildly. She'd found what she was looking for.

Darcy assessed the situation, her breath coming back to her in harsh gulps, her heartbeat steadying. She'd seen suicides before, but this was bad. There was blood everywhere. The woman sat on a stump, slumped over against a branch. The gun was on the ground below her outstretched hand, blood dripping from her fingertips.

The only way to deal with a horrific situation like this was to follow procedures. The subject was obviously beyond help. She'd decided to kill herself, and she'd made a mess of it. Instead of a quick shot through the head, which seldom left much blood, the victim had aimed for her chest. And it had obviously taken more than one shot to finish the job.

Darcy reached for her radio and took several more deep breaths before pushing the transmit button.

"Base, this is Unit 14. I have a confirmed black tag."

Dan, their base operator, was cool and professional. "Message received, 14. Confirming your black tag at 1:27 p.m. Secure the area."

Darcy shook her head wearily. Her blond hair, plastered to her head with sweat, felt like a damp helmet. She gazed at the limp body and sighed. "You know, you could have found a more convenient place to kill yourself."

The woman opened one eye. "Yes, but what fun would that have been?"

She sat up, wiping away a glob of stage blood that had dripped in her eye. "Besides, a real suicide isn't going to make it easy for you."

The victim was Ellen Westheimer, a member of the Vermont K-9 Search and Rescue team, a master at hiding herself, and an essential part of the team's training days. The word was that if you could find Ellen, you could find anyone.

She looked at her watch. "Damn, forty-three minutes. You are hard core."

"High heels slowed me down," Darcy said. "I'll do better next time."

The first fat raindrops began to fall as Pepper circled Darcy, gazing expectantly at her. Darcy grabbed a tennis ball from her pack and threw it a few feet. To search dogs it was always a game, whether training or a real search, and the reward at the end was a chance to play with their favorite toys. Even dogs that specialized in cadaver work wanted their reward after a job well done. It was not unusual to see them cavorting playfully around human remains, completely indifferent to the horror nearby.

Darcy had joined the K-9 search and rescue team a year earlier, shortly after moving to Vermont. Before the move, she'd had a husband, a job at a prestigious Boston law firm—the same one where her husband worked—and an equally prestigious mortgage in the suburbs. Three years into the marriage she discovered her husband's secretary was providing him with services that weren't exactly covered in her job description.

They were divorced a short time later, after which the atmosphere at Lessard, Sterling and Jacobs cooled glacially. She was passed over for promotion, while her ex was made a partner. The whispers among the senior partners—whispers that were not-so-subtly allowed to leak out to the staff—suggested that Darcy might want to consider what her next career move would be. She had beaten them to the punch, announcing that she was moving to Vermont to open a private practice.

"Vermont?" her colleagues had said. "What the hell is in Vermont?"

To begin with, she had told them, her father. Upon his retirement, he had moved to The Village, an exclusive retirement community in Eastham. Not long after moving in, he'd been diagnosed with Alzheimer's. Then came Darcy's divorce. All in all, it hadn't been a great year.

She had moved to Eastham because it was as good a place as any to escape to, and because she was damned if she was going to let her father slip into the twilight of dementia without getting to know him better.

But Eastham, Vermont was a world away from Boston and the adjustment hadn't been easy. The night life in town consisted of pool at the Rusty Gate Grill, the ladies' book group at the library, and the occasional concert at the church. The locals were friendly once you got to know them—it just took twenty years to know them.

Then, out for a run with Pepper one day, she'd met Janis Levine, who headed up the area's K-9 search and rescue team. Janis invited her and Pepper to join them for a training session.

It had been one of the most physically demanding days of Darcy's life, and she loved every minute of it. For eight hours, she and Pepper—who seemed born for search and rescue work—climbed hills, forded streams, and tramped through dense thickets of underbrush. She did not think about her father, her struggling law practice, or her ex-husband.

Within months, Darcy had become a full-fledged member of the team, and search and rescue work became an antidote to her law practice, which increasingly felt like an exercise in drudgery—filing papers, placating clients, and arguing with opposing lawyers about whose fence was over which line. Rescue work, on the other hand, was straightforward and elemental: Find a missing person before they died.

Ellen removed her stained shirt, stuffed it in a plastic bag and pulled a fresh one from her pack. "Nice day, huh?"

"Lovely," Darcy said, mopping the back of her neck.

"Make you wish you were back in that air-conditioned high-rise?"

"And miss all this? No way."

Ellen took a long tug from her water bottle. "How's Marshall?"

Darcy snickered. Not many people called her father by his first name—another thing she appreciated about the people on the search and rescue team. Unlike other folks in town, they didn't seem impressed that her father was famous, nor exhibit a morbid curiosity about his condition.

"The same. Sharp enough to come up with a lame excuse for blowing me off."

"Bingo?"

"Bridge. Which he doesn't even play." Although The Village offered a full schedule of social events and activities for residents, her father rarely took advantage of them except, she suspected, as a reason to avoid seeing her. "Sometimes I wonder why I even moved here."

Ellen gazed at her levelly. "You moved here to be close to him, even if he doesn't appreciate it."

"Thanks," Darcy said, forcing a smile.

The rain began to fall in earnest now. The women

pulled out waterproof ponchos and donned them. As they did, Darcy's radio crackled. "Unit 14, this is base. Return to base immediately."

She hit the call button. "It'll take us a while. The going's rough and we're about a quarter mile from the trail. We need to take a break first."

"Just return to base, Darcy."

Darcy glanced at Ellen. There was genuine tension in Dan's voice, and he'd used her name instead of her unit number—a breach of protocol that was unlike him. She pressed the transmit button again. "What's the story?"

"Darcy, this is not a drill. This is a code 2." Code 2 meant a real search.

"We're on our way."

By the time Darcy and Ellen returned to base—a clearing just off a dirt road at the foot of Mount Connell—the rain had begun to let up. Most of the other team members had already arrived and were packing up, throwing equipment into vehicles, putting dogs in their crates. There was no time for the usual banter that came after a successful training session.

Darcy called to Dan as she headed for her truck. "Where are we going?"

Dan acted as if he hadn't heard her, slamming the door of his ancient Subaru and tearing off down the road, spattering mud as he did.

She shook her head, wondering what that was about, and pulled down the truck's gate. "Pepper," she called. "Come on, girl."

Pepper hopped up into her crate. Janis Levine trotted over as Darcy pulled off her backpack and tossed it into the truck. "Where's the search?" she asked. "Apparently Dan couldn't be bothered to tell me."

Janis put a hand on her shoulder. "Darcy."

Darcy turned to face her. Janis was normally all business on a search, the last person to waste time with small-talk.

"What?"

"We're going to The Village."

Darcy's heart sank. "Oh, God."

Janis nodded. "It's your father."

Ned Epstein took the last gulp of lukewarm coffee and turned back to his computer. It was shaping up to be another slow news day in Vermont, another evening newscast filled with background video of cows grazing and stories about the record-breaking Girl Scout cookie seller.

The police scanner crackled in the background. For the most part, the scanner was useless—the police chief trying to locate his one officer or someone complaining about a noisy neighbor—but once in a blue moon the chatter turned up something interesting.

Ned tuned in as the dispatcher was saying something about a missing person. He cranked the scanner up. An elderly man with Alzheimer's was missing from a retirement complex in Eastham. Search and rescue workers were being called to the scene.

He grabbed a pen to jot down the details, but it was dry. "Great. Just great." He dug through the loose jumble of writing implements in his drawer, muttering about the station's inability to provide its staff with anything as complicated as a working pen.

At one time, Ned Epstein had been the dean of the Boston news scene, the only one viewers trusted to deliver the news to them, good or bad. For ten years, he had covered scandals at the state house, disappearing crime bosses, and evaporating budget surpluses. He was as much a fixture as Faneuil Hall or the swan boats.

Then came Rachel Wilder, a rising star from a small Buffalo affiliate, one of the new breed of anchorpersons—tough, attitude-laden, and of course, drop-dead gorgeous. If Ned had doubts about her experience or reporting abilities, he was too much the gentlemen to share them with anyone.

Ned and Rachel became a team, and Ned admitted to himself that they made a good one, a balanced pair—the beautiful young woman with the intense eyes and sympathetic manner for the younger audience, Ned's reassuring presence for the station's long-time viewers.

He'd had a passing moment of concern when he suspected the news director was assigning Rachel the best stories, but he decided to hold his fire. She was young and needed the experience, and it was no skin off his nose. He was Ned Epstein.

Then came signs of trouble, little things at first: The makeup person hurried through Ned's makeup because Rachel's required more time. A light burned out in Ned's office and the maintenance people took three days to replace it because they'd been supervising the addition of a private bathroom to Rachel's office.

Magnanimity only went so far. He'd just decided it was time to speak to the news director about the situation when he got a call from the station owner himself, Dexter Buchanon. As a rule, Ned only saw Buchanon occasionally, at the company party in the fall when profits were announced, or when Buchanon wanted a celebrity to MC one of the many charity functions his wife oversaw.

But Ned suspected another reason for Buchanon's summons. The company now owned four television stations, and there had been talk of developing a magazine show to be aired by all the stations. If the show was a success on a local level, there was a good chance it would be syndicated, and Ned was the obvious candidate to anchor the show.

Meanwhile, he would use the occasion to bring up the matter of Rachel. Nothing heavy-handed, of course, just a hint that perhaps it was time for her to move on to something more fitting her obvious talents. He felt a little guilty about going over the news director's head, but why not go right to the top? After all, he was Ned Epstein.

The meeting took place in Buchanon's corner office in Boston's John Hancock Tower, looking out over Copley Plaza and the Charles River beyond. There was the usual small talk, then Buchanon explained that the company had recently purchased a station in Vermont and needed someone to anchor the news there.

Ned instantly thought of Rachel. It would be a nasty trick, dispatching her to the wilds of Vermont, but it was time to play hardball. "I've got the perfect person—"

Buchanon shook his head. "This is an important new market for us. We need someone with experience, someone who isn't going to drop the ball."

The realization hit Ned like a cold wave at Revere beach. He was being moved down to the farm team. They'd been grooming Rachel to take his place.

He argued briefly, and considered marshaling his forces to fight back. He still had his fans. A write-in campaign might make the bastards see how ridiculous this was. But he knew that underneath the kid gloves, Buchanon was wearing brass knuckles, and in the end he'd gone quietly.

Channel 34 in Rutland was even worse than Ned had imagined, a decrepit facility in a concrete building at the edge of a strip mall parking lot. Before arriving, he had entertained a fantasy of elevating the station to award-winning status, making it his springboard back to the big time. It didn't take him long to realize that as far as the Buchanon Media Group was concerned, WOFB was not a springboard. It was a pasture.

He considered quitting, escaping to Cape Cod where he still owned a small house, the last remnant of a failed marriage. Unfortunately, the other remnants of that marriage included a hefty alimony payment and child support. So he hung on, biding his time till he could retire and write his memoirs, in which he planned to get complete and vicious revenge.

Of course, before he could do that, he'd have to find a working pen.

He finally unearthed a pencil and scribbled the details as they came over the scanner. The missing man's name was Marshall Cameron. Ned hesitated for a moment, then put in a call to The Village, where a woman who called herself the Community Affairs Director said, "Can I help you?"

"I understand you have a missing person there?"

"That's right."

"And his name is Marshall Cameron?"

The woman sighed. "Yes it is."

"Not *the* Marshall Cameron."

"Yes, sir. I'm afraid so."

"*And that's what's happening in the world tonight?*" he said. "That Marshall Cameron?"

"Yes, sir. That Marshall Cameron."

A bell had been ringing in the back of Ned's mind and now clanged loudly. There had been a rumor that Marshall Cameron had retired to Vermont and was living in seclusion at an undisclosed location. Now he knew why. Cameron had Alzheimer's.

That settled it. Normally, the story of a missing senior citizen would only rate a brief mention during the noon report and a follow-up later. But this was Marshall Cameron. He was a household name. Hell, he was an icon. And even though he'd retired years ago, anything that involved him was news. On top of that, he had Alzheimer's, which gave the story a sympathy angle.

The more Ned thought about it, the better the story got. The Village was a five-star retirement community that catered to retired colonels and Westchester executives, people who could afford the best money could buy. A place like that should be able to take better care of its well-heeled residents. Which made this the perfect story: a well-known celebrity, a tragic disease and a potential scandal.

Ned grabbed a limp tie hanging from a nearby coat rack and headed for the back of the station, bypassing the office of WOFB's news director, Jack O'Brien. He was supposed to ask O'Brien for permission whenever he wanted to use the satellite truck, but he didn't feel like getting into an argument about it today. This was a story that cried out for a live remote, but satellite uplink time was expensive and it was the end of the month, when O'Brien always had his eye out for unnecessary expenses. Ned decided to do the story first and answer questions later. The German defense.

He stuck his head into the engineering closet, where Jim "Granny" Granucci, the station's cameraman-engineer-Mr. Fixit was hunched over a printed circuit board with a soldering gun. Granny was usually up for an adventure.

"Come on," Ned said. "Get a driver for the truck and grab a camera. We're going out."

Granny shook his head without looking up from his work. "Truck's in the shop."

"What? What the hell's it doing there?"

"Brakes are shot."

Ned groaned. "I don't believe this." Did nothing around this two-bit station ever work right? "How am I supposed to do a remote without a satellite truck?"

Granny, who spent most of his time arguing with the management about the sad state of the station's equipment, wasn't inclined to be sympathetic. "Good question."

Ned considered his options. A live update was out, but he could still do a segment for the evening news. "OK, just grab a camera. We'll take the van."

"Where we going?"

"The Village, over in Eastham."

Granny's eyebrows shot up. "Whoa. Breaking news. Pilferage from the petty change jar. On the trail of Metamucil junkies."

"I'll explain on the way. Just get the camera."

2

Darcy drove furiously, tailing the other searchers, muttering under her breath, "Come on, come on." She drove as if she could make up for lost time, time that had passed years ago, long before they'd gotten the call about the search. They were only a few miles from The Village, but it was still taking too long. Every minute counts when a person is lost, especially an elderly person. Especially your father.

Normally the radios crackled with chatter as the team neared a search, but not this time. The radios were quiet, and Darcy knew why. This wasn't just any search, they were searching for Darcy's father. They were searching for Marshall Cameron.

For twenty years, Marshall Cameron had hosted the television news magazine TimeLine. His calm demeanor had comforted viewers through international crises and economic hard times, terrorist attacks and Washington scandals. Everyone in the country knew who Marshall Cameron was. Sometimes Darcy thought they knew him better than she did.

For most of her childhood, her father had been on the road, traveling the world and providing the networks with stories from whatever hot spot he could lie, cheat, or bribe his way into. His career left little time for family, and even his sporadic visits to the states ended when he and Darcy's mother divorced just before Darcy's seventh birthday. Later, after landing the TimeLine assignment, his life was more settled. But his increasing fame left even less time for a personal life, or so it seemed.

When he retired, Darcy had hoped they'd be able to build the relationship they'd never had. The results were disappointing, to say the least. For the most part, her father rebuffed her attempts to visit him, saying he didn't have time. The few times he could not put her off, they dined quietly at the Eastham Inn and Darcy returned home, no closer to understanding who her father was or what made him tick.

The caravan of searchers roared off the state highway onto The Village's tree-lined driveway. The Village was laid out like a college campus. At its heart was a palatial administration and community building known as the Village Square. On either side were the residences, luxury apartments in separate buildings designed for independent living, assisted living and total care. Around these were gardens—English, Japanese, French—and nestled in the trees at the edge of the grounds were million-dollar private homes for people who couldn't countenance the idea of sharing a wall with neighbors.

Onto this idyllic setting, the barely-controlled chaos of a search had descended. Fire and rescue vans, police cruisers and searchers' vehicles were already packed into every available space and crammed in at odd angles beside the reflecting pool and Japanese garden. The groundskeeper, an elderly, red-faced man in green work clothes, paced the driveway, shaking his head as he surveyed the damage.

Darcy drove past the Village Square, where the press had already begun to arrive. A half-dozen television vans and satellite trucks had been sequestered away from the action in a parking lot beyond the gardens. She was surprised they were there already, and just hoped the idiots wouldn't get in the way.

Darcy and Janis wedged their vehicles into the last available spaces on the lawn. Darcy glanced back at Pepper, who was curled up in her crate, exhausted after the morning's training. She would be fine for awhile.

The rest of the team had gathered at the front entrance of the Village Square, waiting for instructions. Janis sprinted toward them with Darcy following close behind.

"Stand down, people," Janis hollered. "Save your energy. You're going to need it." She didn't need to say more.

Darcy began to follow her into the building, but Janis stopped and turned to her. "Take a break. I'll be back with the details as soon as I can."

Darcy shook her head. "Oh, no. There's no way I'm going to stand out here twiddling my thumbs."

Janis glared at her. Members of the team rarely challenged her authority. But Darcy wasn't backing down this time. "All right," Janis said finally. "Let's go."

The lobby of the Village Square was an atrium, sunlight sparkling down from skylights onto hand-made Italian tiles. A seating area featured matching Tuscano leather loveseats, the oak coffee table between them bearing neatly-placed copies of The Robb Report and Executive Traveler. It looked like the lobby of a five-star hotel.

Generally, the atrium was busy with people coming and going, signing up for bridge games, debating which of the Virgin Islands was the best for vacationing. Today, it was vacant except for a massive state trooper at the entry, who momentarily barred the women's way until he saw their search and rescue badges and waved them towards a brightly lit hall.

The Vermont State Police, the agency with the

ultimate responsibility for finding missing people, had commandeered The Village's main conference room as their command post. The room was dominated by a huge oval conference table and floor-to-ceiling windows framing a perfect view of Mount Connell.

At present, the elegant atmosphere of the room was marred by the horde of law enforcement personnel crowded into it. The conference table was piled high with forms, maps, radios and other search paraphernalia. To one side was a bulletin board with a topographic map, concentric circles forming a bull's-eye around The Village.

Barked commands and bits of cell-phone and radio conversations filled the air. At the center of the chaos was Sergeant Jacqueline Bradley—Jackie, to those who knew her well enough—the state police's incident commander for the search. Bradley was talking intently with Eastham's police chief, Harvey Warren, a hefty man whose girth attested to too many coffee breaks spent at the Donut Hutch.

Darcy saw Warren and groaned inwardly. When she arrived in Eastham, Harvey Warren had been one of the first people she'd met. She'd quickly sized him up as a self-important blowhard who was ingratiating to those he respected and condescending to those he didn't. He was forty-two, divorced, and gave off the unmistakable signs of a man on the make.

Darcy had fended off his not-so-subtle advances as politely as she could—it didn't pay for a small-town lawyer to get on the wrong side of local law enforcement. Eventually though, she'd had to tell him bluntly—thanks, but no thanks. She'd tried to be nice about it, explaining that she was recovering from a painful divorce and wasn't looking for anyone right now. She avoided telling him he wouldn't be in the running even if he were the last available man in Vermont. Possibly on the planet.

Chief Warren wasn't used to being turned down or ignored, and his attitude toward Darcy had been surly ever since, especially after she began dating one of his officers. And although she'd stopped seeing the guy, Warren still acted like a jilted lover around her. He was the last person she wanted to deal with in a search for her father.

Janis and Darcy threaded their way through the maze of bodies toward Bradley and Warren. Bradley wore a look of thin-lipped annoyance as she spoke to the chief. "Why do we have to go through this every time? We keep telling you to call us right away."

Warren looked like a pitcher who had been reluctantly hauled from the mound. "We did call you—"

Over his shoulder, Bradley saw Janis and Darcy approaching them. She gave Darcy a hard, sympathetic look. "Don't worry. We'll find him."

"Sure," Darcy said, not meeting her eyes. They both knew that no search was a sure thing.

Bradley led them to the topo map of the area, circles showing half-mile and full mile distances from The Village. The one-half mile circle had been broken into irregular shaded areas that indicated where search teams would be sent. "Chief Warren has just been filling me in on the initial search," she said. "They began with a hasty search of the immediate area—"

"When was that?" Darcy asked.

Bradley frowned. She didn't like to be interrupted, and they all knew what Darcy was getting at. Local police often tried to find missing persons by themselves without calling in the state police and search teams. It was an ego thing—the police never wanted to admit they might need help with anything that happened on their turf. Occasionally, they were lucky and found the person. More often they ended up calling the state police hours later, no closer to success and having wasted precious time.

Bradley ignored Darcy's question. "Marshall Cameron didn't show up for his usual 7 a.m. breakfast," she said. "The Village staff checked his apartment and then the other buildings, but failed to find him. They informed the Eastham police department at 7:50."

Janis closed her eyes and shook her head, but said nothing.

Darcy turned on Warren. "You guys have been screwing around here since 8 o'clock this morning without calling us?"

Warren raised a hand. "Now look—"

"No, you look. Do you have any idea what happens to an elderly person who gets lost? An elderly person with Alzheimer's? They get cold, even in warm weather. They travel, sometimes for miles."

Janis positioned herself between Darcy and Warren, her hands raised. "Darcy, calm down—"

"Calm down? That's my father out there. He's been missing for God knows how long, and this nitwit is acting like Barney Fife going after a moonshine still."

Warren's neck reddened like a Roman candle about to go off. "We have our own K-9 unit," he said through clenched teeth. The Eastham police department had recently acquired a German shepherd. Darcy knew about the shepherd. She also knew that Warren hadn't had a chance to show the dog off yet.

"That's great," she said. "Did he find a track?" The German shepherd, like most police dogs, was a tracking dog and had been bred to follow scents on the ground. Tracking dogs were great if you had a starting place where they could pick up a scent, such as the scene of a crime. But for open-ended searches—lost children, people in avalanches, and most other search and rescue operations—air-scent dogs like Pepper were better. They could detect the most minuscule amounts of human scent in the air, even just a few scent molecules in millions of air molecules.

Warren glanced away. "No, he hasn't picked up anything. Yet."

"So how long were you planning to—"

"All right," Bradley said. "That's enough." A few heads turned in their direction, though most people went about their business; searches tended to make for short fuses and arguments were common. "Chief, your men have their assignments. I suggest you go brief them and get cracking."

Warren started to open his mouth, then changed his mind and left.

As Warren disappeared into the mass of swirling activity Bradley said, "Here's where we're at."

She briefed them as if the missing person were a total stranger. "The subject is a seventy-six year old man with early-stage Alzheimer's missing since 0700 hours. The place last seen was his apartment. According to the staff, the last person to see him was an express deliveryman who was seen outside his apartment yesterday afternoon."

"Have you talked to the deliveryman?" Darcy asked.

"Still trying. The staff couldn't identify which company it was, so we're calling them all to see if we can find him."

"I thought visitors were supposed to check in at the reception desk?"

"They are. But this one managed to slip by. We're not sure what happened."

Bradley studied a clipboard and said casually—too casually, Darcy thought—"We'll have a POD for you later on."

The POD—probability of detection—was a formula based on the weather, wind speed, angle of the sun and other factors. After years of experience, rescue workers had found it to be a reliable gauge of whether a missing person was likely to be found or not.

Normally, Bradley calculated the POD before they began searching. If she hadn't—or if she didn't want to share the results with them—there was only one good reason.

Before Darcy or Janis could speak, Bradley said, "Eastham Police called us in at 1330 hours." The police had already searched Cameron's apartment, the other buildings and the grounds, but found no trace of him or clues to his whereabouts. In addition to Chief Warren's dog, the state police had their own tracking K-9s, none of which had been able to find Cameron's track.

Darcy calculated backwards. "So it's possible that he's been gone for over twenty-four hours."

They all knew what that meant. After twenty-four hours, the chances of survival for a lost Alzheimer's patient grew thin.

Bradley fixed Darcy with a hard look. "Hang in there. You're one of the best searchers we've got. We're going to need you."

Darcy closed her eyes, nodded, and took a deep breath. "All right."

3

By the time Ned and Granny got to The Village, the rest of the media had already arrived, a hive of satellite vans with giant dishes aimed at the sky like upside-down umbrellas. The groundskeeper waved frantically, directing latecomers to a freshly-mowed field away from the Village Square, the administration building and the main residential complex.

"Slow news day in Hooterville," Granny said, following the groundskeeper's directions to the parking area.

"Show some respect," Ned said. Someday, *he* would be the famous retired newsman.

They parked as close as they could and trudged across the pasture, slivers of wet grass clippings sticking to their shoes and pant legs. It was a good thing the camera only showed people from the waist up.

They headed for the main office, but a massive state trooper intercepted them. "All media personnel this way," he said, pointing to the area where the press had been sequestered, like chickens in a pen, away from the action.

Ned glanced at Granny, who read his signal and hefted the camera onto his shoulder. Ned turned to the trooper. "Can you tell us what happened?"

The trooper covered the lens of the camera with a meaty hand. "You'll have to talk to the information officer." He indicated another trooper, who stood talking with a young woman in a business suit and tennis sneakers. Ned recognized her as the news-Barbie from Channel 7 in Burlington.

As they approached, Ned's cell phone rang. "Epstein here."

"Where the hell are you?" It was Jack O'Brien.

Ned took a breath. "We're at The Village, in Eastham. It turns out that Marshall Cameron lives here. *The* Marshall Cameron. He has Alzheimer's, and he's lost. Would have been a great live feed if we had a working satellite truck."

"Were you planning on being back for the 6 o'clock?"

"Shouldn't be a problem, if people don't keep interrupting me in the middle of an interview."

"Right. I'm sure your agent's been hounding you with offers."

Ned considered telling O'Brien what he could do with which orifice, but decided against it. "We'll be back in plenty of time," he said and hung up.

The information officer was a square-jawed young trooper who smiled as he explained to the Channel 7 bimbo that the search team was just now receiving their briefing.

Ned positioned himself beside the Barbie. "Ned Epstein, Channel 34. Do you know how long Mr. Cameron has been missing?"

The trooper's smile faded. "I'll be with you in a moment, sir," he said, managing to make the "sir" sound like an insult. The woman didn't even acknowledge Ned's presence.

"I understand," Ned said. "I just wanted—"

"*I'll be with you in a moment.*"

Ned read the trooper's expression, glanced at the young woman and got the message. As far as the trooper was concerned, this wasn't an information session, it was a mating dance.

Ned and Granny retreated to a white rail fence beside the Village Square. "I'll grab some cutaways of the grounds," Granny said, and wandered off with the camera.

A side door of the building opened and a man in a tan uniform emerged, took up a place next to Ned and lit a cigarette.

"You a friend?" he asked, blowing smoke away from Ned.

"Excuse me?"

"You a friend of this Cameron guy?"

"No," Ned said curtly, turning to face the man full on and raising an eyebrow—the look he'd used to greet New England viewers at the start of the evening news for years. Without makeup, the face bore the ruddiness of too many whiskey sours, and there were the beginnings of crow's feet around the eyes. But the chin was still strong, the eyes sparkling green, the curly reddish-brown hair all his own.

"Oh, sorry," the man said, a dull spark of recognition flickering across his face. "Should'a recognized you."

"Not at all," Ned said. Now that the man had acknowledged him, he was prepared to be gracious.

"Get so many people coming and going around here, visiting folks, I forget when I've seen someone before."

Ned glared. The idiot still thought he was here to visit one of the residents. "I'm not—"

"Yeah, that's what's funny about this whole thing. With all the people coming and going, they have to keep pretty close tabs on the loonies. Got this fancy alarm system and all. So how come it wasn't on when this guy walks out?"

Ned's annoyance evaporated. "The alarm wasn't on?"

"Nah. Someone shut it off just before he disappeared. Pretty smart, huh?"

"Yes, indeed," Ned said, trying not to sound too

interested. He gestured to the clutch of satellite trucks and hovering reporters. "Do *they* know about this?

The man chuckled. "You kidding? The cops aren't gonna tell those vultures any more than they have to."

Ned calculated his approach. If he were a visitor, how much would he know about the alarm system? Probably not much. "Well, someone must have forgotten to turn it on," he said.

The man looked at Ned as if he'd just stepped off the boat. "Ain't a matter of forgetting. That thing's always on, unless someone turns it off."

"Oh. Who's in charge of the alarm system?"

The man blew smoke, gazing out across the manicured lawns. "You're looking at him."

Ned nodded. "I see." He was already writing his piece for the evening news.

Janis and Darcy headed out to join the rest of their team. As they crossed the atrium, an oak door on one side opened and two men emerged, both in suits, one short and compact, frowning deeply as he strode a step ahead of a younger, taller man.

The first man was Leonard Wakefield, the executive director of The Village. Darcy had only spoken to Wakefield once or twice and wasn't greatly impressed by him, a small man who dressed big: Armani suits, Rolex watches and Italian shoes. He also suffered from a severe case of bad hair, with implants that looked as if they'd been set in barren soil during a severe drought. She didn't recognize the other man, who spoke softly to Wakefield, words that the director apparently didn't want to hear.

Wakefield's highly-polished shoes clicked over the tiles in the direction of his office. As he passed the two women, he looked up and stopped. "Are you with the search and rescue team?"

"That's right. I'm Janis Levine, team leader. This is Darcy—"

Wakefield didn't bother introducing himself. "Is there any sign of Mr. Cameron?"

"Not yet. We just—"

"You haven't spoken to the press, have you?"

"No," Janis said slowly. The only people who spoke to the press during searches were the state police. She took a deep breath, and Darcy could tell she was losing patience with him. "We were just about to do our team briefing and get our people out searching."

"Good. I don't know why the press has to be here anyway. As if we don't have enough problems without them poking their noses into it."

"Right. Now if you'll excuse us—"

"We run a tight ship around here. We don't want people to think we're not looking out for their loved ones."

"That's very reassuring," Darcy said, planting herself in Wakefield's face. "I'm Darcy Cameron. Marshall Cameron's daughter."

Wakefield stared at her, confused. Then, slowly, the light dawned. He hadn't connected the bedraggled specimen in front of him with the professional woman he had seen visiting Mr. Cameron. Under other circumstances, it would have been amusing.

"Oh, yes. Yes, yes, yes, of course." His manner changed abruptly. Now he was the fawning servant, the man her father had summed up as a sycophantic ass. "I want you to know we're doing everything we can to find your father," Wakefield said.

If the situation hadn't been so serious, she would have laughed. This idiot was trying to reassure her, when it was her own team that would be doing the searching.

"We pride ourselves on security here," Wakefield

said, as if he were giving a sales pitch to prospective residents.

She considered asking him why, if he was so proud of The Village's security, they couldn't do anything as simple as identify the delivery person who had last seen her father. But she didn't want to waste time now. Later, if anything happened to her father, she would sue the Italian pants off him.

"That's great," Janis said. "But we've got a search to conduct."

They headed for the door, Wakefield babbling in their wake. "Of course. Very good. Let's get right on it."

They stepped through the door and Darcy muttered, "Dimwit."

"So he's the boss around here?" Janis said.

"Right. His name is Wakefield."

"And the other guy?"

"I'm not sure. But I'm willing to bet he was a lawyer."

"How can you tell?"

"I can tell," Darcy said with a smirk. "I can tell."

4

Scott Tannenberg, one of a dozen attorneys for The Village's parent company, followed Wakefield into his office and closed the door. The room was as extravagantly outfitted as its occupant: overstuffed leather chairs, glass and chrome surfaces, built-in bookcases and a picture window that overlooked the peaceful campus of The Village. Tannenberg chose a stiff leather chair and opened his briefcase on a glass coffee table.

Wakefield paced to the window and stared out at his once-stately grounds, now swarming with police and volunteers. He looked pale.

"What's wrong?" Tannenberg asked.

"I just remembered something. She's a lawyer."

"Who?"

Wakefield gestured toward the lobby. "Mr. Cameron's daughter."

"And she's also a search and rescue worker?"

"Apparently."

Tannenberg shook his head. "What a mess."

Tannenberg's law firm had been retained by The Village's parent company—a company that he frankly knew little about—for its expertise in representing retirement communities. In recent years the industry had been criticized for putting profits above people, and reports of abuse were widespread. The last thing The Village needed right now was a messy, expensive liability suit involving a high-profile resident like Marshall Cameron.

Tannenberg pulled a legal pad from the briefcase. "Tell me exactly what happened."

As Wakefield gave him the run-down on Cameron's disappearance, Tannenberg scribbled furiously, only interrupting to ask, "Who was the last person to see Mr. Cameron?"

A petulant frown creased Wakefield's brow as he turned away to the window. "Apparently some express deliveryman."

"From what company?"

Wakefield's neck flushed crimson above the white collar of his shirt. "I'm not sure. For some reason, he didn't sign in at the front desk." He turned to face Tannenberg, sputtering now. "The receptionist says she didn't see anyone come in, but the maid swears she saw a deliveryman at Mr. Cameron's apartment."

"I see." This was exactly the kind of negligence that would get The Village in trouble if they were brought to court. Tannenberg made a note to interview both women. "You said the staff noticed Mr. Cameron was missing after breakfast. You didn't mention any alarms going off."

"No," Wakefield said, hesitating. "Apparently the system wasn't on at the time."

Tannenberg's pen stopped in mid-sentence. "What?"

Wakefield rubbed the back of his neck. "Security checked the system as soon as we realized he was missing. It seems the system had been turned off temporarily."

Tannenberg closed his eyes and exhaled slowly. "Who did that?"

"I don't know," Wakefield said, his voice rising. "Security says they didn't do it, but they don't know who did."

"Who else knows how to turn it off?"

The correct answer would be "nobody." According to company policy, the access codes for security systems were to be closely guarded, but Tannenberg knew that most facilities were lax about the rules.

"Just the senior staff and I," Wakefield said. "I've already checked, and they say it wasn't them."

"Of course," Tannenberg said. He knew how it went. If you were giving a tour to prospective residents and wanted to show them the back gardens, it was easier to go out the back door than walk all the way around the building, so you shut the alarm off. Just for a few minutes, of course. And if you forgot to turn the system back on and a confused resident happened to wander off, suddenly everyone on the staff developed amnesia.

He took off his glasses and rubbed the bridge of his nose with a thumb and forefinger. "Did the police ask about the alarm?"

"No."

"Good. Don't say anything about it unless they ask." Wakefield's eyebrows went up a notch and Tannenberg added, "I'm not telling you to lie to them. Just don't offer any information they don't ask for. We want to keep this as quiet as possible."

"All right," Wakefield said, nodding slowly. "I suppose that makes sense. There's no sense in getting the other residents worried about security unnecessarily."

"Exactly." Tannenberg tossed the pad in the briefcase and snapped it shut. After all, it was the residents they were worried about.

Leonard Wakefield saw Tannenberg out and breathed a sigh of relief as he returned to his office. It was bad enough having to worry about The Village's residents without lawyers breathing down his neck.

Wakefield's assistant waved a batch of pink message slips at him. "I put the urgent ones on top—"

He waved her off. "Hold my calls," he said, entering the inner office and locking the door behind him.

He fell into the leather chair behind his desk. Until yesterday, the hardest part of this job had been keeping track of his social engagements. The wealthier residents of The Village loved to throw parties, and he had cultivated their friendships assiduously. Despite the negative press other retirement communities had received, The Village was a model of corporate efficiency, keeping its nose clean while making money hand over fist.

Suddenly, the damn place was falling apart. Residents were wandering off. Security had gone to hell. Delivery people waltzed in without anyone paying attention, the alarm system was turned off for no reason. Meanwhile, the local police had proven to be a bunch of bumblers who couldn't find their own asses without a compass.

Of course, the missing man had to be Marshall Cameron instead of one of the wealthy nobodies. And to top it all off, Cameron's daughter was a lawyer.

At any other time, that kind of connection might come in handy—say, when you were applying for a zoning variance or looking for a tax break from the town. Just now, it was the kind of information that came back to haunt you.

Wakefield kicked himself for not recognizing Darcy Cameron immediately. Of course, that was hardly his fault. If she wanted to be good citizen all well and good, but what kind of woman let herself look that way in public? He would have to find some way to get back in her good graces when this was all over. It wouldn't do to have a local lawyer—not to mention the daughter of Marshall Cameron—think ill of The Village.

But that would come later. There was something else

he had to do first, a task he'd been putting off all day.

He drew the drapes, turned on his desk lamp and walked to the Picasso hanging on the wall. He removed the painting from the wall, placed it carefully on the floor and turned to the safe hidden behind it. The safe openly noiselessly and he removed an envelope marked "Marshall Cameron."

Wakefield had been given the envelope two years earlier, just after The Village was sold to new owners and shortly after Marshall Cameron had moved in. Two men in dark suits had shown up and instructed him gravely to open the envelope "in the event that anything should happen to Mr. Cameron." He had assumed they were lawyers for the new owners, though they hadn't actually identified themselves as such. Perhaps they were from the network, or even people Mr. Cameron had hired himself.

In any event, the last thing he wanted to do was to admit to them that The Village had botched things and didn't know where Marshall Cameron was. So he had stalled, hoping Cameron would be found, until he didn't dare put it off any longer.

He tore the envelope open. Inside was a sealed plastic pouch. Unable to tear the pouch open, he found scissors in his desk and cut the top off. There was a quiet whoosh as air entered the pouch, followed by a faint but unpleasant smell.

Wakefield removed the single piece of paper inside the pouch and unfolded it. The only thing on it was a telephone number with an unfamiliar area code.

Wakefield reached for the phone, took a deep breath and punched in the number. It was answered on the first ring.

A pleasant female voice said, "Operator 19."

He hesitated, not sure to whom he was talking, wondering if he had dialed the right number. "This is

Leonard Wakefield, executive director of The Village in Eastham, Vermont. I was instructed to open the envelope if anything happened to Marshall Cameron and—"

"Thank you, Mr. Wakefield. If you'll just give me some information. At what time did Mr. Cameron pass away?"

"He's not dead," Wakefield protested. "He's missing."

There was a noticeable pause. "I see." Wakefield heard the sound of a keyboard clicking. "When did you first notice he was missing?"

"This morning."

"This morning?" There was doubt in the voice. It was now four o'clock. "What time this morning?"

"Eight AM."

"Eight AM?"

Sweat formed on his brow. "I know, I know. I should have called earlier, but I couldn't. The police haven't given me a minute's peace." He wasn't about to tell her that he'd hoped Cameron would show up and the whole thing blow over.

"You did receive instructions to open the envelope immediately if anything were to happen to Mr. Cameron?" the woman said.

Was this a cross-examination? "Yes, but—"

"If you could just provide me with the details, Mr. Wakefield."

He gulped several times, his confidence deteriorating rapidly. He covered the details of Cameron's disappearance, continually interrupted by the woman's probing questions. Eventually, the grilling came to an end and he asked, "Do you want me to call you back when he's found?"

There was a pause and Wakefield had the sense she was checking with a superior. "That won't be necessary."

"It won't? But—"

The line went dead.

Wakefield leaned back in his chair, pulled out his handkerchief and wiped his brow. It took several minutes to calm himself.

He reached for the paper with the number on it. It hadn't occurred to him before to wonder where he was calling. Maybe the area code would give him a clue.

The paper was blank.

5

Jane Chandler needed a cigarette. Badly. Unfortunately, no one else on the campaign staff smoked, and it was a non-smoking suite. She could have used a drink, too, but the strongest thing in the mini-bar was raspberry-flavored sparkling water. When this election was over, she was going to have a large glass of scotch and the biggest cigar she could find.

Chandler stood by a picture window overlooking the Chicago skyline. Downstairs, in a crowded conference room, the press corps was waiting, their patience wearing thin. The cameras were ready to roll. The pundits had notepads on their knees, poised to record words of wisdom or folly from Senator John Wagner, the leading presidential candidate. Meanwhile, here on the 23rd floor, Senator Wagner was still in his room, doing God knows what.

Chandler paced to the bedroom door, ready to knock, but stopped herself. Wagner hadn't brought his wife along this time—when Dawn went on the road with him, there was no telling what they might be doing in the minutes before a meeting—but even without her, the candidate hated to be rushed, no matter how late they were running.

She took a deep breath and turned away from the door. Two Secret Service agents, stationed just inside the suite's entryway—a position they'd maintained ever since Wagner walked away with the New Hampshire primary—

stared impassively into the room. One of them spoke briefly into his cuff microphone, probably telling his cohorts downstairs that Turtle-1—their code name for Wagner—was still on the pot. Chandler frowned, knowing that behind their bland expressions, they were probably laughing at her as well.

She crossed her arms over her chest and stared out the picture window again, fuming. She could have forgiven Wagner if his chronic tardiness was just a power-play. Keeping others waiting was one way of asserting your importance. She'd certainly done it herself often enough.

But Wagner wasn't playing games. The man was too damned relaxed about this election. "You are not president yet," she had warned him just the night before.

"I will be," he'd said, flipping a commemorative coin with the image of his father on it. The portrait of President John Wagner Sr. had landed on the tabletop facing Chandler, where it seemed to be saying, *He damn sure will be.*

Wagner had reasons to be confident. Most of the influential voices in the party had given their blessing to his candidacy. His background was spotless—Chandler made sure of that before signing on with him—two years in the Army Rangers and decorations for bravery during the Gulf War. His family life was under control: a good-looking wife who did the grab-and-gab with the best of the Washington crowd, two cute kids who were too young to cause any embarrassment.

"Let's face it," Wagner had confided to Chandler one evening after too many whiskeys. "Unless I rape someone, there's no way they can stop me from becoming president. Hell, they might not be able to stop me even if I did rape someone."

The press, searching for reasons to criticize Wagner, had settled on his indifferent attitude toward schedules.

His lack of punctuality had become a running joke in the press, and it grated on Chandler. She'd told him repeatedly that he needed to stay on message, and the tales of his overly-relaxed approach to the campaign were overwhelming her carefully scripted campaign.

She glanced at the TV monitor, which showed the conference room downstairs, where technicians stood next to their cameras sipping coffee. Reporters from the major dailies scrolled their smartphones or tablets. A couple of them looked as if they were nodding off. Everyone was used to the drill by now.

It was a full house today, comprised of the usual suspects from the major outlets plus a smattering of locals —in an era of tight cost-controls, local newspapers and broadcast outlets couldn't afford reporters to follow a candidate across the country. They were happy to run the canned stories Chandler provided them and take credit for the "reporting." So the campaign's own camera crew was at the center of the pack. That evening, hundreds of local stations around the country would be carrying the campaign-provided video, carefully edited by one of Chandler's people to put Wagner in the always-positive light of the front-runner.

At the head of the conference room, the mayor of Chicago stood next to the podium, glancing occasionally at the introduction Chandler had provided him. He looked at his watch and scowled. Clearly, he too was wondering where Wagner was.

Chandler looked away from the monitor as the door to the bedroom opened. John Wagner strode forth, his full head of graying hair perfectly combed above the tanned and deeply lined face. "All set?" he asked, as if everyone hadn't been waiting for him.

"Let's go," Chandler said, and took up her place at his side. The entourage of assistants and hangers-on followed them to the elevators. As they rode down, Chandler gave Wagner final notes on who would be there, what they were likely to ask, and how he should respond.

Jane Chandler had been preparing for this role for a long time. Fresh out of law school, she had become an aide to Congresswoman Anne Reinhardt of Rhode Island. When Reinhardt decided to run for the Senate, Chandler spearheaded a spectacularly successful campaign that swept Reinhardt into office and drew the attention of another newly-elected senator: John Wagner of New York. Chandler hadn't even moved into her new office when Wagner called to ask if she'd like to join his team.

Senator Reinhardt hit the roof. Didn't that arrogant SOB know that Chandler had been with her for three years? Didn't he know anything about loyalty? Didn't he understand the importance of Reinhardt's role as one of the minority of women in the Senate?

Jane Chandler knew all that. She also knew that Anne Reinhardt was an abrasive feminist from the smallest state in the union, while John Wagner was the heir to a political dynasty and represented one of the largest and most influential states.

It had taken Chandler about two minutes to make her decision. She'd given Reinhardt her notice and walked down the hall to become Senator Wagner's executive assistant.

After a successful first term, Chandler engineered Wagner's landslide reelection for a second term. By that time, his presidential candidacy was a foregone conclusion. Chandler's title had been changed to Special Assistant, an amorphous designation that encompassed everything from writing Wagner's speeches to approving his daily schedule.

It was a job that called for 18-hour days beginning at 6 a.m., dry sandwiches eaten on planes, and constant pressure. But the results were worth it. Wagner had swept the New Hampshire primary, and the boost had given him an early lead. He was the clear favorite to lead the party to victory in November, and polls showed him beating any of the possible opponents by a comfortable margin. If he kept it up, avoiding any disasters, he would be in the White House by January. And Jane Chandler planned to make sure there were no disasters.

With a refined ding, the elevator arrived at the conference level. Chandler shot Wagner her final instruction as they entered the meeting room: "No ad libs."

Wagner strode to the podium as Chandler headed for the back of the room. In the early days of the campaign, she had strategically placed herself next to Wagner during every photo op—stepping off the plane in New Hampshire, signing the forms to enter the race in California. It hadn't taken the press long to notice the stunning blonde at Wagner's side. Aside from simply looking good on screen, Chandler knew how to give reporters what they wanted—quotable quotes and inside information from "a source close to the senator." Now, whenever she appeared, reporters converged on her like sharks circling for chum, and she never disappointed them. They all knew that Jane Chandler gave good sound bites. But today was a day to watch and analyze, not a day to be seen.

Approaching the podium, John Wagner was at the top of his form, an actor absorbed in his part. He moved like a man who was used to being revered and deferred to— comfortable, but exuding confidence, waving at one or two familiar faces, stopping to shake hands with a wealthy contributor and exchange a private joke.

The mayor's introduction was brief and adulatory, just the way Chandler had scripted it. Wagner took the podium and launched into his by-now-familiar stump speech.

The speech was short. Reporters liked short speeches. As he wrapped up, Wagner pointed to one of the waving hands. "Yes. Bob."

"Senator, would you respond to Senator McCallister's comment that the White House is not a sinecure to be passed down from one member of a royal family to another?"

George McCallister was among the leading contenders hoping to oppose Wagner in November. As far as Chandler was concerned, he was an egotist with a messiah complex. He'd made the comment about the royal family during a speech earlier in the week, and they had known the question was coming.

Wagner nodded slowly, looking down, a sly grin creasing his face. That was good, Chandler thought—humble, but clearly telegraphing that he was in control. "I'll tell you," he said, looking up. "I'm not exactly sure what 'sinecure' means."

That was a lie, of course. Wagner had graduated from Harvard—the college and the law school—but it helped establish him as a regular guy, a man of the people who didn't throw around words like sinecure. "All I know is, my dad told me I could have the job."

Grateful laughter rippled across the room. Everyone knew they had their sound bite for the evening news.

The follow-up question came from Malika Chakraborty of NPR. "Senator, what do your parents think about your campaign?"

Another grin. "Well, my father told me to watch out for you guys." He looked down at his folded hands—another nice touch, as if the very thought of his father made him reflective. "Seriously, though, he told me to do the best I could, to tell the truth, and to say my prayers." He took a beat. "My mother told me to buy a new suit."

Another beat—Wagner's timing was perfect. "And my brother..." Here came the punch line. Wagner's brother was the junior senator from California, who would probably be mounting his own presidential campaign someday. "My brother told me not to leave a mess in the White House."

The press corps was completely in his hands now, having forgotten how long he'd kept them waiting.

The remainder of the conference went well, with only one glitch. Once again, Lorraine Englehardt of the New York Times insisted on prodding Wagner about his infrastructure rebuilding proposal. As far as Chandler was concerned, it was a great program, and the only problem was the absence of any money to pay for it, a flaw Englehardt persisted in pointing out. Wagner handled the question well, but Englehardt's repeated needling on the subject was clearly getting to him.

As they left the conference room, Wagner's smile disappeared. "What's up with that bitch? What does she want from me?"

Chandler wanted to say that Englehardt was just a reporter doing her job, but kept her mouth shut. She suspected that Wagner's real problem with Englehardt was that she was a woman. Her persistent nagging would have been bad enough coming from a man, but from a woman it was unforgivable. For all his feminist-friendly rhetoric, Wagner was, at heart, a chauvinist.

"Don't worry," Chandler said. "I'll take care of it."

As they walked into the suite, a junior staffer named Stephanski was talking on a cell phone. "Hang on, he's just coming in." He held the phone out to Wagner. "Senator, call for you."

Chandler glared at Stephanski. The entire staff had strict orders to route all calls through her. There was too much potential for disaster with surprise phone calls—

reporters asking questions before she'd had a chance to come up with the right answer, one of Wagner's old girlfriends calling on behalf of the tabloids.

Apparently, Stephanski had forgotten the rules. His face reddened and he headed for the kitchen, away from Chandler's venomous glare.

Wagner took the phone and wandered to the picture window, speaking in hushed tones. Chandler considered taking a bathroom break or sneaking that cigarette, but decided to deal with Stephanski first.

She found him in the kitchen, pulling a can of Diet Coke from the refrigerator. She took the can from him, slammed the refrigerator door and pinned him against it with a gun-barrel finger.

"All right, listen up and get this straight. Nobody talks to him without going through me first. Have you got that? Nobody. Not his wife, not his best friend from third grade, not the goddamn secretary general of the United Nations." She punctuated each phrase with a beat of the finger. "I don't care if World War III breaks out, his dog dies, and Elvis turns up alive in his garage. Have you got that?"

Stephanski nodded mutely.

"Good. The next time you forget, your ass is going back to St. Paul so fast it'll leave a jet trail."

She spun on her heels and returned to the suite, where Wagner was still on the phone, standing by the window, his back to the room. He was arguing now, the staff huddled at the other end of the room pretending to read or go over their notes—no one liked being around when Wagner blew his stack.

"Don't you have your own people?" Wagner said. The caller could barely have had time to answer when Wagner said, "Then use them, damn it."

Chandler grabbed her notes from the press conference and stood by Wagner's side, ostensibly waiting to go over them. Wagner glanced over his shoulder, saw her, and lowered his voice. "Look, I don't care what it takes, just find him." He moved away, shielding the rest of the conversation.

Chandler sat on the sofa and waited for him to finish. A minute later, Wagner punched a button on the phone and threw it on a side table. "All right, where were we?" he said, falling onto the sofa beside her.

"What was that about?" Chandler asked, trying to sound indifferent as she flipped through her notes.

"Nothing important," he said, grabbing a bottle of water from the table. He twisted the cap off and drained it in one swallow, an action that prevented him from having to say any more on the subject. "All right," he said, tossing the bottle into a wastebasket. "Let's go."

Chandler began the play-by-play, analyzing every question from the briefing as if they were the coach and the quarterback of the #1 team in the NFL, watching game films in preparation for the Super Bowl. But in the back of her mind, she made a mental note: *Find out who that was and what they wanted.*

6

The searchers were beginning to show signs of fatigue. They had already completed an exhausting day of training in the heat and humidity, and now there was a real search to handle. Several had grabbed catnaps while Darcy and Janis were inside the command post, but it hadn't helped much; eyes were red, faces drawn and pale.

Janis unfolded the master search map on the hood of Dan's truck, color-coded sections indicating where each dog and handler were to search. She passed around individual maps and a missing person sheet with a photograph of a distinguished-looking elderly gentleman, frowning at the camera.

"This is Marshall Cameron," Janis said. "The photograph is from The Village's official roster." The photo was a formality. Everyone knew what Marshall Cameron looked like.

Darcy studied the photograph. Though she had never seen it before, she remembered her father grousing about the "mug shot" the staff had taken of him on the day he moved in. "It's for our resident's directory," the admissions director had said. But Darcy suspected the real reason was a day like today, a day she had never expected to see.

Janis filled the team in on the time and location where Marshall Cameron was last seen. When the team realized how long the police had waited to call them, they rolled their eyes and shook their heads.

'The state police went over his room with a fine-tooth comb," Janis said. "They didn't find anything. It looks as if he just left for a minute. Troopers and some local fire department volunteers are checking road perimeters and asking people if they've seen him. Law enforcement K-9s have searched the grounds but didn't find a track. However, with the rain last night and today, any track could have easily been washed away. There's no sign of footprints, either. But those would have disappeared, too."

She glanced at her notes. "Mr. Cameron is 79 years old, five-eleven, 175 pounds, and has a full head of gray hair and a mustache. It's unknown exactly what he's wearing, but the staff says he was always neatly dressed, and his typical outfit was light chinos, a light blue sport shirt, boat shoes, and a tweed hat.

She glanced at Darcy. "Can you add anything to that?"

Darcy hesitated. At this point, even the smallest bit of information could be helpful. But the truth was, she did not know her father well. He was one of those people that everyone knows about, but nobody really knows, not even their own families. Marshall Cameron was everybody's friend and nobody's confidante, a personality who was equal parts bonhomie, noblesse oblige and diplomatic immunity. The ordinary rules did not apply.

Darcy wished desperately that she could tell them about her father's habits—what he liked to eat, the television programs he watched, where he went for walks —anything that might give them a clue to his whereabouts. But she knew none of those. She shook her head.

"All right," Janis said, turning back to the map. "We have to assume typical early-to-mid stage Alzheimer's behavior here. One of the things working against us is that

Marshall Cameron is in excellent physical shape."

There were grim nods, an acknowledgment that this was not good news. Even a frail Alzheimer's patient could cover huge amounts of ground. And for reasons no one really understood, they tended to travel in straight lines. There was no telling how far a healthy Alzheimer's victim could have traveled by now. "Obviously, he could be a long way away by now unless he ran into an obstacle."

Pointing to the map, she said "The biggest obstacle is here—the Wantanakee River. It's more a stream, actually, between 12 and 15 feet wide, fairly shallow and slow for the most part, but there are occasional pools that can run several feet deep. With the last of the spring runoff and the downpour from the thunderstorm, it's running very fast and deep in places, and has overflowed its banks in lower areas."

Several of the team members glanced at Darcy then looked at one another, sharing an unspoken understanding: Alzheimer's patients often had a fascination for water, coupled with a deadly inability to understand whether it was still or fast-running, shallow or deep.

"Given all that," Janis said, "I'm most concerned about the heavily wooded area near the stream, which is just about at the limit of our half-mile search radius." She turned to Darcy. "I want you to do that area."

Darcy looked up from the map. Was she kidding?

Janis gave her the barest of nods. She was serious. And suddenly, Darcy knew why. If Janis assigned her to an area where they weren't likely to find her father, she'd never be able to keep her mind on her work, and not just because it was her father. She was a perfectionist—a trait she suspected she'd inherited from her father—and if she wasn't where the action was, she'd probably spend the whole time thinking about that area, worrying that it wasn't being searched well. Call it pride, call it obsessive behavior, but she couldn't stand to be part of anything that wasn't being done perfectly. By giving Darcy the most important area to search, Janis was saying, you're the best we've got, and you'd probably be wasted if I don't give you this area anyway.

Darcy nodded. "All right."

"Good." Janis made the rest of the assignments, then looked around the group. "Folks, we're all tired. It's already been a long day. But let's go to it."

The team members picked up their maps. As Darcy turned to go, Janis took her by the elbow. "Sure you're up to this?"

Darcy hesitated, giving the question serious consideration. Exhausted searchers and tired dogs could make careless, dangerous mistakes.

"Nobody would blame you if you stayed here at the command post," Janis continued. "Or went home and got some sleep. I can do your area."

Darcy pictured herself trying to sleep. It was no good. She couldn't sit around while others did the work, no matter how tired she was. "I'm OK."

"Really? Because you look like hell, kiddo. And you don't smell very good, either."

Darcy forced a smile. "Thanks. I'm fine."

"All right, let's go."

With most of the searchers now out on the job, the noise and confusion of the team's arrival had turned to a spooky quiet. Darcy headed to her truck. Pepper saw her coming, stood up and stretched, her tail thumping against the side of her crate.

Darcy opened the crate and scratched her behind the ears. The feel of Pepper's fur always calmed her. The dog sighed, a look of utter contentment on its face.

"Are you ready, girl?"

The wagging tail told her she was. She grabbed Pepper's search vest. Pepper leaped from the crate and circled excitedly. She was definitely ready.

Darcy looked into her dog's eyes. "Let's go find Marshall."

At the sound of the familiar name, Pepper's ears went up and her tail wound up again. Pepper knew who Marshall was. Early on, trying to bridge the distance between her and her father, Darcy had brought Pepper along on a visit with her father. The two had connected instantly. From then on, she brought Pepper whenever she visited and her father often greeted Pepper before saying anything to Darcy. She wished he showed as much affection to her.

She strapped on Pepper's search vest, pulled her pack on and checked her radio. Then they were off, moving around to the back of the Village Square. In the distance, she caught glimpses of other searchers moving out into their assigned areas, punctuated by the squawks of 2-way radios.

Darcy rechecked her map. Several hundred feet of manicured landscaping stretched behind the Village Square, leading up to the woods on the west side of the property. She couldn't help but think again about how much money had been spent on the place. Instead of leaving the native New England trees on the site, The Village's designers had specified a selection of rare imported trees and bushes to surround the buildings. Unfortunately, they hadn't factored in the harsh New England winters, which killed many of the plantings in a single season. Gradually, the casualties were being replaced with native species, and the dead and dying foliage removed quietly, without fanfare, in much the same way that deceased residents were removed—through a back entrance, at night, so as not to disturb the living residents. Death was a social faux pas at The Village.

The local fauna had taken to the area with a vengeance. The air was thick with the whoosh of wings and the songs of birds. The local squirrel population, chubby with the good life of residents' treats, sprinted across the lawn. Pepper paused and flapped her ears every time a squirrel passed in front of her, but then she moved on. She had work to do, and a search dog that chased animals soon found itself retired to the easy but much-less-exciting life of a family pet.

The park-like grounds ended abruptly, like a knife edge between civilization and wilderness. Darcy had expected to see paths running into the woods, but as far as she could see, there were none. The Village preferred that its residents stay on the grounds.

And for the most part, residents seemed to obey The Village's myriad rules and regulations—several of the residents were her clients, and although she had grown used to hearing complaints from the more independent-minded among them, they still by and large did exactly what The Village asked them to do.

Her father was different. He had spent a lifetime taking the road less traveled. Which made her wonder: Would he wander into the woods? She wouldn't put it past him. Alzheimer's disease or not, he had a strong independent streak and wasn't likely to be stopped by the absence of a visible path.

Darcy took a compass bearing, whistled for Pepper, and keyed her radio.

"Base, this is Unit 14. I'm starting my area."

"10-4, 14," Dan replied. There was a background buzz of conversation and the staccato bursts of radio transmissions from state police units. "Good luck, Darcy," he added.

Darcy stared at the radio. For the first time that day,

she felt like crying. Apparently there was a real person lurking inside their communications officer after all.

Unlike the rough, tangled terrain of the morning's training, the pine forest that bordered The Village grounds was flat and relatively open. It was dark inside, and her eyes took a few moments to adjust to the abrupt change. Fortunately, the heavy canopy of trees kept the underbrush to a minimum, allowing her to see several hundred feet in all directions. Although it would be easy for someone to hide behind the massive trunks, Pepper would take care of that possibility. Intent on her job, the dog ranged back and forth in front of Darcy, occasionally lifting her head high to scent the air.

Every couple of minutes, Darcy shouted encouragement to Pepper. "Find him, girl. Find Marshall." And every time she heard the name, Pepper's tail wagged more furiously and her head scanned from side to side.

Darcy watched Pepper work, once again in awe of her abilities. While humans live in a world defined by sights and sounds, dogs exist in a rich world of scents that humans couldn't begin to imagine. They were, in a way, as alien to our species as any imaginary creature to step off a space ship, with abilities far beyond ours. It was those abilities that Darcy was counting on to find her father.

The line of thunderstorms that had moved through the area that morning had been the harbinger of a Canadian cold front moving in. The front had swept away the heat and humidity of earlier in the day and replaced it with cool, bone-dry air. The temperature, near 90 in the early afternoon, was now in the low 60s. It was almost ideal search weather, the kind that allowed the dogs and their handlers to cover large amounts of ground without the risk of heat exhaustion, while the damp ground from the rain actually intensified any scents.

Of course, there was a downside to the cool, dry air. If her father had been outside during the downpour, he'd likely be soaked to the bone, and hypothermia was an ever-present danger for people exposed to the elements. Even on very warm days, evaporating water from wet clothes could cool the body to dangerous levels in no time. The lower temperatures and dry air brought in by the cold front would only hasten the cooling process.

Worse, elderly people often had trouble keeping warm anyway; problems with the body's temperature-regulating mechanism were one of the myriad complications of aging. On top of that, Alzheimer's victims often didn't realize that they were getting colder until their core body temperature fell several degrees. Then, just as the condition became life-threatening, the feedback mechanism between the body temperature and the brain went haywire, making them feel as if they were burning up. At that point, they often stripped off all their clothes in an effort to cool off, further hastening the effects of hypothermia.

She recalled a search they'd been on last fall. An elderly woman, in advanced Alzheimer's, had wandered off when her caregiver took a nap. It had only been two hours, but it was long enough to end her life. They had found her just a few hundred feet from her home, all her clothes scattered around her.

The conditions had been identical to today's.

At the end of most days, Leonard Wakefield retreated from The Village to his 17-room home on High Street, the oldest neighborhood in Eastham, an avenue of enormous white houses with enough gardens, hedges and ornamental trees to keep an army of groundskeepers busy year-round.

Tonight, however, Wakefield had decided to stay in

his private apartment in Village Estates, the most expensive residential area in The Village. The board of directors hadn't wanted to set aside an entire top-level apartment for his use, but Wakefield had insisted—he needed it for staff functions and occasional receptions to entertain important guests. But events like today's proved the necessity. He wanted to be available immediately in case of developments in the search.

Wakefield poured himself a scotch and soda from the bar, settled into an overstuffed reclining chair and aimed a remote at the entertainment center.

The screen flickered to life on a newscast. The face looked familiar, and Wakefield glanced at the bottom of the screen: "Ned Epstein, Channel 34 News."

Now he remembered the face. It was one of the media pests who had tried to question him earlier. Fortunately, he'd been able to pass the nuisance off to the police. He was about to change the channel when a photograph of The Village appeared on the screen.

"Our top story tonight, famed newscaster Marshall Cameron is missing from his exclusive retirement community in Eastham."

Wakefield winced as the story progressed. He'd been hoping the news of the search would be pushed to the back burner by bigger news, an international crisis or some political scandal. No such luck. He would just have to hope the searchers found Mr. Cameron quickly or the media lost interest.

Now the screen showed The Village grounds swarming with searchers, police and reporters.

"Channel 34 news has also learned that a security system, designed to safeguard residents from accidentally wandering off the grounds, was turned off at the time of Marshall Cameron's disappearance."

Wakefield sat up quickly, collapsing the recliner's leg

rest and spilling the drink on his pants.

"Sources close to the search say that no one among The Village staff has taken responsibility for turning off the alarm, leading to speculation about the disappearance of the Mr. Cameron."

Sources close to the search, Wakefield thought, angry that someone had told the press about the alarm, and also that his linen pants would have to be dry-cleaned.

7

The sun was setting, casting long shadows in the pine forest behind The Village. Darcy and Pepper made their way forward, Darcy's mind fluctuating from confidence that they'd find her father safe, to unsettling images of him dead in the woods or drowned in the river.

Maybe, she told herself, he had simply gone for a walk and gotten lost. Maybe he'd twisted an ankle or broken a leg. Or maybe, she was forced to admit, his Alzheimer's had progressed faster than anyone realized. Diagnosing the disease was difficult enough, but the progression was different in each victim. Some people developed automatic defense mechanisms that made it hard to tell how the disease had affected them. During a search the preceding summer, Darcy had come across an elderly woman in a state forest, binoculars hanging from her neck and a bird book in her hand. She'd greeted Darcy and had been friendly and coherent, talking intelligently about the indigenous songbird species and the weather. It was only when the woman had made a passing reference to John F. Kennedy—whom she planned to vote for—that Darcy knew she was the person they were looking for.

The pine forest gradually gave way to a thicker deciduous growth of maples and oaks. As the ground sloped toward the river, thick leaves and a more-extensive undergrowth made it harder to see. Pepper ranged far ahead and Darcy often lost sight of her for minutes at a time. A breeze rustled the leaves, and the sound of water in the distance grew, like the low growl of an animal. It didn't sound like a shallow stream.

As she picked her way through a thicket of laurel, the ground fell away more abruptly to a large flat area. The view opened up and she could see lines of willows in the distance, delineating the banks of the stream. But her heart sank as she saw what lay between her and the banks. The small stunted trees in the wetland weren't a problem, but what surrounded them was: two hundred feet of lush thick ferns, grown to eye-level in the warm weather. Darcy waded into them and was immediately surrounded by the vegetation, which sometimes grew above her head. Looking down, she couldn't even see the ground. In conditions like this, you could literally step on a person—dead or alive—without even seeing them.

She couldn't see where Pepper was either, except for an occasional glimpse of a fern frond waving in the distance. The growth absorbed sound like a sponge, and she wished she had clipped a bell to Pepper's search vest. Bells were normally only used for night searching, but it would have been handy in this mess.

She whistled again and was startled when Pepper suddenly materialized in front of her. Despite the cool weather, she was panting with the exertion of moving through the ferns. A breeze rustled the leaves above, but it didn't reach into the fern forest. Darcy took a long pull of water, squirted some into Pepper's mouth, and the dog was off again.

Progress was slow through the ferns, and Darcy's hiking boots suddenly came down in water up to her ankles. Here, the stream had overflowed its banks, and she had no idea how much deeper the water would get. Still, she and Pepper had been wet before, and in much colder settings. These were the kind of conditions where

Pepper's retriever heritage came in handy, the outer layer of her coat providing her with a water-resistant barrier.

The radio, which had been unusually quiet, burst into life.

"All units, this is base. Please stand by."

A combination of panic tinged with an edge of hope flooded over Darcy, and she realized that she was holding her breath. She drew in a long pull of air as the message continued.

"All units. We have a report that the Eastham PD has found a string." A string was a physical item, a clue. "Details unknown at this time. Please stay at your present location and await further instructions. Base clear."

Darcy grabbed her radio. "Base, this is Unit 14. Can you tell me the string location?" There was a long pause. "Come on, come on." She'd been involved with enough searches to know that there was a conversation going on at base, and they were deciding whether or not to tell her. Finally the radio came to life again.

"Unit 14, string location is near the river, directly west of The Village."

Darcy checked her map. That wasn't far from where she was standing. "Base, I'm less than five minutes away from there now, directly south. Do I have permission to move to the area?"

There was another long pause. "Affirmative, 14. Keep heading north until you intersect a narrow path. Then follow it toward the river."

She whistled for Pepper and the two of them headed back to the higher ground. They found the path quickly. Once on it, she had to jog to keep up with Pepper. They came around a corner and found Harvey Warren tying off a police-barrier tape, the words "Crime Scene, Do Not Cross" repeated along the tape. The color drained from Darcy's face.

Warren's German shepherd, happy to see another dog, leaped up, his tail wagging.

"Pepper, hold," Darcy yelled. Pepper stopped at the tape and stared expectantly at Darcy.

"What is it?" she asked, looking over Warren's shoulder.

Warren raised his hands and moved to block her view of whatever was there. "I don't think you should—"

"What is wrong with you?" she said, stepping around him.

He moved to intercept her. "Darcy, this is a job for the police, now."

"Well, Harvey, if the police did their job—"

From behind them came the sound of footsteps jogging up the path. It was Jackie Bradley, followed by three troopers in orange coveralls—the crime scene investigative unit. "All right," she barked at Darcy and Warren. "Stop it immediately, both of you."

Darcy backed away, her eyes still locked on the chief.

"Calm down," Bradley said. "We're all under pressure here. I won't have you two taking it out on each other."

Warren stepped around Darcy and spoke in low tones to Bradley, "I was just trying to explain to her—"

Darcy stared past the tape to see what he'd been trying to hide. She frowned, struggling to understand, still angry at Warren for playing CSI: Vermont.

On the bank, leading down to the river, was a neatly folded pile of clothes—chinos, a blue sport shirt and underwear. Next to the clothes was a pair of boat shoes, a blue sock neatly rolled and tucked inside each one. On top of the shoes was a rumpled tweed cap.

8

Jane Chandler prided herself on being the first person in the office every morning. It was, she knew, a control issue. But it was her way of countering Wagner's lax attitude towards schedules.

She scanned the list of Wagner's appointments for the day. There was a 6 a.m. breakfast meeting with some reluctant senators who needed a few more assurances before signing on to the campaign. That was followed by an 8 a.m. session with the campaign staff, which she decided to move to 9. The first meeting was likely to drag on and besides, she liked jerking the junior staff around. It kept them off balance and reminded them who was in charge. Calling them early in the morning also gave her a chance to remind them how early she got in and let her do a quick check on their personal habits.

She speed-dialed the first person on the list. "Connie. This is Jane. Schedule change."

She worked her way down the list, barely giving the staffers time to wake up before moving on to the next one. It was the equivalent of running down the barracks banging on doors and yelling for the troops to get up.

A few of them were already awake, and others were clearly not alone. There was no answer at their programmer's apartment, but Tiffany—the woman who did their travel arrangements and who had headed out to a bar with him the night before—told Chandler in a sleepy voice that she'd tell him about the time change if she saw him.

I'm sure you will, Chandler thought, and punched a button to clear the line.

A phone rang down the hall. Chandler glanced at the dial pad. Who the hell was calling this early in the morning?

The light glowed on Wagner's private line. She watched it for a moment, then put her hand over the mouthpiece and pressed the button slowly.

"So that's the end of it," Wagner said.

"I'm afraid not." The other voice was deep, sour, perfunctory. It was not a tone people generally used with Wagner.

"What do you mean? You said they found his clothes."

"Yes, but they didn't find him." Now the voice sounded like a teacher explaining a subtle point to a not-too-bright student who happened to be from a wealthy family and must not be offended. "Until they find him, or his body, we can't be sure."

Chandler froze, listening. Wagner was silent for a moment, and she could almost see him rubbing the back of his neck, his habit when he was perplexed or angry. "So now what?"

"My people are on their way. I'll be there shortly myself. I'll let you know as soon as we have anything to report."

"All right," Wagner said. "Just try to keep it quiet."

"Of course."

Chandler listened for the click of the line going dead and hung up at the same instant.

She sat back, breathing hard, fluctuating between anger and panic. Wagner was keeping something from her. How was she supposed to do her job if he didn't tell her what was going on?

But another part of her didn't want to know what this was all about. You didn't have to lie about what you didn't know.

She picked up a pencil and gripped it so hard that it snapped in half. Maybe she had left Senator Reinhardt too quickly. Right now, the road to the White House didn't look as smooth as she'd thought.

At 7 a.m., the only place in Eastham to get coffee was the diner, and Ned Epstein needed coffee bad. The press briefing at The Village wasn't till 8, and he was going to need help to stay awake through it. There had been no news since the finding of Marshall Cameron's clothes the previous evening, so this was likely to be a "We have nothing new to report" report. He wished he could have slept in.

Granny pushed open the glass door to the diner. "You should drink ginseng. Helps keep you alert."

"I'll keep that in mind," Ned said, following him in.

A few heads turned to note their arrival, then returned to their conversations and scrambled eggs. Ned and Granny sat at the counter next to a burly young man in a ragged gray sweatshirt.

"Doesn't look good," the man said to his breakfast companion, a scrawny guy in a frayed flannel shirt.

"Nope. Damn shame, too. Her being on the search team."

Ned stared at the menu, pretending to read it.

"Yeah, that's something," the sweatshirted man said. "Having to search for your own old man."

A waitress appeared in front of Ned and Granny. "Help you gentlemen?"

"Coffee, black," Ned said quickly, not wanting to miss any of the locals' conversation.

"Got any bagels?" Granny asked.

"Sorry, honey. No bagels. English muffins, blueberry muffins—"

"I hear she's a pretty tough cookie," the flannel-shirted man said. "Nice, you know, but tough."

"Guess I'll have a banana-nut muffin," Granny said.

"Anything else?" The waitress tapped her pad.

"No, thanks," Ned said, shooting Granny a "shut up" glance that he missed completely.

"She did my divorce," the sweat-shirted man said. "Didn't let them get away with any funny stuff either."

"Good looking, that's for sure."

"Yep."

The coffee arrived. It tasted like diner coffee. In a pinch, you could use it as paint stripper.

Ned sipped at the tarry liquid, staring at the counter and thinking: *Marshall Cameron's daughter is a lawyer. She's on the search team. She's a looker.*

Granny's muffin arrived. "Bananas are good for you," he said, stuffing a large hunk into his mouth. "Potassium."

The Fish and Wildlife boat made its way slowly downstream. At the bow, a golden retriever who specialized in searching for drowning victims stood like an animated figurehead, the front of its body leaning over the water, tail moving back and forth to help keep its balance. The dog's nose was inches above the water, sniffing deeply for the skin oils that bodies in water give off, oils that float to the surface and are easy for a trained dog's sensitive nose to detect. Sometimes, there was another scent, one given off by bodies that had been in water longer, a scent that was even easier for the dogs to detect. It was not a scent they cared for, any more than their human handlers did.

Darcy and Pepper had stopped on the banks of the

river to rest and watch the boat's progress. They had returned to the search after a few hours of fitful sleep, and even now Darcy could not shake the memory of the vivid dream she'd had.

In the dream, she and Pepper were running through thick woods, following her father, who receded farther and farther into foggy twilight. She remembered wondering how a 79-year old man could move so fast. Pepper poured on the speed, followed closely by Darcy. But the forest grew thicker, underbrush and brambles slowing them down. Her father, however, didn't seem hampered, and last thing she saw of him was a flash of a gray shirt. Suddenly, he was gone, as if the earth had swallowed him up. She had called out in her sleep and been awakened by Pepper licking her face.

At 5 am, she had given up trying to sleep and headed back to the search. In the truck on the way there, her cell phone had rung—a reporter asking her reaction to the news about The Village's security system.

"What news?"

"About the alarm being turned off at the time your father disappeared."

"What?"

"The administration says no one there did it."

"That's typical." Count on Wakefield to deny everything.

"Do you think someone else might have been responsible for turning it off?"

"I have no idea," she'd said, and hung up.

Now, staring at the slow-moving water, she wondered about the alarm, but couldn't decide what to do about it, if anything. She picked up her pack again and was about to give Pepper the search command when she heard a rhythmic thumping in the distance: a helicopter.

Her spirits rose—the more help with this search the

better. She peered through the trees at the summit of Mount Connell and saw a flash of reflected sunlight as the chopper appeared over the mountain. She expected to see the state police's small chopper, or perhaps the med-evac helicopter from the medical center in Burlington, which could be pressed into use if it wasn't involved in an emergency elsewhere. On occasion the Vermont National Guard unit even sent one of their Vietnam-era Hueys to help.

But this bird was big, much bigger than any of the local choppers, and she couldn't make out any markings. Then, as suddenly as it had appeared, the chopper veered off and disappeared beyond the mountain. Her spirits sunk. It was probably just a training flight from the air force base across the New York line, nothing at all to do with the search.

The radio crackled to life with Dan Cumming's fatigued voice. "Base to all units. Return to base immediately. Meet the operational leader in the parking area."

Darcy's pulse quickened. They wouldn't be calling people in unless there had been a new development. She grabbed her radio. "Unit 14 to base, situation update."

"Unknown, 14. There will be a briefing as soon as all units are back at base."

She was about to protest, but swallowed it, not trusting what might come out. Her heart pounding, she whistled for Pepper. "Come on, girl. We're going back."

When they arrived back at The Village, most of the other team members were already gathered around Janis, who stood with her arms crossed, staring at the ground. Bradley was also there, and she didn't look happy. Neither of them made eye contact with Darcy as she joined the team. Darcy's glances at her fellow team members were met with shrugs and head shakes. They didn't know what was going on either.

"Okay people, listen up," Janis said. "Sergeant Bradley has an announcement."

Bradley's look was that of a doctor who is trying to pretend the news she's about to give you isn't all that bad. "You folks, as always, have done a terrific job. I've told you many times that we couldn't do our job without you." She looked at the ground for a moment, as if there were a teleprompter at her feet, one that would help her with the next line. "I won't deny that this is difficult, but I have to tell you that you can all go home now. Effective immediately, Vermont K-9 has been relieved of duty on this search."

The team members looked at each other in disbelief, a low murmur of confusion, dismay, and protest rumbling through the ranks.

"Quiet down, people," Janis said.

Bradley continued. "Please understand that this is no reflection on you. But the management of The Village has decided that National Rescue Services will take over the entire search from this point onward."

Darcy said, "Since when does The Village decide—"

"They have made this decision in conjunction with search management at the state police," Bradley said.

The team members exchanged glances again, this time in stunned silence. Finally, someone said, "Who the hell is National Rescue Services?"

In the tightly-knit New England search and rescue community, everyone knew all the other teams. But this was a new one on them.

Bradley crossed her arms over her chest. "They're a group of professional searchers from upstate New York."

There was more grumbling. Bradley waved her arms for quiet. "Look, I know you're confused. And angry. I'll level with you. This decision comes from high up. I don't understand it myself, and I don't have much more information. But I have my orders, and I'm going to follow them. I expect you to do the same."

Janis took a step forward now. "You've all done the best job you could," she said, her voice tense. "I'm proud of you. Now, let's pack up and go home."

She turned and walked away, signaling the end of the meeting. Bradley looked as if she was about to say more, hesitated, and then headed back to the command post.

Bowing to the inevitable, the team members broke up and headed for their vehicles. A few stopped to pat Darcy on the back and offer words of encouragement. But Darcy stood her ground, staring at Bradley's retreating back with disbelief and growing anger. Then she came to life and ran after Bradley, catching up with her at the steps to the Village Square.

"Jackie, what the hell is going on here? None of this makes sense."

Bradley turned to Darcy, frowning. "Look—"

"And don't go into police mode with me. I'm not a bad guy. I just need to know what's going on."

Bradley's eyes bore into Darcy's. "I'm not trying to pull the wool over your eyes. I was telling it straight. I don't know anything more than I told you." She put a hand on Darcy's arm. "I'm sure the group that's coming in will do the best job possible. We're going to find your father."

Darcy's eyes remained locked on Bradley's. "Who's we?" she said, and turned to walk away.

Ned and Granny elbowed their way into the small conference room that had been set aside in the Village Square for the press briefing. As usual for the second day of a search, the press corps had diminished, the story pushed to the back burner by scandals at the state house and a fire in St. Albans.

The reporters and photographers jostled for room as they awaited the state police information officer, the spigot who would dispense whatever dribbles of information the police thought the media could be trusted with.

The Channel 7 news team had already arrived and positioned themselves at the front of the room. The anchor-babe examined her flawless face in a makeup mirror. Granny stared at her and Ned elbowed him wearily. "Come on." He pointed to a spot on the other side of the room. "This will probably be a waste of time, but you camp out over there and get it on tape. I'm going to go check something out."

Granny shrugged. "Fine with me."

Ned found a restroom and dawdled till he was sure the rest of the press corps had arrived. As he stepped out of the rest room he heard the information officer greeting the reporters in a robotic voice that carried no warmth and little enthusiasm.

Easing out the front door, Ned saw a huddle of people gathered around a search and rescue truck. A heated debate seemed to be taking place. As he watched, the group dispersed amidst shrugs and shaking heads.

Ned hailed a young man with a day-old stubble who was walking away from the group. "Excuse me. Can you tell me where Darcy is?" He'd found her name in the phone book. Eastham had exactly three lawyers, only one of whom had the same last name as Marshall Cameron.

The young man looked him over and nodded toward a woman who was arguing with a state trooper. "That's her over there."

As Ned approached, Darcy Cameron broke off the conversation with the trooper and walked away, a black Lab by her side. "Darcy?"

She turned and frowned at him. "Yes?"

He stuck out a hand. "Ned Epstein, Channel 34 News. Wondering if I can ask you a few questions?"

She ignored the hand and kept walking. "You'll have to talk to the police. They have someone to handle questions about the search."

"I know," he said, trotting to keep pace with her. "This is more personal. I'm working on a story on what it feels like to have a family member missing."

She stopped, turned back, and stared at him. For a moment he thought she was going to strike him. "What it feels like? Are you serious?"

"I'm sorry, I know this is probably a bad time—"

"A bad time? Oh, no, not at all. My father has been missing for over 48 hours. He has Alzheimer's. And now..." she waved a hand toward the trooper, then changed her mind about whatever she was going to say. "Just forget it."

She walked to her truck and unlocked the back.

"All right," Ned called, following her. "I said I'm sorry. I'm just trying to do my job. Maybe I'm being a little clumsy about it, but maybe I've got a reason. Do you think you're the only person who's ever lost someone?"

She stood, one hand on the tailgate. The dog sat at her feet, waiting.

"I lost a brother when I was in high school," Ned said. "We were out hiking and decided to race home. He took a shortcut, thinking he could beat me. I got home, but Jimmy never showed up. When it got dark, we went looking for him."

Her face softened, as if this was a tale she'd heard too many times before.

"We found him the next day. He'd fallen in a ravine and hit his head. He never regained consciousness."

She closed her eyes. "I'm sorry."

Even the dog looked sympathetic. Ned knelt beside it and the dog put a paw on his arm and whined softly.

"What's his name?" Ned asked.

"Her. Pepper."

"Good girl," he said to Pepper, massaging the floppy ears. "Great dogs, black Labs. I had one when I was a kid. Best friend I ever had."

Darcy watched him for a moment. "Look, I'm sorry I snapped at you. But this isn't a good time. Things are..."

Ned waited for her to finish the sentence. Around them, searchers were packing up their gear, tossing equipment into trucks and putting dogs into cages. Nobody seemed happy.

He put two and two together. "Are they calling off the search?"

She swung her backpack into the truck. "Not exactly."

"So what's up?" he said. "Off the record."

"Right," she said, glancing at him sideways. "So then you quote me as an 'unnamed source.'"

She had him there. That was exactly what he'd do. "All right, I won't push it. But when this is over..." he hesitated. There were several ways this could end, not all of them good. "When it's over, let me talk to you."

She said nothing, but motioned for the dog to hop into its crate. "Come on, girl."

"And if there's anything I can do to help—"

She shot him a doubtful look.

"I'm serious," Ned said. "If there's anything I can do, call me."

"Thanks." She slammed the hatch shut. "But I don't think—"

The sound of approaching vehicles interrupted their conversation. Darcy turned to see a convoy of vehicles thunder up The Village's driveway: an enormous black van trailing a string of black SUVs. The SUVs were unmarked, but emblazoned on the side of the van were the words "National Rescue Services."

The convoy spun into the parking lot, doors flew open, and a dozen people in charcoal-colored uniforms emerged and began hauling out equipment.

Ned added it up. The search team was packing it in. The team members weren't happy. And Marshall Cameron's daughter was mum about what's going on. He nodded toward the newcomers. "Who are they?"

Darcy nodded, her mouth a hard thin line. "Now that's a damn good question."

9

The hub of the Senate office building's telephone network was on the bottom floor of the building, several floors below ground level, where it was safe from suicide bombers, missiles, or citizens angry over their Senator's latest vote.

Jane Chandler found Tim Jacobi, administrator of the building's phone system, hunkered over a computer screen, programming manual in hand. Tim was young-looking, wire-thin with a wispy goatee. But at least she didn't find him repugnant, which had made it easier to spend a couple of hours drinking beers with him after work one evening, a rendezvous that had secured his eternal admiration and allegiance. The relationship had never gone further than that, though she knew he'd like it to, knew it in the way a female tiger smells fear or lust in the animals around her. It was useful knowledge.

Jacobi looked up at the sound of her footsteps. She gave him a cheery, "Hey there."

A look that combined surprise, yearning and dismay flickered over his face. "Hey. What's up?"

She leaned against his desk, stretching her bare legs out and crossing them at the ankles. "The usual gopher work for Wagner. Do you have a way of looking up the number of someone who called him this morning? He wanted to return the call but forgot to write down the number."

It was a lame explanation for the request and she knew it. But that was OK. It gave him sufficient cover should anyone ever question him about it.

Jacobi gave the briefest of nods, his face blank. "Sure. What's his extension?"

She gave it to him and he entered a few keystrokes.

"Time of call?"

"Early. Say, 6:30 or so."

More clicking. His eyes narrowed at the screen. "Got it." Then a pause. "Odd."

"Problem?"

"Not really. The line was blocked. But I can get around that."

"You can?" You man, you.

"Sure. Just like these mail order companies—you call their 800 numbers and you've got caller ID blocking on your phone so you think they can't collect your number and sell it to telemarketers, right? Wrong. There are ways."

She was sure there were.

A minute passed as he entered commands, staring at the screen. "This is going to take longer than I thought. Why don't I call you?"

She hesitated, calculating how much she was going to owe him for this favor. "OK. Thanks."

Back in the office, she tried to put the matter of the mysterious phone call aside and concentrate on the task at hand. It wasn't easy—the words "find his body" kept forcing themselves to the front of her mind.

The task at hand was her own pet project—tracking potential nominees for the cabinet and other top positions after the election. Among these positions was that of senior adviser, the slot she planned to fill. Campaign staffers were often so focused on winning the race that they didn't have time to worry about whether they would be sitting around the big table after January 20th. By then, it was too late, and the sacrificial lambs who burned themselves out for the candidate found themselves pushed aside by opportunists who had spent the previous months positioning themselves.

Jane Chandler wasn't about to let that happen. Come January 21, she planned to occupy the room next to the Oval Office—a room where speeches were written, legislation hatched, Supreme Court nominees vetted, political firestorms extinguished, and wars planned or parried. It was a room redolent with the aroma of power.

Technically, of course, appointments weren't made until after the election was won. But the internal campaigning began long before, while the candidates were still bloodying each other in the primaries. Recommendations came in a thousand subtle and not-so-subtle ways, from friends, acquaintances, and people who wouldn't cross the street to speak to you if they didn't think you were going to be president. The campaign was already getting a hundred letters a day from people who wanted to serve in a Wagner administration. And for every empty position, there were a thousand considerations to take into account—the ability of the aspiring job-seeker to actually fill the office being only one of them, and far from the most important. There were old friends to remember, political debts to pay off, bargains to strike, statements to make.

With the upswing in their primary results, Wagner's short list had been growing, and by now Chandler had a good idea who he would choose to be Attorney General, Treasury Secretary, and Budget Director. He hadn't said anything about his senior adviser, but Chandler considered herself to have the inside track. Still, she was keeping her eyes and ears open. She wasn't going to leave anything to chance.

The phone rang. "Jane Chandler."

"Hi. It's Tim," he said.

There was a tremor in his voice—the poor guy was so nervous around her that she could hear it in his voice. "What's up?"

"You know that information you wanted?" He paused, and in the space she sensed that his nervousness hadn't been because of her. He was scared. "Maybe you should come down here."

Darcy threw the truck into gear and spun out of the parking space, fuming, trying to decide who to blame for being called off the search. Something told her it wasn't Leonard Wakefield. Wakefield was a stooge who only acted on orders he received from his corporate overloads. Who then?

She roared past the main building and cast a glance at the parking lot. People in SWAT-team attire stood pulling equipment out of the National Rescue Systems van—a lot of equipment. Seeing all that gear, she came to a realization—the helicopter she'd seen earlier had been with this outfit.

But there was one thing missing. Despite all the fancy equipment these folks had, there were no dogs.

That struck her as odd. In her experience, a well-trained dog was the best means of finding a missing person. After all, it was Harvey Warren's goofy shepherd that found her father's clothes, even if it hadn't seemed interested in tracking the trail from the clothes to the water.

She hit the brakes. There was another explanation for the dog's behavior. Maybe it hadn't followed her father's trail to the water because there was no trail.

Since finding the clothes, the searchers had been working on an assumption that no one wanted to say out loud but was easy enough to imagine: A confused elderly man wanders into the woods and is drawn by the sound of running water. He mistakes it for a swimming pool, a pond, or even a bathtub; people with Alzheimer's had made stranger connections. He takes off his clothes, piles them neatly, walks into the water and drowns. It was just the kind of thing an Alzheimer's victim would do.

There was only one problem. If her father had walked from the clothes to the water, he would have left a track. But the dogs had searched along the banks of the stream and had found nothing. It wasn't impossible for them to miss a track. But if her father was naked, he would have been shedding skin cells the entire way. To a search dog, that was the equivalent of a crop duster spray painting a bright red arrow that said, "He went this way."

She spun the truck around and headed back to The Village. She was operating on instinct now, and her instincts told her one thing: Her father was not in the water.

Sharon Davis had worked at The Village for less than a month. Before that she'd been a teller at the First National Bank of Eastham. The pay at the bank was good, but the stress had been too much for her—the responsibility for her own cash drawer, dealing with people's complaints, the managers constantly checking on her. Then she'd found out she was pregnant, and the hours on her feet became unbearable. When the receptionist's job at The Village opened up, she'd jumped at it.

The Village was a haven, full of pleasant, well-to-do elderly people who stopped to chat with her as they passed the front desk to get their mail or make a dinner reservation.

At least, it had been, until yesterday. Then Mr. Cameron disappeared. Now the place was overrun with police, reporters, and rescue workers. The other residents were nervous, and the phone had been ringing off the hook. On top of all that she had to find someone to cover the desk whenever she had to pee, which was about every fifteen minutes these days.

She was approaching the "tank full" state again when a woman in filthy clothes approached the desk. Her face was streaked with dirt and a tiny twig stuck out of her hair. She looked as if she'd been sleeping in the woods.

Sharon eyed her doubtfully. "Can I help you?"

"Yes. My name is Darcy Cameron. I need to get into my father's apartment. Number 12."

"Hold on a moment," Sharon said, turning to the computer to check the security register. The register listed the names of people who were allowed to enter a resident's apartment in case of emergency. Given the events of yesterday, she wasn't about to let anyone into Mr. Cameron's apartment without making sure it was OK. Especially someone who looked like a back-woods psychopath.

"I'm sorry," she said, looking up from the screen. "I'm not allowed to let you in."

Darcy's face hardened. "What?"

Sharon swallowed and pointed to the computer. "We keep a list on the system here. Mr. Cameron told us not to let anyone in. 'Under any circumstances,' it says."

Darcy leaned over the desk, so close that Sharon could smell the dirt and sweat coming off her body. "Let me explain something to you. My father is missing. You may have noticed all the people walking around here with uniforms on? They're looking for him. When he gave you that information, I don't think he knew he was going to be missing."

"I'm sorry, but I—"

Darcy eyes flickered over her name tag. "Sharon—it's

Sharon, right?"

She took a deep breath. "Yes?"

"Look, Sharon," Darcy whispered fiercely. "I'm a member of the search and rescue team. I'm also a lawyer. I'd hate to have to tell Mr. Wakefield that you obstructed this search. And I'm sure you'd hate being responsible for my father's death because you made me stand around here arguing with you about getting into his apartment."

Sharon hesitated, on the verge of tears. She didn't want to get in trouble for holding up the search. But she didn't want to make a mistake and let the wrong person into the apartment, especially after yesterday.

"All right," she said, placing the visitor's log on the counter. The woman scrawled a signature as Sharon entered several keystrokes into the computer. "The door is open. But I can only leave it open for a minute."

"That's all I ask," Darcy said, and strode off in the direction of the apartment.

Sharon turned back to the computer, praying that no one would ask her about this. They'd already called her on the carpet when they discovered she'd let a deliveryman go to the apartment yesterday without signing in.

It wasn't her fault. She'd had to pee and couldn't find anyone to cover the desk. She'd only been gone a few minutes, but apparently the deliveryman had come in while she was in the bathroom, found no one on duty, and gone down to Mr. Cameron's apartment. He was gone by the time Sharon returned from the bathroom. She wouldn't even have known he was there, but then Mr. Cameron disappeared and one of the cleaning ladies remembered she'd seen a deliveryman going to his apartment.

Her supervisor had immediately come to check the visitor's register. Sharon told him she hadn't seen any delivery person and that she'd been there the whole time

—she felt terrible lying about it, but she just couldn't afford to lose this job, not now, not with the baby coming. She couldn't go back to the bank.

She picked up the phone and called the main office. "Ellen, can you relieve me for a couple of minutes?" Now she really needed to pee.

Darcy marched to the apartment feeling like a heel. The girl at the desk was young, obviously very pregnant, and just doing her job. Darcy hated browbeating her like that, but she needed to get into the apartment and she needed to do it quickly, before Leonard Wakefield or anyone else thought of a good reason to keep her out.

She wasn't sure what she expected to find there, if anything. But if her father was not in the water, he had to be somewhere else. And maybe the apartment would give her a clue where.

As she opened the door, she recalled the question from the reporter who'd called her in the truck: What if someone else had been responsible for turning off The Village's alarm system? Her father was famous. He was elderly. And he was well-off—a perfect target for a kidnapper or madman.

She shook her head to dispel the thought. She didn't want to think about that possibility.

In the entryway, she stood surveying the apartment. Like every other time she'd been there, her father's apartment was the picture of pristine orderliness, a photo spread from Better Homes and Gardens, the kind of place that made you wonder where the owners kept their junk.

She circled the living room searching for anything out of order, some telltale item that might give a clue about where he had wandered. But there was nothing. In fact, the most distinctive thing about her father's apartment was what it did not contain.

To begin with, there was no clutter. Most men, she was convinced, were born with a clutter gene firmly affixed to their Y-chromosome. How else to explain the inability to part with worn-out blue jeans that hadn't fit in years, ancient college textbooks, and recordings of groups who had been out of fashion for decades? It had to be congenital.

Older men, especially single older men, were even worse. She had elderly male clients who couldn't find important tax papers because every drawer they owned was filled with old grocery store receipts, losing lottery tickets, and insurance policies for cars they hadn't owned in twenty years.

Her father's apartment, on the other hand, could have been The Village's model apartment, the one they showed to prospective residents. There were no collections of loose coins in jars, no tables overflowing with newspapers, no socks thrown in piles. If that was unusual for most older men, it seemed remarkable for a man in the early stages of Alzheimer's. True, the disease afflicted different people in different ways. Her father had always been organized, and apparently his illness hadn't changed that. But this was more than neatness, the apartment seemed completely free of any personal items that might have given a sense of his likes and dislikes—candy wrappers, magazines, half-read books. Even the artwork on the walls was generic, pleasant landscapes that gave no clue to the personality of the man who lived there.

Darcy had always known that her father was not in the least bit sentimental. After a lifetime in broadcasting, he had nothing in the way of souvenirs—no scrapbooks, no plaques or awards, no photos of him with famous statesmen. In fact, there were no photographs of any kind —not even, she noted bitterly, a single photo of his only child. Over the years, she had given him several beautifully framed photos of herself, but they had all disappeared.

Where had they gone? And what kind of man spent a lifetime in a high-profile career without having any mementos left over at the end? It was as if he had sterilized his surroundings to remove any trace of his own personality. She had suspected, at times, that her father was obsessive-compulsive, but this went beyond garden-variety neurosis.

She wandered into the bedroom, opening closets, pulling out drawers, feeling like a child peeking into her father's desk, fascinated by the contents but worried he might come back at any moment and catch her at it. But there was nothing to feel guilty about. It was as if the apartment had been outfitted by a movie production company, with only the minimal furnishings necessary to suggest that someone lived there: a single disposable razor in the medicine cabinet, a can of shaving cream, clothes carefully placed in drawers, one towel in the kitchen for drying dishes, neatly folded and hanging from a rack.

She opened the refrigerator. It was almost empty, except for a carton of orange juice, a quart of skim milk, a jar of mustard.

And a small brown dish.

She pulled it out. It was an ashtray, the square, brown-glass kind that restaurants and institutions use, perfectly clean. She held it, her hands trembling. In this Disney-perfect apartment, the misplaced ashtray was like the first red leaf of autumn, a harbinger of the downhill slide into dementia her father was facing.

She turned, gazing from the kitchen to the living room where a picture window looked out over a stretch of manicured lawn to a row of small Norway pines.

"Dad," she whispered. "Where are you?"

The question sent her back to childhood. On each of

his rare trips home from overseas, her father had taken her to Franklin's Wild Animal Park, where tame animals and children wandered unhindered, a place where parents and children could easily get separated.

"Where do you go if you get lost?" her father had asked her each time they went to the park.

"To the bench next to the boathouse by the pond," she would reply—proudly at first, and later, when she was too old to need that kind of reminding, with a trace of annoyance.

The memory of the park drifted, and now she was a child staring out the window of their house in Wellesley, waiting for the mailman to bring mail from her father, wondering when it would arrive and where it would come from. The postcards always showed exotic locales—mountain monasteries, temples, market places—the messages on the back mere descriptions of the scene on the front, no more than she could have gotten from a travel book. There was never a word about him or how he was doing.

Aside from the postcards, the only time she heard from her father was on her birthday and at Christmas, in the form of gifts with terse sentiments attached: "Hope you're well, love, Dad." Even the gifts seemed standoffish —checks drawn on a Boston bank, mail-order items from stores she later realized he'd never been in, probably chosen by a secretary.

For a time she had hoped for more—an actual letter with a return address to which she could respond. Once, she'd tried writing to him in care of the network. The response was a form letter thanking her for her interest and assuring her the letter would be forwarded to Mr. Cameron. There had been no further response.

At the time, she had covered for him, telling herself he was a busy man and that he really did love her. And of course, telecommunications weren't what they are now. If it had been today, they could have kept in touch with e-mail, cell phone and express delivery services.

Express delivery services. Bradley had said an express deliveryman was at the apartment the day before. If her father had received anything, it should still be there.

She searched the obvious places—the kitchen table, the desk where he paid his bills, the bedside stand—but there was nothing. No package, no receipt, nothing. If he'd received a package, he'd already thrown it away.

The wastebaskets then. She checked the kitchen, the living room, the bathroom, but there was no package or receipt. She did find food wrappers, tissues, flyers from newspapers, all of which meant the trash hadn't been taken out yet.

Now her instincts told her something unexpected, something she had been so close to that she hadn't seen it.

It wasn't just that there were no clues here. The clues had been removed. Someone didn't want her to find them.

10

Harvey Warren slammed the phone down and lit another cigarette. So far, his investigation had turned up nothing. One more reason to be in a foul mood.

Warren hadn't been sorry to see Vermont K-9 go when the new search team arrived on the scene; having Darcy Cameron out of the picture was one less thorn in his side.

But then Bradley had called him aside. "Tell your people they can go home as well," she said. "You won't be needed further."

"What?"

She repeated it, sounding like his old high-school teachers when he hadn't been paying attention. "Your assistance is no longer required."

Warren exploded. "Just a goddamn minute. Who the hell do you think you are? This is my town, and I decide when my people are through working a case."

The command post became very quiet. Generally speaking, there was no percentage in trying to intimidate a state police officer.

Bradley stood expressionless. "Are you finished?" she asked.

He glared at her but couldn't think of anything else to say.

"Then let me remind you that state law places responsibility for missing-person incidents with the state police. You will be the first to know when Marshall Cameron is found. Good day."

He had left, but he was damned if he'd put his tail between his legs and let a bunch of outsiders solve the biggest case that had come along in twenty years. This was his town, his case, and he planned to keep working on it. Sure, it looked like Cameron had drowned, but the case wasn't closed until they found a live person or a dead body. And there was still lots of legwork to do.

To begin with, there was the delivery guy that had been seen at the time Cameron disappeared. If nothing else, that person should know something about the old guy's state of mind just before he walked away.

After two decades of police work, tracking down leads was second nature for the chief. His initial research turned up a dozen express companies that delivered to Eastham, including a few he had never heard of before. He'd had to sweet-talk some and browbeat others. More than one thought he was a prank caller and he'd had to assure that them he did indeed mean Marshall Cameron, the broadcaster. So far, none of them indicated they had delivered anything to Cameron that day.

His receptionist rapped on the glass partition between the front desk and his office. "Call for you on line two."

He grabbed the phone. "Warren here."

"Yes, this is General Delivery Services calling in regard to your question about a delivery." The woman had one of those hybrid human-automated voices.

"Right. I need to know if one of your people made a delivery to Marshall Cameron in Eastham on May 19."

"Do you have the confirmation number for that delivery, sir?"

"No, you don't get it." He stubbed out his cigarette in an overflowing ashtray. "I'm not trying to trace a package. I'm trying to figure out if someone from your company was at The Village on the 19th."

"I understand, but in order to locate the package—"

He squeezed the phone as if he were brandishing a mallet. "LISTEN TO ME." Now he had her attention. He could hear her breathing hard on the other end. "This is a criminal investigation." He emphasized each word as if he were speaking to a child with a limited attention span. "Marshall Cameron is missing. A delivery person was seen in the vicinity of his apartment just before he disappeared. I need to know if that person was from your company."

There was a brief pause. "Just a moment, sir."

He counted the seconds, deciding that for every ten seconds he waited, a General Delivery Services van would get pulled over for a "routine safety check" when passing through Eastham.

She returned in thirty seconds. "We have not made any deliveries to The Village in Eastham within the last month, sir."

"Thank you," he said, biting off the words and slamming the phone down.

He reached for the pad on his desk. The neat list of twelve companies had all been crossed off except for General Delivery Services. He drew a line through it and swore softly. Somebody may have come to Marshall Cameron's apartment the day he disappeared. But whoever it was, they weren't from any delivery company.

Jackie Bradley paced the command center. National Rescue Services had been on the scene for two hours and nobody from the group had shown up to take her report yet. They were wasting precious time; every minute that passed decreased the odds of Marshall Cameron being found alive.

She had considered going to them, but decided against

it. Her supervisor had told her flatly that National Rescue Services was taking over all aspects of the search. From now on, her role was to act as a liaison between National Rescue Services and the state police. Liaison, she suspected, was French for "sit around with your thumb up your butt."

More time passed, and it occurred to her that the idiots might be waiting for an invitation. She sent a trooper to tell them the command post was ready for their use.

He returned a minute later. "They said they don't need the room."

"What does that mean?"

"They're set up in that mobile mansion. Anyway, it looks as if they're already out searching. And they're all carrying sidearms."

"They're what?"

"Glocks," the trooper said. "Nice new ones."

Bradley's brow furrowed. Search and rescue personnel sometimes carried small handguns as protection against rabid wildlife, usually light 22-caliber weapons. But the Glock was a serious weapon, a 9mm sidearm that could stop a moose, not to mention a man. She had an image of trigger-happy idiots tromping around her woods and she decided to do something about it. If Mohammed wouldn't come to the mountain, she would go to Mohammed—and make damn sure he had permits for those guns.

In the parking lot where National Rescue Services had set up shop, the black SUVs were parked side-by-side in military precision. Each one was equipped for off-road work, with large mud tires, brush guards, and high-intensity floodlights. Each roof sported at least four antennas, including a large black plastic radome that looked like the carapace of a giant beetle that had fastened itself there.

But the SUVs were nothing compared to the large black van parked off to the side, its roof bristling with antennas. In addition to the familiar whip antennas, there were several small satellite dishes pointing to different areas of the sky and a large, flat antenna that turned constantly. The van looked like an air traffic control center on wheels.

Bradley approached the van and noticed that the logo on its side was a magnetic vinyl stick-on. Odd. Why hadn't they painted it on permanently?

She had only a moment to think about that before the door to the van opened. A tall man stepped out and closed the door behind him. As he did, Bradley glimpsed racks of electronic equipment and computer monitors, people wearing headsets.

He strode toward her as if intending to intercept her before she got any closer. His uniform had been pressed to razor sharpness, gray-black with an American flag and National Rescue Services patches on the arms. A Thales tactical radio hung from his belt—an expensive digital unit that was a far cry from the battle-scarred hand-me-down radios most search and rescue units used.

"Sergeant Bradley," the man said, his hand extended, his mouth not quite forming a smile. "Glad to meet you."

She was caught off guard. He knew her name but she had no idea who he was. "Hello, Mr.—"

"I'm Jack Fredericks, incident commander for National Rescue Services." His grip was iron, and his eyes drilled into hers with an intensity that disconcerted her.

She took a breath. "I've been told to report to you on the status of the search for Marshall Cameron. As of eight hundred hours we—"

"That won't be necessary," Fredericks said. "We've been briefed by your captain."

A kernel of annoyance rose in Bradley's throat, but

she swallowed it. "All right. The command post is cleared out and ready for you to move in."

The man's face was a stone. You could have sharpened knives on it. "Thank you. But as I told your trooper, we won't be requiring it. We have everything we need in our van."

Bradley nodded, feeling like a kid who'd been called to the principal's office and had nothing left to say.

"Now, if you'll excuse me," Fredericks said. He turned and headed back toward the van.

Bradley hesitated, then walked to the rear of the Village Square, where her car was parked out of sight of the National Rescue Services command center. She got in, grabbed one of the radios her searchers had used and set it up to scan a wide range of frequencies for any local signals. With all those antennas on the National Rescue Systems van, she was bound to have hours of good listening.

In seconds, the radio locked on a frequency and a whining burst emanated, like the sound from an old dial-tone modem connecting. That meant they were using digital communications, which made it impossible for ordinary scanners—the kind that were so popular with the public—to listen in.

Fortunately, Bradley's radios were equipped to handle digital signals. She pushed a button to decode the transmission. The sound turned into something like Donald Duck speaking Swahili.

"Bastards." They were using encryption on top of the digital data. There was no way she'd be able to listen in without knowing their encryption code. What the hell was so secret?

She tuned off the radio and drummed her fingers on the dashboard. If things were rotten in Denmark, they were getting downright putrid in Eastham.

Ned Epstein stared at his computer screen. As far as he could tell, National Rescue Services didn't have a web site, headquarters, or even a phone number that was listed. Whoever they were, they kept a low profile.

There was one other source he could check. He dialed a number and the phone rang only once before being answered.

"Lieutenant Baker."

Chris Baker was Ned's second cousin, an investigator with the Massachusetts state police.

"Chris," he said, "It's Ned." He explained about the search for Marshall Cameron.

"The TV guy?"

"That's the one. Anyway, they've got some outfit called National Rescue Services looking for him. But I can't find any information on them."

"Doesn't ring any bells." The sound of fingers clicking on a keyboard drifted over the line. "Hang on."

A moment later Chris came back and said, "Seconics Corporation."

"What's that?"

"The parent company. Out of Chantilly, Virginia."

"Really? The vehicles all had New York plates."

"So what else is new? These days, corporations are buying up small outfits all over the place. Is your station owned by locals anymore?"

No, it wasn't. But Ned decided not to tell Chris about his move to the bustling metropolis of Rutland. "What can you tell me about Seconics?"

"That'll take a minute. Let me call you back."

Ned hung up, pulled out a ragged atlas and opened it to the page for Virginia. Chantilly was located in the northeast side of the state, near Maryland.

As he studied the map, Jack O'Brien appeared in the

doorway. "What are you doing?" It was half question, half accusation.

Ned frowned, trying to look busy. "Background on the Marshall Cameron story."

"Is there something new happening there?"

Ned scrambled. As far as O'Brien was concerned, if a story didn't keep developing, it was dead. The "mysterious new searchers" angle probably wasn't enough to keep it alive, and Ned didn't want to say anything about that until he had more information. The risk of looking like an idiot was too great. "I'm working on an angle—"

"Never mind," O'Brien said, tossing a scribbled memo onto Ned's desk. "Get on this."

The memo read: *Fire. Middleton mill #4.*

The Middleton mill buildings were a series of enormous brick structures that ran along the Otter River on the west side of town. The mill companies were long gone and the buildings now housed offices, storage facilities, a gym and artists' studios.

"Probably some wacko sculptor burning the place down with her acetylene torch," O'Brien said. "Get over there with Granucci and grab some footage."

"You know they're still looking for Marshall Cameron," Ned said.

"Great," O'Brien said, talking over his shoulder as he walked away. "They'll still be looking for him when you come back. They'll probably be looking next week."

Ned grabbed his jacket and headed for the door. Unfortunately, the jackass O'Brien was probably right.

The phone rang and Ned stopped to pick it up.

"Ned, it's Chris."

"That was quick. What'd you find?"

"This Seconics outfit has its fingers in a lot of different pies. High-tech companies, biotech, research labs. They even own a retirement community up in your neck of the woods."

"The Village?"

"That's it."

"That's where the search is happening."

"Makes sense, I guess. They probably brought in their own team to cover their asses, liability-wise."

Maybe, Ned thought. But if that were the case, why hadn't they called in their own team immediately? "Got any contact information for them?"

"No. The basic information on Seconics is all there in the system, but when I try to dig deeper I keep running into a brick wall. The detailed information just isn't there."

"What does that mean?"

"In this neighborhood? It probably means someone doesn't want you to know."

Ned glanced at the atlas again. Chantilly, Virginia was located just outside of Washington, D.C.

11

Typically, a search for a missing person was divided into stages: a quick search of the immediate area surrounding the place last seen, then a more intense search of the area up to a half-mile away. If nothing turned up, you broadened the search area. In the woods, that meant expanding your search area. In a populated area, it meant talking to neighbors.

Map in hand, Darcy drove in a roughly circular route around The Village, stopping joggers to ask if they'd seen an elderly man wandering around, showing her father's photograph to shopkeepers, knocking on doors. The photo brought stares and gasps of recognition, but no one had seen him.

The Eastham Airport was her final stop, three miles from The Village if you took Route 115, a mile if you walked through the woods over a high ridge of granite outcroppings and stunted evergreens. It was a Spartan facility with a single landing strip and a metal-roofed hangar that was hidden from the highway by a stand of old pine. A rust-riddled pickup sat just outside the hangar. Darcy called into the cavernous space. "Hello?"

A voice came from beneath the cowling of a Cessna 182. "Yeah?" The speaker hadn't bothered to look up.

"My name is Darcy Cameron. I'm with Vermont K-9 Search and Rescue." She paused, but the only response was the clack of a socket wrench tightening a bolt.

She forged ahead. "We're looking for an elderly man who wandered away from The Village some time yesterday. Wondering if you'd seen him."

Pause. Another bolt being tightened. "Nope."

She wasn't giving up that easily. "I've got a photograph here, if you wouldn't mind taking a look at it."

There was an audible sigh. A thirty-something man emerged, rubbing the back of his hand against a wispy blonde beard, his long hair pulled back in a ponytail beneath a canvas baseball cap, the name "Roy" stitched onto the pocket of his coveralls

His eyes passed over Darcy quickly as he took the photograph. He studied it for a moment and handed it back with no sign that he'd recognized her father. "Nope. Nobody here yesterday 'cept me." He turned back to his work. "And one plane."

"Who was that?" She had no particular reason for asking, but when you were on a search, any detail might prove useful.

"Dunno."

If she was looking for long, windy answers full of helpful details, she'd clearly come to the wrong man. She'd probably come to the wrong state. But she'd dealt with recalcitrant witnesses before. They took persistence and patience, but in the end they were often more valuable than the talkative ones.

Eventually, with bulldog determination, she learned that the plane—a Mitsubishi MU-2 turboprop—had landed, taxied to the far end of the strip and sat for half an hour, idling. Then it had taken off.

"Where was it headed?"

"Dunno."

The taciturn Yankee routine was really wearing thin. "Don't planes have to file a flight plan?"

"Not here."

More teeth pulling followed. He explained that this was an uncontrolled airport, which meant pilots didn't have to identify themselves or file a flight plan. Planes came and went as they pleased, and anyone hanging around would pay about as much attention as they would to someone pulling into a self-service gas station.

"Why would anyone land here?" Darcy asked.

The mechanic pulled his head out from under the cowl with a weary sigh. "Could'a been a student, practicing." He leaned against the cowl with crossed arms, a gesture that seemed to say, that's all I know, and it took a lot out of me to tell you that much.

"So why did he sit at the end of the runway for half an hour?"

A shrug. "Eating dinner, maybe."

"With the engines running?"

"Takes all kinds." He said it with a shake of his head that encompassed not only the mysterious plane but Darcy as well.

She wanted to bite his head off, tell him the missing man was her father and that he had Alzheimer's. She wanted to grab the socket wrench and bring it down on his thick Yankee skull. But she didn't.

"OK," she said simply. "Just call the police if you see anything?"

"Yep."

Driving back to town from the airport, Darcy considered her options. When a secondary search turned up nothing, you had a few choices. You could go back and search the place last seen one more time. You could broaden the search even further. Or, at some point, you decided to give up the search.

With all the people tromping around The Village,

there wasn't any point in going back there. Meanwhile, the state troopers would have alerted the police departments in surrounding towns to be looking for her father, so the residential areas around Eastham were covered. Beyond that, there were hundreds of miles of forested hills surrounding the town, but the newcomers with their helicopter had the best shot at covering that. There was nothing a single person acting alone could do.

Except quit. And she wasn't ready to do that. She wasn't sure she ever would be.

In her crate, Pepper whined. She was hungry, and Darcy realized they both needed some real food. It was a good thing the dog had to be fed regularly. Some days, it was the only thing that reminded her to feed herself as well.

She turned for home, deciding that a break would also give her a chance to figure out what to do next. For a moment, she thought about stopping at her office but decided against it. If she went anywhere near the place, she'd get caught up explaining to little old ladies why she wasn't working on their wills and then listening to their sympathy about her missing father. She didn't have time for that. If anyone really needed her, they could catch her at home.

She turned west and took Route 118 toward Perkins Pond, a body of water that would have been a lake in any other part of the country. Darcy's place was an old summer home that had been winterized, four rooms and bath. It wasn't anything special, but it was on the lake, it was private, and there was plenty of room for Pepper to run around.

A mile outside of town, traffic came to a stop. At the head of the line were police cars, and Darcy assumed it was an accident until she saw state troopers talking to drivers and walking around their cars.

As she came to the head of the line, a beefy young trooper strolled up to her window. Thanks to the search and rescue work, she had a nodding acquaintance with most of the troopers in this part of the state. And for those who didn't know her, the search and rescue decals on her truck usually guaranteed a friendly response. "What's up?" she asked.

"Good afternoon, ma'am," he said with no sign of recognition. "This is a routine safety check. License and registration, please."

She reached for the registration in the glove box. She knew the real reason for most safety checks was to catch drunks and druggies; she'd had more than a few clients pulled in by them. But the chances of catching anyone drinking in the middle of a weekday afternoon were slim, unless you were looking for ladies with sherry on their breath coming home from a bridge party.

"Kind of an odd time for a safety check, isn't it?"

The trooper ignored the question. "License and registration, please."

Fine, then. She handed over the documents, considered making a crack about not having her usual six-pack sitting on the seat, but decided against it. This guy was clearly not in the mood for jokes.

As he scanned the license and registration, a second trooper walked around the truck, ostensibly looking for missing taillights, bad tires, problems with the plates. But she had a sense he was more interested in what was inside the truck than anything on the outside. And he had a massive German shepherd with him.

That was a first. What was the dog doing at a safety check? She imagined the trooper saying, "This is Barnie, the safety dog. He can smell bad brakes."

No, a dog meant they were looking for drugs, a bomb, or a person. Maybe all three.

The shepherd and his handler finished their circuit and moved on to the next car. The first trooper handed Darcy her papers. "All right, Ma'am. Have a good day."

On a hunch, she said, "Officer, I just realized I left something back at my office. Can I turn around here?"

He nodded and held up a hand to stop traffic while Darcy did a respectful three-point turn. As she did, she noticed a muscular young man in civilian clothing aiming a hand-held device at each car that passed through the traffic stop. A radar gun? Maybe—but why aim a radar gun at cars that were barely moving?

She headed back to town. A half-mile away, she turned onto a side road, a back way home that avoided the highway and the roadblock.

As she crested a hill she saw, at the bottom of the hill, two state police cruisers, stopping traffic. She slowed the car, but her mind raced. Her hunch had been right. This was no safety check, it was a manhunt. They were checking every road out of town.

She took a turn and followed roads that took her back to town. Home and food would have to wait. Someone had some explaining to do.

At breakfast that morning, the manager of the QuikMart had drunk an extra-large coffee. By now, it had worked its way through his kidneys and was sitting in his bladder demanding release. At fifty-five, he'd learned to listen to his bladder when it complained.

He called to a chubby woman who was replenishing the bags of pretzels and chips in aisle two. "Sally, take the register, will you? Gotta go see a man."

"You got it."

He opened the men's room door to find an overflowing wastebasket.

"Damn kids," he muttered. He'd told his workers a

thousand times to empty the wastebaskets when they closed up at the end of the day, but they never remembered. Either that, or they just couldn't be bothered, in too much of a hurry to head home and hop into the sack with their boyfriends or girlfriends. The wastebasket didn't look as if it had been emptied in a couple of days.

First things first. He emptied his own tank with a sigh of relief, then grabbed the overflowing trash can and headed out back.

It was only a few steps around the corner to the dumpster—it wasn't as if he was asking these people to go out of their way to empty the trash. He threw back the top of the dumpster and emptied the basket into it.

At the bottom of the wastebasket was a wadded bundle of gray cloth. He frowned, grabbed a stick and plied it apart carefully—you never knew what kind of crap people threw away these days.

It was clothing, like some kind of uniform—a pair of brownish-gray pants and a matching shirt. They looked brand new.

He shook his head. Why would someone throw perfectly good clothes away in a QuikMart rest room?

Darcy pulled into The Village's driveway and passed Harvey Warren going the other way, spraying gravel as he tore out onto the main road. He didn't look happy.

She found Jackie Bradley in the Village Square conference room, talking on the phone. "Yes, sir," she said. "That's what Chief Warren told me. I have my people checking it out right now."

Darcy wondered what that was about, but decided to deal with one issue at a time.

"What's up?" Bradley asked as she hung up the phone.

"That's what I'd like to know," Darcy said. "What are

the roadblocks about?"

"What roadblocks?"

"All right, the safety checks." She could go along with the charade if she had to.

Bradley crossed her arms over her chest. "I have no idea what you're talking about."

Darcy considered this. The state police had dozens of units. Ordinarily, she wouldn't expect Bradley to know what they were all up to. But this was no ordinary operation.

"There's a roadblock on every single road leading out of Eastham," she said. "Did you really not know about that?"

Bradley frowned, saying nothing.

"Look," Darcy said, "I'm sorry to bother you—"

Bradley held up a hand and shook her head. She turned and stared out the picture window as if she were calculating, putting pieces together. Then she turned back and said, "Wait a minute."

She picked up a radio, strode to the window just out of Darcy's hearing, and made a call.

Even with her back turned, Darcy could tell Bradley wasn't happy with the conversation. When it ended, Bradley stood still for a few seconds, then spun around and strode back to the conference table. "It's a routine safety check," she said.

Darcy slammed a fist onto the table "Jackie, don't give me that. We both know it's bullshit."

Bradley sighed. "What makes you think so?"

Darcy studied her face. She knew Bradley well enough to know it was an honest question.

"It's too coincidental." She hooked a thumb toward the parking lot and the National Rescue Systems van. "First these people show up out of nowhere. No explanation, no information about who they are. The next thing you know, Eastham is closed up tighter than Berlin before the airlifts."

Bradley nodded but said nothing.

"And why's everyone so close-mouthed all of a sudden? The trooper at the roadblock acted as if I were a terrorist. They've got dogs sniffing the cars and some radar device like I've never—"

"What radar device?"

"Black. Hand-held. I tell you, it was like something out of Buck Rogers."

Bradley shook her head. Either she didn't know what the device was or she couldn't believe they were using it on a routine safety check.

"Level with me," Darcy said. "Does this have something to do with my father?"

Bradley looked away, still frowning.

Darcy did her own calculations, the kind she did in court when she was faced with a reluctant witness. It was clear that Bradley was wrestling with something. Whatever she knew, she'd probably been told to keep quiet. And what she didn't know was grating on her. Maybe a little pressure would bring things to a head.

"Talk to me, Jackie. Tell me what's going on. It's my father."

Bradley shook her head. "I don't know what to tell you."

"Fine," Darcy said. She turned and headed for the door.

"Where are you going?"

Darcy kept walking. She didn't know where she was going. Right now, she wanted to scream. She wanted to tear someone's head off. She wanted to call someone up and ream them out.

Then she remembered the TV reporter, Ned Epstein. Where did he say he was from?

She stopped in the doorway and turned back. "You know, maybe I'll call up Channel 7. I bet they'd like an exclusive interview with the daughter of Marshall Cameron. In fact, I'm sure they'd be very interested in all this."

"Darcy—"

"Don't you think it would make a great story? Marshall Cameron, beloved television newsman, is missing. The local search and rescue team has been pulled off the search with no explanation. All roads leading out of town are under surveillance. The state police refuse to comment."

Bradley stared at her, then glanced in the direction of the National Rescue Systems van.

"All right," she said. "Stay here. I'll see what I can do."

12

Bradley reappeared a few minutes later and motioned to Darcy. "Come on."

They walked to the National Rescue Services van, neither of them speaking. Bradley knocked and Captain Barry Anderson opened the door.

Darcy's stomach knotted. Anderson was Bradley's supervisor, the officer in charge of search and rescue operations for the entire state. He rarely showed up at searches, and there was only one reason for him to be here now: Somebody had screwed up royally, and he was here to smooth things over.

Anderson gave Darcy a brief sympathetic smile, like a parent about to tell a child bad news. "Come on in."

He motioned for Bradley to wait outside, and Darcy glimpsed a look on her face that she couldn't quite read—anger, frustration, perhaps worry. The knot in her stomach tightened.

She glanced around, getting her bearings, her eyes adjusting to the dim light inside the van. It was a compact version of the command center the state police had set up back at the Village Center, but with better equipment. There were storage areas, lockers, and a bathroom. A row of infrared night goggles sat on a high shelf—Berkhauser goggles, military instruments that cost $10,000 a pair. These folks weren't holding bake sales to pay for their equipment.

One entire wall was a communications center filled with radios, computer displays, GPS trackers, and miscellaneous electronic devices, including what appeared to be a radar screen. Apparently, this outfit spent time searching in places more remote than Eastham, Vermont.

Toward the rear of the van, two operators worked the radios, conversing with the searchers against a background of electronic beeps and clicking keyboards. They wore headsets that masked the usual buzz of radio traffic and gave the van the air of an operating room where surgeons were conducting intense, complicated surgery.

At the other end, the front of the van was a conference area, with a narrow table in the middle and plush chairs along the sides. Television monitors on either wall flashed aerial images of The Village and the surrounding countryside.

Two men stood at the far end of the table, light from the front window silhouetting them. One wore a dark suit, with a jutting hawk-like nose and a receding hairline. He was doing most of the talking, fierce whispers that Darcy couldn't make out over the background noise. The other man was younger, broadly built, wearing a National Rescue Services uniform.

The one in the suit finally noticed Darcy and Anderson, broke off the conversation and came toward them.

Anderson said, "This is Raymond Devlin. He'll be briefing you."

Briefing you, Darcy thought. What did that mean?

"Ms. Cameron," Devlin said, acknowledging her presence with a handshake and not much else.

"If you'll excuse me," Anderson said, and left.

Darcy frowned. She had expected Anderson—the top ranking official on site—to stick around. She didn't like being left alone to deal with Devlin, whoever he was.

She tried to defuse the tension. "Nice place you've got here."

Devlin glanced around. "Oh, yes." He paused as if he were searching for more to say on the subject, but found nothing. "Have a seat."

Darcy waited until he began to sit before pulling out the chair opposite him. She had played power games before, and wasn't going to get caught in an intimidating position.

The other man, the one in the National Rescue Systems uniform, had already seated himself at the other end of the table. A laptop computer lay open before him, the lines of an electronic topo map snaking across the screen. She suspected he was following the progress of the searchers in real time via their GPS devices and satellite tracking.

"This is Mr. Fredericks," Devlin said. "He's in charge of the search for your father."

Fredericks nodded to her, and Darcy's pulse quickened against her will. His eyes were steel blue and his features seemed to be chiseled out of Vermont marble —Harrison Ford, Pierce Brosnan and Brad Pitt all rolled into one—and she was instantly angry with herself. This was no time for schoolgirl crushes. Her father was still lost. Besides, she didn't want anything distracting her during this conversation.

She turned back to Devlin. "I didn't catch your title."

"I'm the head of the Office of Security. For the Central Intelligence Agency."

Darcy's breath stopped short. "The CIA."

"That's right."

She shook her head. "I don't understand."

Devlin folded his hands together on the polished surface of the table. "You may be aware that the Central

Intelligence Agency is constrained from operating in this country except under very specific, prescribed situations. These include..." He waved a hand, as if the details were not that important, "surveillance of foreign nationals that we have reason to believe are involved in covert operations, monitoring the activities of American citizens known to be in the employ of other nations. And, of course, watching out for the welfare of our friends and associates." With this last statement, he gestured toward The Village.

Darcy stared at him, with the odd sensation that she was watching a not-too-believable movie of the week. There was only one possible explanation for Devlin's mini-civics lesson about the CIA, one that was obvious and fit all the facts—and was totally unbelievable. "Are you telling me my father works for the CIA?"

"No, no," Devlin said, waving a hand.

"Oh, god." Now she felt completely foolish. She had been watching too many movies. "I'm sorry—"

"Your father's service to the country ended years ago."

She nodded slowly. "I see. He's *retired* from the CIA." This was on a par with saying her father was not an alien. Just part alien.

"Exactly."

Darcy sat back against the padded chair, feeling like Alice in Wonderland. The last thing she knew she had been searching for her father. Then she'd fallen into a high-tech rabbit hole where people talked utter nonsense and insisted on being taken seriously.

She considered the options. First, Devlin was kidding. That didn't seem likely. She couldn't believe anyone would joke with the daughter of a celebrity who was missing and whose life was in grave danger.

Option two: Devlin was wrong. Some other Marshall

Cameron had worked for the CIA and there had been a mix-up. Again, unlikely. Government agencies were perfectly capable of screwing up big-time, but this wasn't the kind of mistake they would make, especially with someone as well-known as her father, especially if this really was the CIA.

Which suggested option three: Devlin was lying. These people weren't really with the CIA. But the state police were cooperating with them, and surely they'd know if this was the Mafia, or the IRS, or some reality TV show pulling a stunt.

Which left only one other option.

"This is crazy," she said. "My father is Marshall Cameron. He was a newscaster."

"That's true. And during the early part of his career, he was also an officer in the CIA, operating under non-official cover."

"What is that supposed to mean?"

"It means that if he had been caught, he would not have had diplomatic immunity." He did not elaborate, and the implication was clear: Her father would have been in deep shit if he'd been caught.

"What exactly did he do?"

"I'm afraid that information is still classified. I can say that he assisted various overseas bureaus, that he served with honor and earned the gratitude of his peers and his supervisors." He leaned toward her as if imparting a secret. "Your father was a very brave man. He risked his life in order to serve his country. He is a true patriot."

Darcy wasn't sure how she felt about that. If Devlin was telling the truth, her father was also a liar. And he hadn't just lied to her, he'd lied to the whole country.

She shook her head, as if that would make this nonsense go away. "It's ridiculous. If my father had worked for the CIA, I would have known..."

She stopped. No, she wouldn't have. Given their history, her father could have been the Bishop of Rome and she never would have known.

Suddenly, an entire lifetime of questions, losses, and painful memories made sense—her father's aloofness, his world travels, his obsessive behavior, his inability even now to connect with his only child.

The revelation could also explain her parent's divorce. For most of her life, Darcy had skirted around the reasons for her parents' failed marriage, as if it were a toxic sinkhole that would drag her in if she got too close: her mother was not smart enough for her father, her father had had an affair, or affairs. She recalled the one time she had asked her mother about it. "You'll have to ask your father someday," her mother had said, a statement shaded with ominous overtones.

As Darcy grew old enough to understand the ways of men, her mother's comment grew also, taking on a dark shape at the edge of her mind, a specter hovering in the background whenever she thought about her parents' marriage. Later, her own husband's infidelity only made the specter more real.

And now, the specter vanished. Her father had not committed adultery, he had merely worked for the CIA. And although part of her wanted to cry, she resisted that, and gave in to another reaction that surprised even her. She laughed.

"You're telling me that Marshall Cameron, a man who was watched every night by millions of viewers on national television, was actually a spy?"

Devlin frowned, as if he saw no humor in the situation. "He was not in active service during his years on TimeLine. His service took place before that."

"I see." She considered this for a moment. "I thought the CIA wasn't allowed to use journalists as agents?"

Devlin acknowledged this with a brief nod. "You're familiar with the Church hearings?"

"Somewhat." In the 1970s, the Senate held hearings into the CIA's operations, hearings that led to guidelines prohibiting the use of journalists as CIA operatives. But that was all she knew.

"The guidelines that were issued after those hearings do allow us to employ members of the press under special circumstances, " Devlin said. "Especially freelancers, as your father was at the time."

She considered asking what the special circumstances had been in her father's case, but decided it was pointless to ask. "So what are you doing here?" She waved a hand to encompass the van and its equipment. "What's all this about?"

Devlin nodded again, as if acknowledging the incongruity of the setup. "National Rescue Services is a legally incorporated entity, established to provide rapid response search and rescue services."

"And wholly owned by the CIA."

Devlin shrugged. "The company provides services in situations that are of importance to the national interest."

"How exactly is my father important to the national interest?"

He leaned toward her again. "He's important to us. He's one of ours. And we don't forget our own."

"I see." If Devlin was looking for an apology, she refused to give it. She wasn't going to be intimidated by his self-righteous display of fraternal loyalty.

"Ms. Cameron, let me explain something. Our organization is made up of heroes that no one else will ever know about. There's a wall full of stars in the lobby of our headquarters, each one representing an agent who lost his or her life in the line of duty. Most of those people can't be named in public, for security reasons. Some of them never will be. They may be secret heroes, but they're heroes nonetheless. And we don't forget our heroes."

Darcy could almost hear the national anthem playing in the background.

"Let me ask you something," Devlin said. "You're a search and rescue worker. How many operations have you taken part in?"

She searched his face, wondering where he was going with this. "Dozens."

"And what has your experience of the press been?"

Now she knew what he was driving at. This was about her threatening to go to the newspapers. "I get along fine with the press."

"How do you feel about them being at searches?"

She hesitated, then decided there was no reason not to tell him the truth. "At best, they're simply one more thing to do: bodies to work around, questions that have to be answered."

"And at times..."

He was leading the witness, and they both knew it.

"They're a pain in the ass," she said. To be honest, there were times when the press actually jeopardized the success of an operation. The more newsworthy the search, the more likely the press was to show up in force, getting in the way and obstructing the very search they were supposed to be covering.

Devlin gestured toward the Village Square. "Things seem to have calmed down here. What do you think the reaction would be if word leaked out that your father worked for the CIA?"

In other words, she thought, if you go to the press, the chances of finding your father will diminish even further. Up to you. Your choice.

"And of course," Devlin added, "there is the question

of your father's reputation."

"His reputation?"

"Your father's service to the country was a noble sacrifice. But the average person on the street might not see it that way. The public's opinion of the intelligence community is...complex these days."

Darcy wondered if he was more worried about her father's reputation or that of the CIA. At any rate, he was right about the press. The media had already had a feeding frenzy over her father's disappearance. She could only imagine what they'd do if they found out he had worked for the CIA.

"All right," she said finally. "But I have a couple of questions."

"Yes?"

"What's with the roadblocks?"

Devlin blinked, as if that wasn't a question he had expected. He stared at her for a moment. "Standard procedure. We have to cover every contingency."

"What contingency would be covered by stopping every car that leaves Eastham, Vermont?"

He gave a minimal shrug. "We can't leave anything to chance."

She wanted to ask what "anything" meant, but was afraid of the implication: that her father had not left The Village of his own accord.

"OK, another question. What's with the fancy radar gun your people are using at the roadblocks?"

Devlin frowned. "Radar gun?"

She described it, and Devlin looked to Fredericks at the other end of the table. "Are we using any special equipment at the roadblocks?"

Fredericks looked up from the laptop and shook his head. "Not that I know of."

"Check on it," Devlin said, and turned back to Darcy.

"We'll let you know what we find out. It could be something the state police are trying out."

She studied his eyes. If this guy was lying, he was damned good at it.

There was a knock at the door. Devlin nodded to Fredericks, who went to the door. As he opened it and stepped out, Darcy glimpsed Captain Anderson outside.

He said, "We've just learned..." and the door closed before Darcy could hear the rest.

"Is there anything else I can do for you?" Devlin asked.

Darcy leaned back, the fight draining out of her. In the past thirty-six hours she'd only had a few hours of sleep and those had worn off. She had been running on adrenaline, and now her body was calling in the chips.

She passed a weary hand over her eyes. "What can I do to help?"

Devlin's face took on a concerned look, though even in her weariness she could sense it contained relief as well.

"Go home," he said. "Get some rest. We'll let you know as soon as we have any new information."

She thanked him and left. Fredericks was still talking to Captain Anderson as she stepped out of the van. They stopped, and Anderson gave her a look that said: What do you think?

Darcy shook her head. It was all unbelievable, but she was still digesting it.

"Get some rest," Anderson said.

"OK," she said, deciding that she must really look like hell. Everybody was telling her to get some rest.

She headed for her truck and overheard Fredericks thanking Anderson and returning to the van. As tired as she was, she couldn't help wondering what Anderson had stopped by to tell him.

13

Fredericks stepped back into the Mobile Command Center and Devlin immediately said, "I want to know every move Darcy Cameron makes. I want to know where she eats, where she sleeps, and who she sleeps with." He thumped the table with an index finger to punctuate each demand. "If she sneezes, I want to know about it before her neighbors do."

The caring, compassionate Raymond Devlin had evaporated and Fredericks wasn't surprised. The Cameron woman had basically blackmailed Devlin into talking to her. That wasn't the way to make friends, especially with Raymond Devlin.

Devlin's reputation in the company was legendary. He had begun his career in the CIA as the station chief in Beirut at a time when the region was a mess—civilians being kidnapped, suicide bombings at the embassy and marine barracks, general chaos in the streets. Devlin— who had been a Special Forces commander before coming over to the CIA—was known to be ruthless, vindictive, and unforgiving of anyone who got in his way. He worked ungodly hours and had no personal life to speak of. According to the grapevine, he had campaigned relentlessly to head up the Office of Security. In short, Devlin showed all the signs of a man who was clawing his way to the top: the Director of Central Intelligence.

So what was he doing in Vermont, Fredericks

wondered. Devlin's speech about heroes and "taking care of our own" had been a great performance, and if he didn't know better, he would have believed it himself. But the head of the CIA's Office of Security didn't show up at the search for any old Tom, Dick, or Marshall.

Fredericks had been surprised about the operation from the beginning. To begin with, the Mobile Command Center was intended for overseas work—if some terrorist or nutcase kidnapped a diplomat and held him hostage in the mountains of Turkmenistan, the van and the entire crew could be airlifted there within hours. Fully outfitted, the MCC cost ten million dollars, and only a few agents were even qualified to drive the thing. Sending it to search for a geezer who wandered away from his retirement home—even a famous one—was like using a Rolls Royce to go to the corner store for coffee.

When Fredericks got the call, he had assumed Devlin was simply looking for an excuse to put the van through its paces, a sort of shakedown trip. In that regard, the operation had been a success. The command center was working perfectly. Of course, they hadn't found Cameron, but Fredericks had figured that wasn't the point of the operation anyway. Then Devlin showed up and read him the riot act because Cameron was still missing.

Maybe Devlin's arrival had to do with public relations. If news got out that the beloved Marshall Cameron had once been a spy, there would be hell to pay. The media would be all over it, and old questions about the agency overstepping its bounds would be rehashed and served up all over again. It was just the kind of publicity the agency didn't need, the kind Devlin would want to avoid if he was bucking for the DCI job.

It could also explain why Devlin had showed up without an entourage. Section chiefs rarely went anywhere without a small army of assistants, and Devlin's showing up alone meant he was purposely keeping a low profile. It also meant that Fredericks had to act as his personal lackey.

Devlin gestured to the door, indicating the conference with Anderson. "What was that about?"

"New information. The staff saw an express deliveryman at Cameron's apartment just before he disappeared. But apparently none of the area companies sent anyone to Cameron's apartment that day."

"Idiots. Have them check again."

"The state police just confirmed it. They called every single company. Nothing."

Devlin stared out the van's front window, his jaw working as if he were chewing on a hard nut. "All right. Get a description of the deliveryman and start looking. Post the picture locally, but don't give any details. I don't want anyone to know this is related to the search for Cameron."

Fredericks returned to his laptop to initiate the search for the mystery man and put Darcy Cameron under surveillance. Technically, neither activity was within the scope of his division's mission. But these days, terrorist attacks had all but destroyed the distinction between legitimate and illegal activities.

It was a shift that Fredericks had observed with apprehension. As an undergraduate at Vanderbilt, he had majored in history. His senior thesis had been on the development of police states in the 20th century. He knew all about the secret dossiers of Himmler's *Geheime Staatspolizei*, the Red Terror of Stalin's NKVD and the torture cells of Romania's brutal Nicolae Ceausescu. He was wary of the least sign that such things could ever happen in this country.

He also knew that Raymond Devlin felt no such qualms. Even before the 9/11 attacks, Devlin had a tendency to interpret the agency's mission in the loosest possible terms. He would use whatever methods were necessary to make an operation succeed.

Take, for example, the radar gun that Darcy Cameron had seen at the roadblocks. Fredericks and Devlin both knew it was a Carditect unit, designed by the agency's Office of Technical Service—the folks who had invented the exploding pen, the camera in the tie-tack, the microphone in the fake mole. The Carditect could detect a human heartbeat through metal, wood or concrete, within a range of several hundred feet. It could be loaded with a cardiac "fingerprint" and identify an individual whether they were disguised, drugged, or locked up in a trunk.

There was no good reason to use the Carditect to search for a missing Alzheimer's patient. You used it when you were looking for illegal aliens hidden inside trucks, or maybe someone who had been kidnapped.

So what did Devlin really think had happened to Marshall Cameron?

14

Darcy drove home, barely able to keep her mind on her driving.

Her father had worked for the CIA. And now he was missing. His clothes had been left by the side of a rapidly moving stream, but she felt sure he hadn't drowned. Now the CIA was looking for him, and she had a feeling there was more to this than they were letting on.

Other facts drifted into her mind. Someone had turned off the alarm system the day her father disappeared. Someone had swept his apartment to remove anything that might explain what had happened to him.

The pieces were lining up, like a series of sculptures that, viewed from one angle were merely vague shapes, but from another angle combined to form a clear image— a figure perhaps, or an animal of some kind. In this case, the facts of her father's disappearance were lining up and she could no longer push the emerging image from her mind.

Someone had kidnapped him.

She breathed deeply, trying to control her fear. Her instincts told her he was still alive. If they had merely wanted to kill him, if this was revenge for some long ago grievance, they would have done so by now. Instead, they had taken him somewhere.

But why?

Money? That seemed the most likely motive. She

didn't know how much money her father had. He'd been as circumspect about that as everything else in his life. But the network and the media conglomerate that owned it had extremely deep pockets indeed. Would they be willing to pay a ransom to save her father's life?

She wondered about the value of his life now that he was no longer an asset to them. Would the bottom line justify paying ransom for an aged newscaster when there was a new crop of starlets, Hollywood hunks and porcelain-toothed talking heads to look after?

A dark thought drifted into her mind. What if the kidnappers weren't the ordinary, garden variety? What if they were terrorists, planning to use her father as a symbol of the American media, or America itself? She saw an image of her father, unshaven, haggard, red-eyed, sitting on a plain chair, staring at a video camera.

She forced the thought from her mind. She didn't want to imagine what might come after that. She preferred to believe that these were just domestic criminals, and even found some comfort in the thought. But if that were the case, they would be contacting her soon. How would they go about it? And what would she do when they did? Could she tell the police or CIA without endangering her father? How much money would they want, and could she collect it without alerting the authorities?

The questions played themselves over in her mind repeatedly, like flash cards that she wasn't allowed to see the back of. Finally, exhaustion and worry overtook her and she fell asleep on the sofa, expecting the phone to ring at any moment.

That evening, Fredericks held a conference with his searchers—all of them CIA staff—in the command center.

"I'll make this brief," he said as they settled around the table. "We have new information."

He relayed the news about the express deliveryman and the calls to the companies in the area. The searchers absorbed the information like robotic sponges. He wouldn't have to tell them twice.

"So far, an intensive search of the river has turned up nothing. There's every possibility that the clothes left by the side of the stream were put there purposely to mislead us."

The searchers said nothing, but Fredericks knew their pulses were quickening. This was why they'd joined the service, to hunt for bad guys, not to chase some old celebrity around the woods.

"So now we've got a different kind of search. We have to work on the assumption that Cameron may not have left The Village on his own accord."

He entered a command on his laptop and the monitors over their heads came to life with maps of the town of Eastham. Concentric circles radiated out from The Village, encompassing the entire town and the national forest that surrounded it.

"We will maintain a limited presence here at The Village. But from now on, the search area has been expanded, as well as the object of the search."

From a folder, he pulled out a pencil sketch of the delivery man based on the description provided by The Village's staff. "We'll continue our search for Marshall Cameron. But we'll also be looking for this man."

Later, the MCC van was quiet, lit only by dim track lighting and the glow from Fredericks' laptop. Half the team had changed into civilian clothes and checked into the Tarry-Awhile Motel, a row of tired vacation cabins in Eastham that had yet to be spruced up for the season—far from the most comfortable of accommodations, but if they were called into action overseas, they'd see worse. And the middle-aged woman who ran the place didn't ask any questions about what they were doing in Eastham during the off season.

The rest of the team kept working, thanks to night-vision goggles, infrared technology and GPS units. Fredericks had found Devlin a room at the Eastham Inn, a historic tavern listed on the National Register. That wasn't the Hyatt Regency either, but it was big enough for a traveling businessman to pass unnoticed, and at least Devlin could get a drink if he wanted to. Fredericks suspected he would need one.

Devlin had been on edge since they'd gotten the report about the deliveryman, pacing the command center, barking demands for updates. But he hadn't done any of the things Fredericks would have expected him to do in a case like this: checking up on Cameron's history, finding out what cases he had worked on and whose paths he might have crossed. Those were the questions that needed answering if someone else was involved in the disappearance of Marshall Cameron, as appeared to be the case.

But who? That question overshadowed the mystery of Devlin's behavior. Why would anyone care about an old, retired newscaster—or an old, retired CIA operative, for that matter? In the intelligence field, things changed so fast that kidnapping a retired officer would be like stealing an old personal computer—everything about it was bound to be obsolete. Of course, even an old computer could hold important information, but Frederick's instincts told him this wasn't the case here.

No, if someone had kidnapped Marshall Cameron, there had to be another motive, maybe a personal one. Revenge? That was possible—even the most unassuming desk-jockey in the service could become involved in cases that created enemies, extremely nasty ones at times. But it was hard to believe anyone would engineer something this complicated simply for revenge. If that was the motivation, why not simply take the target out—a bullet in the back of the head or a quick cord around the neck?

Ransom, then. Maybe Cameron had been abducted merely because he was famous and the kidnappers didn't know about his service with the government. If that were the case, his team merely had to sit back and wait to be contacted about a ransom—and the kidnappers would find that they'd stuck their hands into a beehive more deadly than they could ever have imagined.

But logic told Fredericks that Cameron's disappearance wasn't motivated by money. If he were being held for ransom, why had the kidnappers worked so hard to make it look as if he wandered away on his own?

No, whoever caused Marshall Cameron to disappear must have had other reasons, but Fredericks was damned if he could think of what they were. It was a giant puzzle and Fredericks had a love/hate relationship with puzzles: He loved completing them and hated being stumped by them. Presented with a brainteaser, his mind would not let it go until he had a solution. And the Marshall Cameron case was a definite stumper.

15

The clock read 4:30 a.m. when Darcy finally gave up the pretense of trying to sleep. She rose, then fed and walked Pepper. By then it was 5:30, still early. She decided to go to the office and see what kind of shambles it was in.

The office was a high-ceilinged suite overlooking Main Street, in a building that was once a bank. She carved a slice of bare desk from the piles of papers to be filed, pulled out a legal pad, and checked her answering machine messages.

Darcy's practice combined all the worst aspects of a large and a small firm—it was exhausting, frustrating, and the money sucked. She had expected small-town law to be nobler than the corporate version she'd left behind, picturing herself as a legal James Herriott, helping storybook Yankees with their amusing legal dilemmas. The reality had proven different. Her new clients were a mixture of the usual human traits—greed, nobility, fear, hope, jealousy—combined in a range of characters from the living saint to the complete bastard.

In a way, she loved them all, even the bastards. At least in Eastham, everyone knew who the bastards were and dealt with them accordingly, in contrast to her old life, where the bastards were witty, urbane and capable of convincing you that the sharp sensation you felt between your shoulder blades was just a friendly pat on the back.

She listened halfheartedly to the messages on the machine, sighed and pushed the pad aside, bowing to the inevitable. She would never be able to focus on work until she got some word about her father.

She glanced at her watch. It was still only 6:30. She hadn't eaten anything, and she wasn't hungry, but the diner was just around the corner. It was something to do.

The entryway to the diner was plastered with notices for dances, spaghetti dinners and pickup trucks for sale. Thumb-tacked over these was a freshly photocopied sketch of a middle-aged man with dark, receding hair. Anyone who had seen him was urged to call the phone number at the bottom of the page. There was no other explanation.

As she studied the poster, a woman called her from behind the counter. "Darcy, sweetie. C'mere."

It was Gloria Westervelt, a fixture at the Eastham Diner. Gloria was a stout, middle-aged blonde who refused to go gray, coloring her hair with something that left an orange sheen under the harsh lights of the diner. She stood in the space between the two halves of the counter, arms extended to Darcy.

"How you doin'?" Gloria said and threw her arms around Darcy. Gloria had once been married to a jerk who saw her as the solution to his gambling and drinking problems. Darcy had helped her escape, and Gloria had treated her like a second daughter ever since.

"I'm OK," Darcy said and took the stool nearest the cash register. "I could use some coffee."

Gloria poured a black stream into a cup. "Any word?"

"Nothing yet."

"Oh, sweetie." She put a hand on Darcy's arm. "Don't worry. They'll find him."

The man on the next stool turned to Darcy. "You still looking for your old man?" It was the mechanic from the airport, Mr. Helpful.

"Yes," she said, trying hard not to frown at him.

"Sorry I couldn't help. Didn't know it was your old man."

She hadn't expected the change in his attitude, and it touched her. Even the rock-ribbed Yankees were becoming sympathetic. She nodded, a lump rising in her throat.

"I did find out something," he said. "Don't know if it could help."

Her mind cleared instantly. "What?"

"That turboprop? The one I didn't know where it came from?"

She fought the urge to grab him by the throat and shake the information out of him. "What about it?"

"Charlie Emerald saw it too. Said he noticed the tail number 'cause it was the same as his son's initials."

Gloria refilled the mechanic's cup. "What a coincidence, huh?"

"Yup. C, H, E—same as Charlie's. The kid is Charlie junior, and the tail number was CHEJR. Weird, huh?"

"Wow," Gloria said. "He ought'a send that into Ripley's Believe It or Not."

"Yeah, but it's not like his son was on the plane or anything. He just noticed it because it was the same—"

Darcy grabbed his arm. "What was the license again?"

"C, H, E, J, R. The C means it was a Canadian plane."

Darcy jotted the numbers on a napkin and stuffed it into her jacket. "Gloria, put that on my tab." She headed for the door.

"Aren't you going to eat?"

"Later."

It hadn't taken long for Fredericks to assemble a background report on Darcy Cameron, the outlines of which he read to Devlin; Devlin could never be bothered to read reports himself.

"Darcy Cameron, thirty-two years old," Fredericks said. "Daughter of Marshall Cameron and Barbara Hampton Cameron, socialite, deceased. Parents divorced when she was eight years old. Educated at Philips Exeter, Tufts, and Yale Law School."

"Good grades?" Devlin asked.

"Very good." Far better than his own had been, in fact. "After graduating she joined the law firm of Lessard, Sterling and Jacobs in Boston."

"Track record?"

"So-so," Fredericks said. "Apparently, she was drawn to the tough cases—liability cases against corporations poisoning water supplies, workers' rights, that kind of thing." Those probably weren't the kinds of cases that would help a person climb the legal ladder, nor was there a lot of money in them. "Her husband worked for the same firm. They were married for three years."

"Happily?"

"For a while." From what his researchers were able to learn, the Cameron-Pointer marriage had been outwardly successful—matching BMWs, vacations in Provence, and private secretaries who cared for their every need. In the case of Darcy Cameron's husband, apparently that meant *every* need.

"Where is he now?"

"Still with the firm. But now he's a partner." In contrast to Ms. Cameron, her ex-husband had focused on the more profitable aspects of corporate law. The choice had paid off, apparently.

"And she moved to Vermont."

"Right. She runs a small, not very successful practice in Eastham. A mix of domestic, criminal and small-time liability work. Takes on more than her fair share of child guardianships for wards of the state, spousal abuse cases, farmers fighting government bureaucracy."

"She can't be making much money at that," Devlin said, and Fredericks wondered if he heard a note of disdain.

"No, not according to her tax returns." Still, as far as Fredericks could determine, Darcy Cameron paid her bills on time, didn't run large credit card balances, and didn't overcharge her customers. "She writes checks to the Girl Scouts, Salvation Army, United Way, Eastham Animal Shelter—"

"Basically, anyone with their hand out."

"It looks that way."

"What does she do when she's not working?"

"Active member of the Vermont K-9 Search and Rescue team and not much else." Apparently, whatever spare time and energy Darcy Cameron had left at the end of the day went into the search and rescue team. It was a non-profit, volunteer organization, but its members appeared to be well-trained and dedicated to the work. They also paid for most of their own equipment, which was not cheap. Fredericks imagined they hadn't been happy to be pulled off the search for Marshall Cameron, and he couldn't blame them. These were clearly good people.

"What about her social life?" Devlin asked.

"None to speak of."

"Dating anyone?"

"Apparently not." Although she had dated a few times after moving to Vermont, her social life seemed to be dormant at present. Fredericks imagined it wasn't easy for a woman of her caliber to find suitable company in Eastham, Vermont.

"Is she a lesbian?"

"Not that I know of." It would never occur to Devlin

that a woman might not be dating simply because she didn't feel like it, or because there were no available prospects. If Darcy Cameron had a partner it was, to all intents and purposes, her dog. He decided not to mention that to Devlin, whom he didn't expect to understand the bond between a dog and its owner.

"All right," Devlin said. "Keep watching her."

Diane Schecter, in-coming charge nurse on the surgical floor at Eastham Community Hospital, took notes as the night nurse gave her report.

"Room 214, Mrs. Anderson, complications following appendectomy..."

It was the usual mix of post-op and medical patients: hip replacements, pneumonias, infected wounds, patients who would sleep through a hurricane and others who demanded their pain medication every four hours on the dot.

"Room 218," the night nurse said. "Mr. Adams, fifty-five year old man in for observation." She shook her head. "He's a strange one."

"Yeah?"

"Came in the night before last from the ER. He was crossing the road out by the highway and got hit by some kid in a Volkswagen. I'd sure like to know how a teenager can afford to drive a new Beetle."

"How's he doing?"

"A little shaken up. He just got his license and it's his first—"

"The *patient*," Schecter said, wondering how some people ever got to be a charge nurse.

"Oh. He's fine. Vital signs stable throughout the night. No signs of concussion. He's pretty quiet, hardly made a peep all night. I think he might be foreign."

"Why's that?"

"He hardly speaks when you talk to him. It's like he's ashamed of his English and doesn't want to say the wrong thing. Anyway, Dr. Beronis says he can be released this morning if he's stable. Just make sure he checks with billing before he goes. I guess he doesn't have insurance."

Schecter finished taking the report and did her rounds. She walked into room 218 and was surprised to find Mr. Adams up and dressed, sitting in a chair by the window and peering around the edge of the drapes.

"Well, good morning. Aren't you the early bird?"

He turned slowly, eyeing her. Despite a receding hairline, he was a handsome man, with a ruddy complexion and piercing dark eyes.

"I'm Diane Schecter, I'll be your nurse this morning," she said, swiping the digital thermometer across his forehead.

He nodded, still silent.

"Cat got your tongue, huh?"

No response. He turned to look out the window.

OK, she thought, be that way. She took his blood pressure and typed his vital signs into the digital chart, a brief document with sketchy details of the accident and no previous medical history. He must not have been from the area—if he had been, the computer would have included it automatically.

Fingers poised over the laptop she said, "How are you feeling now?"

"Fine."

It wasn't much, but it was a start. "No dizziness, no pain anywhere?"

He shook his head, lapsing back into silence as she skimmed the report from the radiation department. His right leg had been bruised in the accident and they had x-rayed it, but apparently nothing was broken.

She slapped the laptop shut. "All right then. The

doctor says you can leave if you're feeling OK. Would you like us to call someone for you?"

Another shake of the head.

Schecter sighed. Maybe he didn't have anyone to call. But if he wasn't going to communicate with her, there wasn't much she could do. Besides, she had other patients to attend to.

"OK, then. Let me get a wheelchair and give you a ride out. We'll have to stop at the billing office on the way so you can make some arrangements with them."

The wheelchairs were stored in the utility room at the other end of the hall. She grabbed a chair and was headed back when a physical therapist stopped her to talk about another patient. When they had finished, Schecter spun the wheelchair down the hall into room 218. "Here we go."

The chair by the window was empty.

"Mr. Adams?"

The bathroom door was closed. She leaned an ear against it. "Are you in there?"

She knocked, but there was no response. She opened the door. It was a shared bathroom and the door to the next room, which was vacant, stood open.

She stepped out of the room. The hallway was empty. Behind her, at the far end of the hall, the fire door to the stairway closed with a soft thunk. She turned, too late to see who it was.

That afternoon, when her shift ended, Diane Schecter stopped at the market to pick up broccoli for supper. She had not given much thought to Mr. Adams—it had been a busy day, with three patients going to surgery and returning—but now she couldn't get him off her mind. There had been something mysterious about him, his manner, and the way he had skipped out without talking to the billing department.

She had called security, but they hadn't seen anyone leave the building—not that those dimwits would have noticed if a pink elephant walked out of the hospital.

As she left the store, she passed a bulletin board by the door that held posters for flower shows, choir concerts, the stock car races in Chester. Tacked over the posters was a pencil drawing of a man.

She stopped to examine it closer. It was not a great likeness, but there was no mistaking it. It was Mr. Adams.

Fredericks was at the hospital within fifteen minutes. He scanned the chart of the missing patient while the chief radiologist pulled up the man's x-rays. At first, the hospital's administrator had been reluctant to give Fredericks access to the records, citing privacy concerns. Those concerns evaporated when Fredericks put him on the phone to Devlin. The color drained from the administrator's face, and Fredericks could only imagine what kind of consequences Devlin was threatening him with. He hung up and told Fredericks they'd help in any way possible.

The patient's chart didn't reveal much. George Adams, if that was his real name, had been an amazingly healthy individual who apparently dropped out of the sky just before being clipped by a car as he crossed Route 115 near the QuikMart gas station.

There was a knock at the door. The administrator entered with Devlin behind him. "Here we are," the administrator said, the picture of the helpful public servant. "This is Dr. Kazarian, the head of our—"

Devlin brushed past him and said to Fredericks, "Is it the same person?"

"We're not sure yet. The nurse's description matches, but there wasn't much else to go on. We're just looking at his x-rays."

The radiologist pressed a button. An x-ray of a leg appeared on the large computer screen. "This is Mr. Adams' right leg," he said, tracing the long bones with a finger. "You can see there were no breaks, no fractures."

Devlin pointed to a pattern of white fragments just below the knee. "What's this stuff?"

"Hard to say. Metal obviously, from some traumatic event. Could be shrapnel from an explosion."

"Pull up the other file," Fredericks said.

A second x-ray appeared in a split screen beside the first. This one was also a leg, but it appeared to have been taken on a different system.

"Can you correlate them?" Fredericks asked.

The doctor typed a command. The images disappeared, then reappeared one line at a time, from top to bottom.

"What the hell's it doing?" Devlin asked.

"This is image correlation software," the radiologist said. "It's similar to fingerprint analysis. You give it two digital images and the software compares them on a number of parameters. Then it gives you a correlation index. The higher the index, the more likely it is that the two images represent the same object."

His voice betrayed the delight of a man with a new toy. Image correlation software wasn't cheap, and Fredericks figured this guy had a lot of pull in the hospital. In an area full of wealthy retirees, anyone who did hip and knee replacements was probably a very busy man.

With a soft beep, the software completed its task. A line at the bottom of the screen flashed: "98% correlation."

"So what does that mean?" Devlin asked.

"It means these x-rays came from the same person,"

the radiologist said. "98% is about as close to absolute certainty as the program gets."

Devlin pointed to the second x-ray. "Where did this come from?"

"One of our own people," Fredericks said. On a hunch, he'd requested the digital file from headquarters and had it uploaded directly into the hospital's system. "It was taken in a hospital in Lebanon. The agent was caught in a fight between warring factions and took shrapnel from a home-made hand grenade."

Devlin leaned closer to the screen, his face red, the veins in his neck standing out. "It's one of our own? Who?"

Fredericks pulled out the drawing of the delivery man they'd been searching for. His hunch had been correct. The hairline was higher and darker, the mustache gone, the nose larger—putty perhaps. It was amazing that such small changes could make such a big difference. But now that he knew, it seemed obvious.

He studied Devlin's face, watching for his reaction. "Marshall Cameron."

16

John Wagner's private line rang, awakening him from the cat nap he was taking at his desk. "Yes?"

"Good afternoon, Senator."

Wagner frowned. He was getting tired of hearing bad news from Devlin. "What is it?"

"The situation has changed. It appears that our man did not simply wander off. Nor was he abducted."

"What the hell does that mean?"

"At this point, Senator, we suspect that he engineered his own disappearance."

"He what?"

"He faked his disappearance." Devlin reconstructed the scenario based on the information they'd collected: the clothes by the water, the phony delivery man, the accident on the highway, the hasty departure from the hospital.

"Why would he..." Wagner stopped.

"I think you know why, Senator." He let that sink in for a moment. "Of course, there is another explanation."

"What's that?"

"Given his behavior, there's a very good chance that he was, at some point in time, compromised."

"What makes you think so?"

"He's certainly behaving like a man who has something to hide."

Wagner considered the implications of that for a moment. "That makes things simpler, doesn't it?"

"I suppose it does, Senator."

The voice on the phone, from a small airport north of Toronto, was filled with Canadian courtesy, but was nonetheless firm. "Sorry, miss. Much as I wish I could help you, that's confidential information. I hope you'll understand that the privacy of our clients is as important to us as it is to you."

Darcy stared at the bookcase of dusty law tomes across from her desk and paused. She was getting a headache and couldn't bring herself to snap into attorney mode and push back. Besides, her instincts told her that she'd reached the limit of this particular dead-end alley. "I understand. Thanks for your time."

"G'day, miss."

She hung up the phone and rubbed her eyes. She'd spent several hours wandering the nooks and crannies of the Internet and finally tracked the turboprop's registration down to a small Canadian air charter company. And then she'd hit a wall.

Aeroflights Limited refused to tell her what their jet was doing in Eastham. She did learn that the company was small, with a fleet consisting of a dozen very expensive, very fast aircraft, including several Learjets. Charter operations of this type, especially those outside the United States, catered to clients with very big bucks. Renting a private jet cost thousands of dollars an hour and there were a limited number of clients who considered that to be pocket change. Darcy had the feeling that it was also a business where few questions were asked, or answered.

She bounced the eraser end of a pencil on her desktop. Maybe the turboprop's appearance at the exact time her father disappeared was a coincidence. There were plenty of wealthy retirees in Eastham who sat on the boards of corporations. Maybe the jet was supposed to pick someone up for a meeting. But if that was the case, why hadn't they made their flight?

She bounced the eraser a few more times, then picked up the phone and punched out a number.

"Will? It's Darcy Cameron."

Will Webster was a recluse who lived north of town in a cabin heated by wood and solar energy. He was also, paradoxically, a four-star hacker. Will's computers ran off his own generators and his connection to the Internet was via satellite. Darcy had gone to bat for him several times in cases involving town ordinances, the IRS and a patch of cannabis that mysteriously appeared in the state park a mile from Will's cabin. He owed her.

"What's up?" Will said.

"I'm trying to track down some information." She told him about the Aeroflights plane and their reticence to share its flight plan.

"Shouldn't be a problem. Might take me awhile. But I'll get back to you."

As she hung up, her cell phone chirped the arrival of a text message. She tensed. At this point, any news could be good news, or the worst possible news.

The message was brief, from an unknown caller. She stared at it, her pulse racing. For a moment, she considered the possibility that it was a joke. But that was impossible—even if anyone were that cruel, there were only two people on the planet who would even understand the message.

Where do u go if u get lost?

Across the street from Darcy Cameron's office, a grizzled Yankee sat behind the wheel of a battered Chevy S10 pickup. He adjusted the earpiece to the eavesdropping device—which had been disguised to look like a hearing aid—and glanced up at the window to the office.

It had been laughably easy to plant the bugs. Both Darcy Cameron's home and office had simple doorknob locks that had opened in seconds. After that, it had taken only a few minutes to plant the listening devices on her phones and in strategic locations around her home and office.

Then they began listening. They had expected her father to get in touch with her, but so far there had been little activity in the office, just the ticking of a clock and the tapping of her fingers on the computer keyboard. The phone conversation with the aircraft charter company had been interesting, but didn't seem related to her father. Still, the folks back in the van would check it out. They were following everything she saw or typed on her computer, thanks to what looked like a TV antenna on the roof of the building across the street. The antenna tapped into the radio-frequency energy of Darcy Cameron's computer monitor, transforming it into, essentially, a low-powered TV station broadcasting a live picture to a very limited audience.

Through his earpiece, the agent heard the unmistakable sound of a text message arriving on her cell phone. That wasn't something he could intercept, but he was sure the command center van's frequency sweeping equipment would pick it up.

There was silence for a moment, then a rush of activity in the office. A minute later, Darcy Cameron and her dog rushed out of the street-level door. They sprinted to her truck and she pulled out with barely a glance to see if there was any traffic coming.

The agent tapped a VFW pin on his flannel shirt. "Delta three to base. Little Bird is in motion."

Darcy broke every speed limit driving to Williston

Park, the only park in Eastham with a pond. She dared anyone to try pulling her over.

Where do you go if you get lost? To the bench next to the boathouse by the pond.

The parking area was dotted with cars—an SUV with a "My child is an honor student" bumper sticker, a small blue sedan, an electrician's van.

She peeled into a space, hopped out and jogged with Pepper toward the pond.

The boathouse was a small wooden building with green doors. Beside it was a dark green two-sided bench, one side facing the pond, the other the park. Both sides were empty.

Darcy fell onto the bench, breathing hard, and scanned the park. Two mothers talked as their children played on a swing set. A lunchtime jogger passed on the path that wound around the pond and into the woods. In the parking lot, a young man in the electrician's truck gnawed on a sandwich.

Pepper, tail wagging, stared up at Darcy. "Sorry girl. Can't play now. We still have to find Marshall."

Pepper collapsed at her feet. A noise came from behind and Darcy glanced over her shoulder. An elderly man shuffled out of the woods, a dusty overcoat clutched around him, misshapen fedora pulled down over his forehead. He walked unsteadily toward the bench and Darcy beamed telepathic signals: Don't sit down. I'm waiting for someone. Don't sit down.

The man lowered himself onto the other side of the bench, facing the pond. Go away, she pleaded. Her father might not show up if he saw anyone else there. She considered asking the man to leave, but she couldn't bring herself to do it. What kind of person would kick an old man off a bench?

Pepper stood, tail wagging, and moved as if to

investigate the stranger. Darcy yanked her leash. "No, girl."

Pepper whined and strained at the leash. Before Darcy could scold her again, the stranger spoke.

"Hold the dog."

A split second of annoyance evaporated, her heart pounding. She knew the voice.

"Don't turn around," her father said. "And don't speak."

Darcy fell back against the bench, her heart racing.

"Don't nod, or shake your head, or do anything to acknowledge that I'm talking to you. Let me do the talking. If you want to say anything, say it to the dog."

If she wanted to say anything? There were a hundred things she wanted to say, a thousand. She leaned forward and scratched Pepper behind the ears. "Are you all right?"

"You mean, am I in my right mind? Yes."

She had meant more, but he'd read her correctly, answering the question she couldn't ask. And now she knew. He knew what he was doing, had known all along.

"You planned this whole thing," she said.

His silence was confirmation.

Slowly, the pieces fell into place. The alarm mysteriously turned off. The missing delivery man. The neatly piled clothes. "That's why there was no trail from the clothes to the water," she said, thinking aloud. "You walked back along the same path just to fool the dogs."

There was no answer. A paper bag rustled and she turned her head enough to see a handful of bread crumbs fly out from his side of the bench.

"I didn't want to drag you into this," Cameron said. "And I couldn't take a chance that you'd find out and tip someone off, even accidentally."

A squirrel darted cautiously down from a nearby maple, assessing the crumbs.

Darcy scratched the top of Pepper's head. "Please—just tell me what's going on."

"I can't. It's a long story and I don't have much time."

"If you mean about working for the government"—somehow, she couldn't bring herself to mention the CIA, as if even now it was too unbelievable—"I already know."

"Then you know this is serious. I have to get out of here, and I need your help. By now, they'll have the area sealed. If I try to leave by the normal routes, they'll know."

She was about to accuse him of being paranoid when she remembered the radar device at the roadblock. "What makes you think they're after you?"

The bag rustled again and more bread crumbs flew. "I can't tell you that. You're in too much danger as it is."

"Me? Why?"

"I don't expect you to understand. Just trust me. You're being followed."

"That's crazy. I'm not—"

"Look around. It could be anyone. Those women at the swing. The young man in the van. The red pickup that just pulled in. Maybe all of them."

Darcy scanned the park, frowning. "Why would they follow me?"

"To get to me."

"And why are they after you?"

"Because I know things."

It was a line from a second-rate spy movie, and if she hadn't been so tense she might have laughed. "What kind of things?"

"I can't tell you."

She wanted to throttle him. It was like talking to a Magic 8 ball.

"I don't expect you to understand," he said. "But the less you know, the better."

"What else is new?" She'd never really known her father. The fact that he thought he was protecting her didn't make that any easier.

Still petting Pepper, she said, "So what do you want?"

"I need your help. I have to get out of here and I can't do it alone."

"How do you propose to do that?"

"I'll come to your house tonight. They'll be watching the road. But they won't be watching the lake."

What was that supposed to mean? A midnight row across the lake? A mad dash through the woods to the next town? The whole thing was crazy. She had just spent the last two days looking for him, and now he wanted her help getting lost again. "And just where did you plan to go?"

"Somewhere they can't find me."

"Such as?"

Silence.

"Were you at least planning to contact me when you got there?"

Silence.

She leaned back, rubbing her temples. What was she supposed to do? Her father was asking for help. He seemed to be in his right mind. And there wasn't much time. But it was all so incredible. If she hadn't met the others, she'd think her father was completely delusional. She wanted to call someone and ask for help with the million-dollar question. But there was no one to phone. She had to make this decision on her own.

"Can I ask you something?" she asked.

"Yes."

"Do you really have Alzheimer's?"

"What do you think?"

What did she think? What was she supposed to think? Could a man who was unbalanced pull off a stunt like this? Alzheimer's victims could fool you, but an escapade like this took long-term planning. It wasn't something you could do spontaneously.

She played back the tape of her father's life at The Village: the occasional memory lapses, the all-too-typical symptoms of early Alzheimer's. The ashtray in the refrigerator. They were classic signs, just what you might find in a textbook. And then she knew. It was possible.

"How long have you been planning this?"

"Ever since they bought The Village."

"Who?"

"The company."

"Which company? The network?"

"No. The agency."

"The CIA? You're telling me they own The Village?"

"They do now. They bought it after I moved in. Or one of their paper corporations did."

"What makes you think that?"

"It doesn't take a great deal of skill to learn that kind of thing."

It sounded like the height of conspiracy thinking. Next, he'd be claiming the CIA was broadcasting messages to a metal plate in his brain. "And you're saying they bought the place just because you moved in? To keep track of you?"

"You have no idea what they're capable of."

That was true. This was all new to her, and she was flying by the seat of her pants, trusting her instincts.

The last of the bread crumbs flew.

"Will you help me?"

Decision time. She took a deep breath. "All right."

"Good. You leave first. Look at your watch as if you had been expecting someone and then go. Don't look back after you get up. Spend the rest of the day doing whatever you would normally do. When you go to bed tonight, don't leave any lights on. I'll arrive after dark."

"All right."

"There's one more thing."

"What's that?"

A breeze came up off the pond, rustling the bread bag. "If I don't make it," he said, the sound muffled by the wind and the noise of the bag, "If anything happens to me, it's because of Al Beaker."

She wasn't sure she'd heard him clearly. "Who—"

"And don't say anything to Darcy about this. When she's old enough, you can explain it to her."

Her breath caught in her throat. "What?"

"Tell her I love her. Tell her I did it for her sake, because I never wanted them to be able to use my family against me. And Barbara?"

She took a deep breath to steady herself. Barbara was her mother's name. "What?"

"Tell her I'm sorry."

With that, her father's tale collapsed like a house of cards, a mirage that dissolved as it was approached. And she had almost believed it. She felt sick, as if someone had punched her in the stomach.

"Did you hear me? Tell Darcy I'm sorry."

"I'm sorry too," she said. She stood and tugged on Pepper's leash. "Come on, girl."

Without looking back, she walked to the parking lot, scanning the vehicles there. The electrician's van had left. More mothers and children had arrived. But a red pickup was parked at the edge of the lot, and she realized she'd seen it outside her office that morning.

The driver looked up from his newspaper as she approached. "Howdy."

"Do you work for them?"

"Beg pardon?"

"Skip the cornball farmer routine. Do you see the man

on the bench?"

He looked past her. "Yeah?"

"That's my father."

She turned, following the agent's gaze to the bench, where her father looked at her with an expression that combined anger and sorrow. It was a look that said: You just killed me.

17

Senator Wagner stuck his head in Jane Chandler's office. "Quitting time. Let me buy you a drink."

Chandler glanced at her watch. 7 p.m. She usually didn't leave the office till 9 at the earliest. But when the boss said it was time to quit, it was time to quit. And something told her this wasn't the usual after-work bull session.

The early primaries had gone well. Wagner had pulled well ahead of McCallister. She had stopped listening in on the mystery phone calls—she didn't want to know about missing people, or bodies, or what this had to do with Senator John Wagner—but she had learned to recognize the signs: the call on the private line, the closed door, the distracted look on Wagner's face.

Then, suddenly, the calls stopped. Wagner was his cocky, overconfident self again. Apparently the storm had passed, whatever it was. Chandler just hoped that was the end of it.

Meanwhile, there was work to be done—a campaign to win, appointments to plan. And the obvious place for Wagner to begin was choosing his senior adviser.

Wagner suggested the Dubliner, an upscale Irish pub near Union Station frequented by senators and those who wished to be seen with them. He ordered a Chivas and Chandler did the same.

"I've been thinking about appointments," Wagner

said.

Chandler nodded. This was it.

"Goodrich wants Veterans Affairs," Wagner said.

He was starting near the bottom—the Secretary of Veterans Affairs wasn't exactly one of the power positions. "Goodrich would be fine," she said. Herb Goodrich was a wealthy manufacturer of plastic tubing who had poured millions into the Wagner campaign. If he wanted to be in charge of a bunch of nursing homes and cemeteries, good for him.

"And I got a call from McHue today." Senator Jane McHue of Wisconsin had been one of Wagner's early supporters. "She wants State."

"So does Senator Hathaway."

Wagner snorted. "Oh, he's got a chance."

Chandler gave him the smile she knew he was looking for. Wagner was himself again—playing the game, looking for the angles, deciding which favors needed to be repaid and which ones could safely be postponed or ignored. The dark cloud that had hovered over him for the past few days was gone. He acted like a man who'd just gotten good news from his doctor: the tests were negative. He was going to be all right after all. In fact, he was going to live a long, happy life as president of the United States.

She twirled the bottom of her glass on the mahogany tabletop, waiting for him to say, "You know, Jane, I'm going to need someone to help me..."

Instead he said, "I also got a call from Phil Koch at NAMS." The National Association of Military Suppliers was one of the most powerful political action committees in the country. "They like David Pendleton for CIA."

At the sound of those initials, a chill ran down her arms. "Pendleton would be good."

But he shook his head. "I've already got someone in mind for CIA."

"Who's that?"

"Ray Devlin. He's in the security division. A good man. Career guy."

Chandler put the swizzle stick in her mouth and chewed on it. The Director of Central Intelligence was a notoriously political position. Candidates were often business leaders whose only qualification for one of the top intelligence posts in the country was a history of generosity to politicians. Occasionally the job went to a favored party hack who needed a place to park while planning his next career move. For the most part, the people chosen to head the CIA wouldn't know a dead drop from a lunch box.

But Devlin was none of those, which meant Wagner must have some other reason for thinking of him. "It's about time we had someone in there who knew how the organization works," he said.

"Sure." She wasn't about to challenge him. She had no idea what Raymond Devlin did at the CIA or what his qualifications were. But someone at the CIA had been calling Wagner, calls that had thrown him into a panic. Now the panic had passed, and Raymond Devlin was being considered for the top job at the CIA. Which raised the question: What did Devlin have on John Wagner?

With her father safely in the hospital, Darcy went home and cried for three hours. Exhaustion, relief and thirty years of anger poured out in an emotional waterfall. Then she slept.

At 3 a.m., the phone rang, a wrong number. After that, she was fully awake. There would be no going back to sleep.

She wrapped herself in a quilt and sat by the picture window, staring at the moon on the smooth surface of the lake and remembering the events at the park.

She had been stunned when she first saw her father, his mustache gone, hair darkened and forehead shaved to simulate a receding hairline. It was hard to believe such simple changes could hide such a famous face. It was also hard to believe a person with Alzheimer's had done it.

"I'm afraid it's fairly typical of early Alzheimer's," the doctor at the hospital had said. "At times, patients will be completely lucid. Then suddenly, for no apparent reason, they will become delusional."

"This didn't come on suddenly," Darcy said. "He must have been planning it for months."

The doctor shrugged. "Your father is an extremely intelligent man. Alzheimer's doesn't necessarily strip a person of all their skills and abilities. Just their reasoning abilities."

The doctor had suggested they keep her father at the hospital overnight for observation and Darcy agreed. When he returned to The Village, he would need round-the-clock supervision.

As she left the hospital, Raymond Devlin had taken her aside and assured her that the company would pay for the 24-hour nursing care.

"Which company? The CIA, or the one that owns The Village?"

Devlin cocked his head. "The agency, of course."

"I just wondered. Because my father told me the agency owns The Village."

Devlin looked amused and concerned at the same time. "He told you the CIA owns his retirement community?"

It was only when she heard the words spoken aloud that she realized how ridiculous it sounded, on a par with a person who thought the government was tracking him via the metal fillings in his teeth.

"Trust me," Devlin had said, "we have enough

problems without owning retirement villages."

Now, as she stared out at the liquid-black surface of the lake, Darcy remembered her father's words and wondered what else he had been delusional about.

I have to get out of here.

Why? What was he afraid of? He had clammed up after she'd turned him in, refusing to speak to her, treating the agents like prison guards. Maybe he still imagined he was protecting her, or was trying to sort out his confusion behind the closed door of his silence.

I need your help.

Had she done the right thing? What else could she have done? However confused her father might be, she couldn't get past the nagging sense that she'd betrayed him.

I couldn't take a chance that you'd find out.

He had been planning his escape for a long time, perhaps as long as he'd been living at The Village. For whatever reason, he felt he couldn't trust her. Now, he would probably never trust her again.

If I try to leave by the normal routes, they'll know.

Who did he imagine was after him? Old adversaries? And where did he think he was? In a rest home for retired spies?

You're being followed.

At least he'd been right about that. They had followed her. In all her years of practice, despite all the odd characters she'd dealt with, nothing like that had ever happened.

On the other hand, she wasn't surprised that they had followed her. It might have been nice if they'd told her. But this was the government, and the government was only as considerate as the people who worked for it.

If anything happens to me, it's because of Al Beaker.

And here the conversation with her father became a

skipping record, playing the same line over and over:
>*It's because of Al Beaker.*
>*It's because of Al Beaker.*

18

The conflagration at the Middleton mills turned out to be a bust. A painter had fallen asleep on a sofa in his studio while smoking. The smell of cheap upholstery burning woke him and he pulled the fire alarm. By the time Ned arrived, firefighters had the blaze well under control. Fortunately, only a small section of the mill had been damaged; unfortunately the artist had rescued most of his paintings. Ned was pretty sure the world would have been better off without them.

Meanwhile, the Marshall Cameron story was over. Cameron had been found, safe and sound. Another reporter had done a brief wrap-up for the late news. National Rescue Services, whoever they were, had packed up and gone home. And Ned had missed his chance for a story that might have gotten him noticed outside of East Overshoe, Vermont.

But something about the story still bothered him. Someone had orchestrated an intensive high-tech search for Marshall Cameron. And the search team was connected to an elusive company located outside Washington, D.C. Maybe that was just coincidence. Cameron's old bosses at the network could simply be watching out for one of their retired personalities. But every journalistic nerve in Ned's body told him that wasn't the case.

So why would the government be interested in

Marshall Cameron? Ned did a quick online search for Cameron's biography. According to the NewsDex entry, Cameron had graduated from college in 1949 and begun traveling immediately, writing news stories for UPI and the Associated Press. In the early 50s, he'd seen the writing on the wall and made the jump to broadcast journalism. He became a freelance stringer, traveling the world and providing stories for the fledgling television networks, a position that suited his passion for travel and his disdain for reporting to bosses. The picture that emerged was that of a Lone Ranger, a man who didn't like reporting to higher-ups or dealing with the office politics that came with a full-time job.

Then, in 1983, Cameron's career had taken a dramatic turn. He was given his own news magazine called TimeLine, and overnight his name became a household word to the millions of viewers who tuned in weekly to hear his warm, fatherly take on international events.

It was a plum assignment, though it seemed like an odd one for a man who had previously been such a loner. The TimeLine spot was a high-visibility position, the kind that would require a lot of ass-kissing, politics and corporate nonsense.

As Ned wondered about that, Granny stuck his head around the corner. "Someone here to see you" he said, his eyebrows raised.

Darcy Cameron appeared in the doorway. She hesitated a moment, then entered with her hand extended. "Hi. Darcy Cameron."

"I remember." Ned's mouth was suddenly dry. In truth, if she hadn't spoken, he might not have made the connection. The last time he'd seen Darcy Cameron, she looked like a refugee from a soldier of fortune magazine, someone who'd been wrestling with a briar patch and lost.

Today, Darcy's blonde hair was pulled back into a

loose ponytail. She wore a denim skirt and an off-white sweater—definitely not business attire. Her eyes were the deep blue of a summer sky just before rain and she had a smile that would charm the pants off any man who was lucky enough to be so charmed. It occurred to Ned that if Darcy Cameron had chosen to follow in her father's footsteps, she could have written her own ticket with any broadcasting company in the business.

"What's up?" he asked.

"You said you could help me out if I ever needed anything."

Ned's pulse shot up a notch. Maybe the story about Marshall Cameron wasn't dead after all. Or else she had something more personal in mind. Either way, things were looking up.

"Sorry about this mess," he said and shoved a stack of press releases off a chair so she could sit.

"I've decided to write a biography of my father," she said, sitting and crossing her legs. "But there are so many things he doesn't remember at this point."

Ned forced himself to ignore her legs. "Of course."

"I've been going through his papers and I came across a name I didn't recognize. Probably an old coworker, or someone he did a story on. Al Beaker?"

"Wasn't he a character on the Muppet Show?"

She smiled faintly. "Right. Anyway, I wondered if, being in the business, you might have heard of him. Or know someone else who knows him?"

Ned's chest swelled like a week-old balloon that had just been given a fresh shot of helium. He had never heard of Al Beaker. But by God, he was going to find out who the guy was if it killed him. After all, that's what newsmen did, especially for the beautiful daughters of fellow broadcasters.

Of course, if Al Beaker did have anything to do with

broadcasting or the print media, locating him might not be that hard, and Ned didn't want it to seem too easy. "There is a database I can check," he said. "It's supposed to be for the media only..."

Darcy leaned closer and said softly, "I'd be really grateful."

"Well, what the heck," Ned said, spinning around and tapping a command on his keyboard.

The NewsDex logo appeared on the screen. "This is a database for professional journalists." He clicked on an icon. "I'll check the personnel database first. It lists anyone who ever worked in the industry."

He entered the name. As the computer churned, Ned decided to do some trolling of his own. "Did you ever find out where that other search team was from? National Rescue something, wasn't it?"

She gave a minimal shrug. "The Village called them in. That's all I know."

"Sure. I just wondered because it seemed like overkill for..." That wasn't what he meant to say. "Not that your father doesn't deserve the best..." He was digging himself deeper. "Not that your own team wasn't capable—"

"It's OK," Darcy said, and he heard a trace of amusement at his discomfort. "I didn't really understand it either."

The system beeped.

BEAKER, AL NOT FOUND. SEARCH AGAIN?

"How about Albert?" Darcy said. "Or Allan?"

"Nope. It would have found them, along with Alphonse, Alonzo, and Alcibiades."

He clicked to another area. "I'll try the biographical index. It lists anyone who's ever been covered in a major news story."

As the system searched Ned said, "You know, it's funny. I found myself wondering. What if that other team was actually from the government?" He glanced at Darcy to see if she found that amusing.

Her face was a blank. "I'm afraid I don't—"

"You know, maybe in the course of doing a story he stumbled on something he shouldn't have. Daniel Ellsberg and the Pentagon Papers. That kind of thing."

She looked uncomfortable, so he decided to back off. "I know, just a wacky thought."

Darcy said nothing and the system responded again.

YOUR ENTRY "BEAKER, AL" WAS NOT FOUND.
THE CLOSEST MATCH WAS BECKMAN, ALAN.

Ned shook his head. "Did you ask your father about this Beaker guy?"

There was a pause. "I'm not able to communicate with my father right now."

"Oh. Sorry. I didn't realize his condition was—"

"It's not that. He just feels like a prisoner in his own home. And he blames me for that."

Ned tried to think of a way to comfort her—God, how he wanted to comfort her—but she cut him off, pointing to the computer. "Is there any way to look at actual broadcasts?"

"We could go to New York," he said with a shrug and a slight grin. "There's a place called the Paley Center that keeps copies of most programs that have been aired."

Darcy said nothing and Ned turned back to the computer. OK, he thought, bad timing. Don't overplay your hand.

"This system does have abstracts of most broadcasts," he said. "I can search through those."

He entered Al Beaker's name and the system chugged

away for half a minute.

BAY OF PIGS
BEACH BOYS
BEADLE, GEORGE W.
NOT FOUND. YOUR ENTRY "BEAKER, AL" WOULD
BE HERE.
BEARD, JAMES
BEATLES
BECKER, BORIS
BEEKEEPING

"Nothing," Ned said. "Let's try it with the first name first, just for the heck of it."

AL ALAMAYN
AL BANNA HASAN
AL BASRAH
NOT FOUND. YOUR ENTRY "AL BEAKER" WOULD
BE HERE.
AL BIQA
AL FAYED, DODI
ARAFAT, YASIR

"Mostly Arabic names," Ned said.

Darcy stared at the screen.

"I can call some friends," Ned said. "If this guy is in the business, I'm sure someone—"

"That's OK," Darcy said. "It wasn't that important."

"It would only take a minute."

"No, no. I've taken up too much of your time already." She stood to leave, but hesitated a moment, noticing a photograph on his desk. It was a picture of Ned's son, Parker. "Is this Jimmy?"

"Who?"

"Jimmy. Your brother?"

"My brother? I don't..." He caught himself. "Oh, no, no. That's my son."

A killing frost fell over Darcy's face. She stared at him for a long moment. "Did you even have a dog?"

"Sure," Ned said quickly. "Lucky. He was a great dog."

"What kind?"

Ned shuffled papers on his desk. "Retriever. Golden."

"Right," Darcy said and headed for the door. "The last time you told me it was a black Lab."

"Oh, well I—"

"Thanks for your help," Darcy said, and left.

Ned stared at the door, wondering how long it would take Granny to appear and how far out of his mouth his tongue would be hanging.

Fifteen seconds.

"What was that about?" Granny asked.

"I don't know. Some lame excuse about writing a book," Ned said with a shrug. "I think she wants me."

19

Darcy told the cab driver, "The Paley Center for Media on West 52nd."

She fell back against the seat and closed her eyes. The drive to Boston had taken longer than the actual flight to La Guardia. She still wasn't sure why she was doing this. But she couldn't stop thinking about what Ned Epstein had said.

Epstein was a class-A jerk, but his instincts were good. He had already figured out that there was something odd about National Rescue Services. Then there was his comment about the government searching for her father. Maybe that was just a lucky guess. But the idea that her father had stumbled onto something he shouldn't have kept coming back to her. Maybe that something had to do with Al Beaker.

Or Al Biqa. If she hadn't been staring at Epstein's screen so closely, she would have missed it. She didn't know who or what Al Biqa was, or even how it was pronounced. But she had an idea that if it was spoken by an elderly man who was facing away from you on a blustery spring day, it could sound like "Al Beaker."

The cab pulled up to a curb. "Paley Center," the driver said.

The entrance to the Paley Center looked like a church, with an art-deco Roman arch atop heavy stone columns. Darcy checked in with the receptionist, who directed her to the Scholars Room, a special area for researchers. She had told them she was writing a biography of her father and they quickly approved her request. If nothing else, being the daughter of Marshall Cameron opened doors.

An assistant explained how the system worked. Each of the study carrels was equipped with a TV screen, headphones, and computer link to the museum's electronic archives. The broadcasts were catalogued by title and key words.

Darcy typed the phrase "Al Biqa" and hit Enter.

1. ARMY OF ALLAH KIDNAPS MISSIONARIES
2. STANDOFF WITH HOSTAGE TAKERS CONTINUES
3. HOSTAGES SLAIN IN CLASH BETWEEN RIVAL TERRORIST FACTIONS

Beside each entry was a video icon. She clicked on the first one and a new window opened, a blank screen with a title.

CBS World News
Aired April 3, 1983 7:00 P.M. ET

A young Dan Rather appeared on the screen.

"Islamic terrorists kidnapped five missionaries from their compound in Lebanon today. Here is Marshall Cameron in Lebanon."

At the sound of her father's name, Darcy's heart thumped. Her hunch had been right.

The image of a lush valley filled the screen, with her father's voice providing the voice-over. He sounded strong, confident, and twenty years younger.

"This is the Al Biqa, a fertile valley in central Lebanon that provides half of the agricultural products grown in the country. It has also, unfortunately, become a hotbed for growing a new breed of terrorist."

A small cluster of stucco buildings appeared on the screen.

"This morning, a band of heavily armed men from a group calling themselves the Army of Allah kidnapped five missionaries—three Americans and two English citizens—as they attended a prayer meeting at their headquarters in the town of Bourj El Moulouk."

Her father appeared on the screen, a well-tanned man in his fifties. She stared at the screen, her eyes filling—he was so strong and handsome.

"The kidnappers contacted U.S. authorities through intermediaries and are demanding freedom for several Palestinians now held in Israeli prisons."

The story was brief. The United States, Israel and their allies were demanding that the missionaries be released unharmed, with no conditions. The Army of Allah, as usual, wasn't listening.

Darcy clicked on the next story. Dan Rather led off again.

"The hostage standoff continues tonight as members of the Army of Allah hold five missionaries at an undisclosed location in southern Lebanon. Here's Marshall Cameron in Al Biqa."

Now her father stood on a dusty street, gripping a microphone and frowning into the camera.

"American and British negotiators have arrived at the town of Rashaya in Lebanon, but so far, attempts to free the three Americans and two English missionaries have failed."

Grainy photographs of the hostages appeared on the screen.

"The hostages are being held in an undisclosed location by the Army of Allah, which is demanding freedom for a dozen Palestinians held in Israeli prisons. However, Israel says it will not negotiate with terrorists. Earlier today, CBS obtained this exclusive statement from a spokesman for the terrorists."

A man wearing traditional Arab garb sat cross-legged on a dirt floor, his words translated by a voice-over.

"Unless our brothers are freed, we will begin to execute those in our custody, whom we consider to be prisoners of war. We will begin executing them in 24 hours from the release of this message."

A spokesman for the Israelis appeared and reiterated that they would not budge on the question of the Palestinian prisoners.

"Meanwhile, American and British authorities grow increasingly worried about the fate of the hostages. Marshall Cameron, Lebanon."

Darcy clicked on the final story in the list. Rather looked even more somber than usual.

"A tragic ending to the hostage situation in Lebanon tonight, as Marshall Cameron reports from the Al Biqa valley."

Her father's fatigue jacket was dirty and wrinkled. Deep lines creased his face and his hair was barely combed. Beyond that, there was something in his attitude that Darcy couldn't identify—anger at the outcome of the situation, or simple exhaustion perhaps.

"It began at 3 a.m. local time, when the compound where the five missionaries were being held by the Army of Allah was attacked by a rival militia group."

A video showed a small farm that bore evidence of a battle. Even on the low-resolution television image, she could see bullet holes in the walls, broken windows. And bodies.

"According to American military sources, the missionaries were caught in the crossfire between the militia groups and all were killed, as were all the members of the Army of Allah present.

The camera returned to her father.

"The rival group that staged the attack has not been identified, and none of the other militant organizations that operate in the area have claimed responsibility for the attack. There is speculation that the rival group may have been composed of members of the Sunni militia, a group opposed to the Shiite Muslims who make up the Army of Allah.

As he spoke, Cameron stared at the screen, his eyes flat, face expressionless. Darcy had never seen her father play cards, but she knew a poker face when she saw one.

Dan Rather appeared again.

"That report from Marshall Cameron. There was another tragedy in the region today as three American soldiers..."

The clip ended abruptly with a CBS logo and copyright information. She stared at the screen for a moment. Another tragedy. What was that?

She clicked back to the main menu and searched for all the stories that had been broadcast that day.

1. HOSTAGES SLAIN IN CLASH BETWEEN RIVAL TERRORIST FACTIONS
2. LAND MINE TAKES LIVES OF THREE SERVICEMEN
3. SENATE DEBATES SOCIAL SECURITY LEGISLATION
4. ANTI-NUCLEAR PROTESTS CONTINUE IN EUROPE

She clicked on the second story. After the CBS World News logo, Rather appeared.

"There was another tragedy in the region today as

three American soldiers were killed in an accident involving a land mine in the Golan Heights."

A map of the Middle East appeared on the screen. The camera zoomed in to show the Golan Heights, a stretch of Israeli-occupied Syria next to Lebanon. Darcy paused the video and studied the map. It looked as if you could throw a rock from the Golan Heights to Al Biqa, where the missionaries had been killed. Clearly, this was not a good place to let your guard down.

"According to Army spokesmen, the soldiers were taking part in a training exercise in the Golan Heights when their jeep ran over a concealed land mine. All three were killed instantly.

Photographs of the soldiers appeared on screen.

"The three soldiers were Robert LeJeune of Sacramento, California, Jesus Rodriquez of Fort Worth, Texas, and Mark Herriman of Newport, Rhode Island. In Newport today, the parents of Mark Herriman remembered their son as a caring young man who had always wanted to be a soldier."

Darcy fast-forwarded over the interview with the parents. An army officer appeared on the screen, his name flashing by too quickly to read. She resumed the video.

"These young men were among the best and the brightest," the officer said. "Their loss is a great blow to the country, as well as to their friends and families."

The officer's face was familiar—a younger, less-fleshy version of a face she recognized but could not place. She rewound the video to the point where the officer's name appeared at the bottom of the screen.

Major Raymond Devlin, US Army

She stared at the screen. On the same day as the massacre at Al Biqa, three soldiers had been killed in an accident not thirty miles away. Raymond Devlin had been there.

She felt a sudden chill, as if from a draft. She stood and walked to the large windows that looked out over 52nd street. The street below was filled with passersby, but she recognized no one—at least, no one who looked like a government agent. But that no longer gave her any peace of mind.

Fredericks handed the update to Devlin. "She's in New York."

Devlin scanned the paper quickly. "What's she doing there?"

"Research at the Paley Center for Media."

"The what?"

"Formerly the Museum of Television and Radio. Apparently she's working on a biography of her father."

It made sense, Fredericks thought. With Marshall Cameron failing, there was no time to lose if she was going to tell his story.

Devlin considered that for a moment. "All right," he said, handing the paper back to Fredericks. "Keep watching her."

Fredericks returned to his office, wondering why they were still watching Darcy Cameron. Marshall Cameron was safe and sound back at his retirement home, so there was no good reason to continue surveillance of his daughter. At this point, following her was clearly outside the agency's legitimate jurisdiction—unless there was more to the case of Marshall Cameron than Devlin was saying.

To Fredericks, the Marshall Cameron puzzle, rather than being solved by his recovery, had only grown more complicated. The old guy apparently thought he was a prisoner in his own retirement home. His daughter was suddenly fascinated with his background. And Devlin insisted they keep watching her.

Fredericks decided to do some research of his own. Darcy Cameron wasn't the only person who wanted to know what was going on.

In Hardwick, Maine, there was really only one place to get coffee: Shirley's Stop 'n Go.

"More coffee for you?" Shirley asked the stranger, a slight man with dark skin. He nodded.

"Nice day for traveling, huh?"

The stranger smiled but said nothing and turned back to his paper. He had been reading the paper for an hour, and Shirley wondered how anyone could find that much of interest in the Hardwick Ledger. In a town the size of Hardwick, the most interesting thing was the police report, and even that only took up half a page.

The front door creaked open and Earl Tulley, a bulky middle-aged man in a green windbreaker, stomped in.

"Earl, where the heck have you been?" Shirley asked.

"Fixing the garage door opener at the fire station. I tell you, one of these days somebody's house is going to burn down because that damn thing won't open."

She poured him coffee. "Why don't they just buy a new one?"

"'Cause this town is too friggin' cheap, that's why."

"They cost that much?"

"Nah. Hell, Gardner's sitting in his cruiser out on the highway right now. He could pull over the next three Massachusetts drivers and they'd have enough for a new door opener like that." He snapped his fingers.

"Gary?" Shirley snickered. "If I know him, he's too busy talking to Cathy on the squawk box."

"You got that right."

The stranger put money on the table and left. Earl went on complaining about the town fathers as Shirley headed to the empty table with a rag.

"Son of a gun," she said. The stranger had left a five dollar bill. She'd never seen anyone leave a five dollar bill for a cup of coffee, even with refills, even if he had been sitting there for an hour.

She pocketed the bill and wiped down the table. It took all kinds.

Cathy Gardner's voice came through the CB, thin and distant. "So I told her we'd try to get there by five, but I have to pick up Jason first—"

A green Camry with New York plates flew by. Gary Gardner glanced at the radar. *92 MPH.*

"Gotta go, babe," he said. "Call you later."

He clicked off the CB, flicked on his lights and pulled onto the highway. The genius behind the wheel of the Camry didn't even notice the cruiser until it was practically in his trunk.

He pulled over. Gardner did the same and approached the car. The driver was a small man, dark skinned.

"License and registration, please."

The driver nodded, reached to the glove compartment and retrieved the registration. He pulled his license from his shirt pocket, which struck Gardner as odd. Most men carried their licenses in their wallets.

The man held out the papers. "Gary Gardner?"

Gardner leaned to look at him closer. He didn't recognize the man, whose voice had an odd, foreign sound to it. "What?"

The hand with the gun came up quickly and fired three rounds into Gardner's chest. He fell backward onto the road. As the Camry sped away, something fluttered from the open window and landed by Gardner's side.

Gardner gasped for breath and turned his head. As darkness closed in he saw something on the pavement beside him: an eagle feather, long and white with a dark tip.

20

On the plane from New York to Boston, Darcy came to a decision. In for a dime, in for a dollar. If she was going to chase wild geese, she might as well chase them all the way.

She retrieved her car from the Logan airport parking garage and headed back through the Sumner Tunnel. But when she hit Rt. 95, she headed south instead of north.

She drove for an hour, glancing in the rear view mirror periodically, wondering if she was just being paranoid. But she remembered the old joke: Just because you're paranoid, doesn't mean they aren't out to get you.

A gray drizzle fell as she turned off the exit for Newport, Rhode Island. Several cars took the exit with her. That probably meant nothing, but you never knew. Call it intuition, a suspicious nature, or an overactive imagination.

She headed for the center of town. At one time, Newport had been a playground reserved for the rich and famous. These days, it was another tourist destination, a theme park dedicated to conspicuous wealth. The downtown area was a paradise of shops for those with no real needs and an excess of disposable income: delicatessens that charged New York prices for a plate of rice and curry, galleries selling ersatz African art, antique shops, and clothing stores that carried denim and flannel for people who would get no closer to the woods than a

Discovery Channel program.

Darcy parked and walked to the Ginger Thistle, a tiny shop that offered "casual clothing for professional women." In the window, an anorexic mannequin modeled a forest green suit. As Darcy gazed at the outfit, the window reflected the street behind her: passing cars, mothers and children in strollers, a young couple entering a deli.

And a man in a plaid shirt and blue jeans, his back turned, looking into the window of a dry cleaner across the street. What could be so interesting about a dry cleaner?

She wandered to a cross street that had been made into a pedestrian mall. Stepping into a coffee shop called Brew Heaven, she ordered a latte and grabbed a newspaper from a coffee table. Positioning herself at a tall table that looked out to the street, she sat and opened the paper.

The man in the plaid shirt strolled by, glanced into the coffee shop, then crossed the street and walked into a music store with loud signs advertising thrash and punk CDs. He didn't look like the thrash type.

Darcy stared at the newspaper but didn't see a word printed there. Her heart thudded in her chest and she heard her father's voice.

You're being followed.

Ned Epstein dialed Darcy Cameron's number. He had decided the only way to keep the lines open was to make a clean breast of it, apologize, and hope for the best.

"You've reached the office of Darcy Cameron. I'll be out of the office today. Please leave your name—"

Ned hung up. He didn't want to talk to a machine, though he'd probably get as much out of it as he would from her, given the mood she was in the last time he'd seen her.

Then it hit him. If Darcy Cameron wouldn't talk to him, why not talk to Marshall Cameron? He could just swing by The Village. If he saw Darcy's truck in the parking lot, he'd keep going. But if she wasn't there, she couldn't very well object to him talking to her father. And based on what she'd told him, old Marshall might just welcome the chance to get out of the house for awhile.

Fifteen minutes later, he was knocking on the door to Marshall Cameron's apartment. A nurse opened it.

"Hello," Ned said briskly. "I'm here to take Marshall to lunch."

The nurse frowned. "I'm sorry, Mr..."

"Epstein. Ned Epstein, Channel 34 news."

"Oh, of course. I thought you looked familiar."

"Is Marshall ready?"

She opened the door a bit further. "I'm afraid we weren't told—"

Ned elbowed his way in the door, shaking his head. "Don't tell me—Darcy forgot to tell you I was coming. That poor girl has been so busy. She told me she was headed off for the day, and she must have forgotten."

Over the nurse's shoulder, Marshall Cameron looked at Ned as if he were a festering wound.

"Marshall," Ned called cheerfully. "Darcy told you I was coming, didn't she?"

Cameron stared at him for a moment, then nodded slowly. "Yes. Yes, she did."

"There you go, " Ned said. He leaned closer to the nurse, "I promise not to wear him out too much."

In the end, the nurse acquiesced. "Just make sure he's back for his 2 o'clock meds."

As the door closed behind them, Cameron murmured, "I don't know who the hell you are, but here are the ground rules. I'm not doing any god-damned interviews. We go where I want to go. And no pictures."

"Fine," Ned said. Whatever he'd been told, Marshall Cameron certainly seemed like a man who was in control of his faculties—and his surroundings.

As they walked to Ned's car, Cameron looked him over. "You really are in television, aren't you?"

Ned flushed, pleased at the recognition. "You've seen my work?"

"No. It's the clothes. Decent jacket, lousy shoes. You'd have better clothes if you were a..."

Ned waited for him to finish. "If I was a what?"

"Never mind."

Ned opened the car door for him. "Where would you like to eat?"

"La Finestera."

"Where's that?"

"Costa Rica."

"Right," Ned said, chuckling. "How about the diner?"

"Fine."

They drove in silence for a few minutes. Then Cameron said, "What do you want?"

Ned shrugged. "I just wanted to meet you. You're kind of a hero of mine, and—"

"Stow it. I'm not that far gone yet. What do you really want?"

OK, Ned thought. The old guy wasn't interested in bullshit.

"I've been reading about your career and I'm curious," he said. "In the early days you were a Lone Ranger, working for yourself, foot-loose, making your own rules. Then in 1983, you took the TimeLine job, which seems like quite a change. What made you go from being a loner to being a company man?"

Cameron stared at Ned as if he were x-raying his head it to see what was inside it. Then, turning his gaze back to the highway he said, "It was time to settle down. My daughter was heading to college and I needed the money."

"I see." He wasn't buying it. If Darcy Cameron had been going anywhere in 1983, it was kindergarten, not college. He decided not to challenge Cameron about it. So he backpedaled. "What was it like, working on TimeLine?"

Cameron snickered. "A bundle of laughs." He began talking, and slowly seemed to relax into this topic. After a few minutes, he was sharing anecdotes about guests who showed up drunk and well-known politicians who arrived with their "nieces" hanging off their arms.

The conversation continued at the diner, where they had burgers and onion rings. Cameron ate with gusto and Ned had the feeling that diner fare wasn't exactly on his approved diet.

By the time they were headed back to The Village, Cameron seemed more comfortable. Ned decided to try again. "So where were you just before you took the TimeLine job?"

Cameron glanced at him and lapsed into silence. A minute passed. "All that stuff is pretty fuzzy now," he said. You'd have to talk to Art Keene."

"Who?"

"Art Keene. He was in charge of the international assignment desk at the network. He might be able to help you."

"OK. I'll give him a call." Now Ned felt sorry for the old man. If he couldn't remember what he'd been up to just before taking the TimeLine job, maybe he was further gone than Ned suspected.

"If you do talk to Art, tell him we should go fishing some time." Cameron said.

"Sure. I'll do that."

A light drizzle fell as Darcy drove toward the

Newport visitor's center. She passed a thrift shop, pulled over, and entered the shop. From a rack of second-hand clothes, she chose a long raincoat and floppy hat. She paid, donned the jacket, and continued on to the visitor's center.

The Newport Information Center was a low-slung brick building that served as the gateway to the city's attractions. Inside, tourists gathered brochures from a circular desk manned by perky young people who sold tickets to the city's attractions. Outside, a line of buses ferried visitors to the mansions that lined the city's shoreline like jewels around a dowager's neck: the Breakers, the Elms, Kingscote, Château-sur-Mer.

Darcy skirted the information desk and slid into the bathroom. She sized up the women around her. Too old. Too short. Too timid-looking.

She pretended to examine her makeup in the mirror. A group of women came into the restroom en masse, chattering like blue jays. One of them had Darcy's hair-color and build. She looked poised, confident, and most important, sympathetic.

Darcy splashed water in her eyes, reddening them. She turned as the woman approached the sinks. "Can you help me? I'm desperate."

The woman stared and her group fell silent. "What is it?"

"I'm being followed. It's this guy..." She ran a hand through her hair, disheveling it. "I don't know, I went out with him once, and now he won't leave me alone."

She poured out an incoherent tale of a blind date arranged by a coworker and a man who had been stalking her ever since. "Everywhere I go, there he is." Her voice trembled, her eyes searched the group for sympathy. "Can you help me? Please?"

The agent studied a brochure for the Rosewood estate, constantly moving around the information desk to avoid being asked if he needed help. The Cameron woman had been in the bathroom for several minutes, longer than he thought it should take for her to do whatever women did in restrooms.

He watched the bathroom door closely, wondering if there was a rear exit. It hadn't occurred to him to secure the rear of the building, but Darcy Cameron was a civilian and it hadn't seemed necessary.

A constant stream of women emerged from the restroom. That slowed to a trickle and for a minute, no one came out. Then came a cluster of women, talking animatedly. Cameron was at the center of the group, rain hat pulled tightly around her head. The women left the building and headed for a waiting tour bus.

The agent glanced at the number of the bus, jumped into one of the information lines and purchased a ticket for that tour. He boarded the bus as the driver revved the engine. The door closed behind him.

He took a seat and gazed out the opposite window, scanning the other passengers from the corner of his eye. Across the aisle and two rows back, the woman he had followed removed her rain hat. She looked—as did each of the women around her—like the cat that had just swallowed the canary.

It was not Darcy Cameron.

21

Not all of Newport is mansions and park-like estates. Morningside Lane was a narrow street of houses squeezed together like chocolates in a box, each with a yard barely larger than its porch. Peeling paint, crooked mailboxes and loose shutters told of owners who were growing too old to take care of their homes and children who no longer cared because they were too far away.

Or dead, Darcy thought. She glanced at the slip of paper again before ringing the bell at 118 Morningside Lane.

An elderly man answered the door. "Yes?"

"Mr. Herriman?"

His face was pleasant, open, and it didn't change at the sight of a stranger intruding on his privacy. "Yes?"

"My name is Darcy Cameron. I'm working on a biography of my father. Marshall Cameron?"

The man's eyebrows went up a notch. "The newscaster?"

"Yes. I wonder if I could talk to you for a moment?"

"Sure. Come in, come in." He called into the house. "Anne, come out here. Company."

Mrs. Herriman appeared and urged Darcy into the living room, a compact space dominated by a flower-print sofa and a reclining lounger. A painting of Jesus beamed compassion, his heart glowing burgundy-red through his robe. Atop a small piano were color photographs, faded blue with age—the Herrimans standing at the altar as newlyweds, a boy in altar clothes and a girl dressed for her first communion. Then the same girl—older now—with a prom date, and a young man leaning against a Mustang. In the place of honor on top of the television was the standard military portrait of their son alongside a framed letter with a presidential seal on it.

Darcy sat, a notepad open on her lap. "I wanted to follow up on some of the stories that especially touched my father during his career. Your son's death was one of those." She hoped they wouldn't remember that her father hadn't actually reported on their son's death.

Anne Herriman looked at her husband, then nodded, her eyes glistening. "OK."

"Can you tell me about those days?" Darcy asked.

"It wasn't easy," she said. "For the longest time, we couldn't even talk about it." She slipped a hand into her husband's. "Eventually, we got some counseling. That and prayer helped us get through."

Darcy glanced at the photo on the piano. "He was a handsome young man."

"Mark was a hero," Mr. Herriman said, taking the framed letter from the television and handing it to her. "He gave his life for his country, as surely as if he had died in battle."

The letter conveyed official condolences from the president. Darcy wondered if the signature was genuine.

"Being a soldier was Mark's lifelong dream," Mrs. Herriman said. "When he was a little boy, he spent all his time playing army with the other boys on the street." Her voice cracked. "He was so proud when he made the Special Forces."

Darcy looked up from her notepad. "Your son was in the Special Forces?"

"Green Berets," Mr. Herriman said. "They couldn't

talk about that in the press, of course."

"National security," Mrs. Herriman said, as if the phrase explained all lapses in communication on the part of the government.

"Of course," Darcy said. She scribbled "Special Forces" on her pad and underlined it. "I know this is probably painful for you, but can you tell me exactly how your son died?"

Anne Herriman glanced at her husband. "That was the hardest part for us. Nobody knows exactly what happened."

"It was a training exercise," her husband said. "Their jeep was passing through a mine field..." His lip quivered, and he was unable to finish.

"Do you have any idea what kind of training exercise it was?"

Mrs. Herriman shook her head. "That was classified information, too."

"Does anyone know what happened?"

"Probably the other men in his unit," he said. "But of course they couldn't say anything. National security."

Mrs. Herriman stared out the window, past lacy curtains with ball fringe, as if she could see the event happening in the street outside. "Paul knew."

"Who?" Darcy asked.

"Paul Menard," her husband said. "He was Mark's best friend in his unit."

"Poor boy," Mrs. Herriman said. "He was never really the same after Mark's death."

"Where is he now?"

"Somewhere near Boston, I think." She opened a desk drawer and pulled out a letter. "He wrote to us right after he was discharged. He didn't say much, just how sorry he was about Mark. We haven't heard from him since then."

Darcy read the return address on the envelope Mrs.

Herriman held—she had long ago learned the trick of reading upside-down, a skill that came in handy when sitting across the table during a difficult negotiation: *41 Wilmington Avenue, Roxbury, Mass.*

Ned Epstein scanned the NewsDex entry on Arthur Keene. Keene had run CBS's foreign assignment desk from the 1960s to the 80s. In that position—working with stringers and freelancers—he'd probably had a great deal of contact with Marshall Cameron. Now he was retired and living in Ridgefield, Connecticut.

A quick Internet search turned up Keene's phone number. The voice that answered the phone was still strong, though no longer that of a man in his prime.

"Keene here."

"Mr. Keene, this is Ned Epstein from WOFB in Rutland, Vermont."

"Yes?"

"We're doing a documentary—" At that moment, Granny walked into the office and Ned waved him into a chair—"about Marshall Cameron. You may have heard that he's battling Alzheimer's. We thought it was important to capture his story before he slipped away."

Granny rolled his eyes and played a mock violin. There was no such story in the works.

"I heard about him going missing," Keene said. "I was glad they found him."

"We all were. It was quite the effort they put into the search."

"I'm sure it was."

"They pulled out all the stops. Helicopters, geo-trackers. It was very impressive."

"I see."

"It almost made me wonder if the government was involved in looking for him."

"I beg your pardon?"

"I mean, does the network provide that kind of service for all its former employees?"

"I wouldn't know," Keene said. "He *is* Marshall Cameron."

"Right." Ned sensed there was nothing to gain by barking up that tree, so he changed tack. "I wonder if you can tell me about Mr. Cameron's early career. I get the sense that he was a free spirit."

"I suppose he was. The life of an overseas correspondent requires a great deal of self-reliance, especially if you're a freelancer."

They talked about Cameron's early work—the Cold War, Korea, Vietnam, the Middle East. From the sound of it, Cameron had been everywhere and seen everything.

"But then he took the TimeLine assignment," Ned said. "Wasn't that a bit out of character for him?"

Keene cleared his throat. "Oh, I don't know. He was getting older. He was probably tired of working for himself, tired of other people getting all the glory. You can't be a wanderer forever."

Maybe, Ned thought. But lone wolves don't become lap dogs overnight either.

He asked about the TimeLine years and Keene repeated some of the stories Cameron had already told him. As the conversation wound down Ned said— casually, he hoped—"I'm trying to track down another associate of Mr. Cameron's. Someone named Al Beaker?"

Keene was silent for a moment. "I'm afraid I don't know anyone by that name." His tone was noticeably cooler now.

Ned shuffled papers as if looking through them. "Oh, sorry, I was looking at the wrong paper. I think Al Beaker was part of a story Mr. Cameron worked on once."

"I'm sorry," Keene said. "I can't help you."

Ned thanked him for his time and was about to sign off when he remembered Cameron's request. "Oh, Mr. Cameron wanted me to say that you two should go fishing some time."

"Did he?"

"Yes. We have some great fishing up here. If you ever get up this way, you should give me a call. I'd love to show you—"

"I'll do that," Keene said, and hung up.

As Ned put the phone down, Granny said, "Who's Al Beaker?"

"I have no idea. But I'm willing to bet Arthur Keene does."

Keene stood by his desk for a moment, pondering the call.

"Who was that?" his wife asked.

"Some reporter. Trying to dig up dirt on Marsh Cameron."

"I hope you didn't give him any?"

"No, of course not."

Keene poured himself a Scotch and returned to his leather chair by the fireplace. The call had disturbed him, more than the dim-witted reporter would ever guess.

Not that he had lied. Everything he had said was perfectly true. He'd merely omitted a significant detail: that he and Marshall Cameron had both worked for the CIA. In fact, it was Keene who had introduced Cameron to the agency in the first place.

Maybe that was why the call troubled him. He'd always had a proprietary feeling for Cameron. From their earliest days together in college, Keene had known that Cameron was destined for great things. Marsh had been driven, fearless, and instantly likable. People trusted him —a personality trait that came in handy later, when he needed to talk his way through a war zone or deal with tribal leaders haggling over drug profits. Cameron had been one of the agency's top assets, with a brilliant career record, until the debacle at Al Biqa.

Even now the name touched a sore spot in Keene's memory. He had never believed the massacre was Marshall Cameron's fault. But Cameron had been there, ostensibly to cover the story of the kidnapping, in reality to act as the CIA's liaison with the Army of Allah and negotiate the release of the hostages.

Was it Cameron's fault that things had gone so badly? Keene didn't know. But if Cameron felt responsible, perhaps that explained his disease. Maybe Alzheimer's was caused by guilt, eating away at the brain's synapses like rust corroding the connections in an old, damp radio.

Guilt could also explain why Cameron had accepted the TimeLine job. Despite what he'd told the reporter, Keene had been surprised when Cameron took the position. It was essentially a desk job—a high-profile, highly-paid desk job, but still a desk job, one that would preclude Cameron's ever being of service to the agency again. It didn't fit with Cameron's personality, nor did it make sense. People who screwed up assignments didn't get major promotions, either from the CIA or the companies that provided their cover.

But Keene had never had a chance to ask Cameron about that. After they left the field, the two had little contact—a passing word at a broadcaster's conference, a toast at Keene's own retirement. Keene blamed the separation on the high-society circles in which Cameron was traveling; he simply didn't have time for old friends. Or maybe old friends reminded him of something he would rather forget.

"Did you ever hear back from Marsh?" his wife asked.

"No."

After learning of Cameron's retirement and his diagnosis, Keene had tried to contact him, but there was no response. On one level, he was relieved. What did one say to an old friend diagnosed with Alzheimer's? Sorry to hear you're losing your mind?

After that, he had not thought about Cameron much, until he'd gotten word of his disappearance. Now this call from a reporter, asking pointed questions and relaying a message: Marshall Cameron wanted to go fishing.

Keene swirled the remaining Scotch in the glass, pondering his next move. He did not want to look like a fool. But that parting comment would not let him be. He went to his desk and dialed a number in McLean, Virginia. When it was answered he said, "Howard. It's Art Keene."

Howard Chase was Keene's exit contact. Every retiree from the CIA was assigned a contact within the company, someone to call if you had a problem—an old case that came back to haunt you, or just having trouble getting your retirement check deposited in the right account.

"Art," Chase said jovially. "How are you? How's retirement?"

Keene lied and assured him that retirement was wonderful. "Howard, I'm wondering if you could check on something for me?"

"What's that? Don't tell me—they're raising your insurance deductibles, the bastards. If I—"

"No, no. It's...this is going to sound foolish, but I'm worried about Marsh Cameron."

"Cameron? I heard he got lost in the woods or something. But didn't they find him?"

"Yes, yes. He's fine now. I get the feeling that our people were involved in finding him."

"Really? News to me."

Keene didn't know whether to believe that or not. "I

just had a call from a reporter. He passed on a message from Marsh. Said that we should go fishing some time."

"Uh-huh." There was a shuffling of paper; Keene suspected Chase was only half listening to him.

"I'm worried because that was his XFC, back when he was active."

"His what? Ecstasy?"

"His exfiltration code," Keene said, not bothering to hide a note of exasperation. "If he needed to be pulled out, he was to send me a message that we should go fishing some time."

"Oh, right. I thought you said 'ecstasy.' I wondered what the hell you were talking about." More paper shuffling.

"I didn't know if I should do anything about it," Keene said. "I mean, given his condition."

"His condition? Oh, right. Alzheimer's. Isn't that a kick in the pants? Work your butt off for a lifetime, finally get to retire, and then you come down with that."

Keene waited for Chase to get back to the point. When it was clear he wasn't going to, Keene said, "Should I do anything?"

"Well, I don't know. I mean, it's probably just the disease, right? Picking up bits and pieces of stuff from the past?"

"I suppose. Still, I wonder if you could have someone check on him? Just to make sure he's all right." There was a pause and he added, "Just in case, you know."

Chase was silent for a moment and Keene knew what he was thinking: One more damned thing to do, on top of everything else.

"Sure, sure," Chase said finally. "I'll see what I can do."

"Thank you, Howard. Thank you."

He hung up, feeling foolish. Chase would probably

spend the rest of the day regaling his workmates with the story of old Art Keene, sitting up there in Connecticut, so bored that he was dreaming up conspiracy plots involving Marshall Cameron.

He poured himself another Scotch. Well, he had done his duty. If Marsh Cameron really was in trouble, someone would check it out.

22

Darcy drove from Newport to Roxbury, a part of Boston that urban renewal seemed to have skipped entirely. Store fronts were encased in steel grates or bore plywood patches over broken windows. Garbage collection was spotty at best, and there was little evidence of any other form of municipal interest.

41 Wilmington Avenue was a boarding house. Darcy knocked at the door and a woman appeared, cigarette smoke blurring her features. "Yeah?"

"I'm looking for Paul Menard."

"Won't find him here."

"He doesn't live here?"

The woman flicked her ashes into the street. "He sleeps here. And picks up his disability check." She pointed down the street with the cigarette hand. "Where he lives is at the Sportsman's Lounge. Also where he spends his check. Might as well just sign it over to them every month."

The Sportsman's Lounge, on the corner of Wilmington and Biscayne, had survived a dozen economic cycles by catering to men whose idea of a fancy drink was a twist-off bottle. It was a narrow room with barely enough space for the bar running down one side and four booths opposite it. The only light came from a jaundiced fluorescent bulb over the bar and daylight that leaked in around the Budweiser and Miller signs in the windows. This was not Cheers.

Darcy entered, trying not to look out of place, which was impossible. Clearly, this was a place where strangers seldom came, women never.

"Help you?" the bartender said.

"I'm looking for Paul Menard," she said, her eyes still adjusting to the gloom.

The bartender nodded to the far end of the bar, where a man in a plaid shirt leaned on it, his back to the door.

She approached and understood why Menard sat at that end of the bar. The right sleeve was empty, folded and pinned to his shirt. It also explained the disability check.

She had expected him to be about fifty years old. He looked older, his eyes red sockets in a lined face, the flesh stretched across a thin frame, the look of a man who drank too much and ate too little.

"Mr. Menard?"

He glanced in her direction, then back at the row of dusty bottles behind the bar. "Yeah?"

"Your landlady told me I might find you here."

Menard acknowledged this with the briefest of nods but said nothing.

"Can we talk? Privately?"

"Sure."

He made no effort to move, so she pointed to a lone booth at the back of the room. "How about over there?"

He nodded to the bartender, who refilled his mug, then he followed Darcy to the booth. A television overhead blared an afternoon game show.

"I wanted to ask you some questions about your time in the service," Darcy said.

For the first time, Menard looked directly at her. "Who are you?"

"My name is Darcy Cameron. Marshall Cameron is my father." No response. "The newscaster?"

"Lucky you."

She ignored the slight and pressed on. "I'm writing a book about my father and I wanted to follow up on some of the events he covered. You know, where the people are today, what they're doing." Here, amid the cigarette-stale air and insipid chatter from the television, the story seemed particularly thin.

Menard lowered an eyebrow. "What do you want from me?"

"I understand you were in the Golan Heights in 1983, in the unit that lost some soldiers to a land mine?"

Something flickered in Menard's eyes, but he turned away before Darcy could decide what it was. The bartender aimed a remote at the television and switched it to a football game.

After a long moment, Menard looked back at her. "Yeah, I was there. But before you even start, I'm gonna save you some time, because I don't want to talk about it."

She had expected that. A man didn't see his best friend get blown up without having it affect him. "I understand. I'm sure it's hard for you—"

"Hard nothing," he said. "I just got nothing to say." He took a long drink from his beer.

She hadn't come this far for a 30-second conversation. "All I need is a little background—"

Menard's mug hit the table with a thud. "What do you want? Do you want me to tell you what a hero he was? Do you want me to tell you he was a fag? What's your angle?"

She had underestimated the man's pain. Decades after the event, he was still suffering, in a way that even Herriman's parents were not.

"OK, we won't talk about your friend."

Menard snorted. "He wasn't any friend of mine."

"Really? His parents told me—"

"Whoa. Whose parents?"

"Mark Herriman's."

He frowned. "You came here to talk about Mark?"

She hesitated. Who did he think she was talking about? "Well no, not specifically. The Herrimans were just my first contact. I'm interested in anyone who can talk about what happened there."

"Good luck," Menard said, and in his face Darcy saw a door closing.

"I mean, in order to tell the story, I need a little more background. The government reports are sketchy—"

He snickered. "There are no government reports."

This was getting her nowhere. There was only one more angle to try: the truth.

"All right then, here's the deal." She told him about her father, about his being lost, and the revelation of his CIA connections. She told him about Al Beaker and Al Biqa and about being followed. As she told the story, Menard stared up at the football game on the television.

When she finished, Menard nodded once and said, "Interesting story. Did you write that yourself, or did your editor come up with it?"

"I'm not a reporter—"

"That's OK, don't bother." He stood up. "I'm done talking anyway."

Menard went back to his stool at the bar. Darcy pulled a business card out of her pocket. "That wasn't a story," she said and slid the card onto the bar in front of him. "Call me if you change your mind."

A political ad came on the television. Against a background of waving wheat, a square-jawed man with the barest touches of gray at this temples said, "Hello, I'm Senator John Wagner."

"Turn it off," Menard said to the bartender.

From the other end of the bar a voice complained, "Hey, the game is still—"

"Turn it off," Menard growled.

With a glance at Menard, the bartender aimed the remote at the screen and silenced it.

Darcy left, wondering about Menard's sudden animosity toward the television. But other questions elbowed that one aside. Why had he assumed she was a reporter? And who was he talking about when he said, "He wasn't any friend of mine"?

Fredericks gave Devlin the day's report. "Marshall Cameron went to lunch with a Ned Epstein today."

Devlin frowned. "Who the hell is that?"

"A local broadcaster. Used to work in Boston but got sent down to the farm team."

"What did they talk about?"

"Shop talk, mostly. It was noisy, but our source says Cameron spent most of the time telling old war stories."

The lines in Devlin's forehead deepened. "What kind of stories?"

"Celebrities. Amusing incidents at the studio."

"Oh," Devlin said, and Fredericks thought he relaxed a little. "Let me know if this guy crops up again."

Eleven across, Fredericks thought as he returned to his office. Another clue to the puzzle of Marshall Cameron: *What was Ned Epstein talking to him about?*

Jane Chandler had arranged to meet Ernie Kessler at Heaven and Hell, a trendy bar in the Adams Morgan neighborhood where she was unlikely to be seen by anyone she knew. Heaven was the upper level, a dance club with blaring techno music that made conversation impossible. Downstairs was Hell, a pub and pool room complete with satanic decorations. Given the company, the name seemed appropriate.

Ernie Kessler was an overweight, balding reporter with roaming hands—a proven jerk, but he'd been covering the capital for over twenty years and knew everything there was to know about anyone worth knowing. He also knew how to keep his mouth shut in exchange for a favor.

"Jane," he said as she slid into the seat opposite him, his eyes passing over her like a metal detector. "Looking as delicious as ever."

"Thanks." She grabbed a menu, mostly to keep him from staring at her breasts. "I guess clean living pays off."

"I'm sorry to hear that."

They ordered drinks and she got to the point. "I need a favor. Deep cover here, all right?"

"For you, my love, anything."

She ignored that. "What do you know about a guy named Raymond Devlin at CIA?"

"Devlin? Head of the Office of Security, a.k.a. the Keystone Cops—the folks who specialize in harassing U.S. citizens under the pretext of internal security."

"What about Devlin himself?"

"Career guy, been at the CIA since he got out of the army. He's got a reputation for being a bull-dog. No friends, no family, so he spends his time climbing the ladder. No class."

She sipped her margarita, hoping the next question would sound casual. "What do you know about Devlin and Wagner?"

Kessler raised his eyebrows. "Wagner the first? Or Junior?"

She ignored the dismissive nickname. "Senator Wagner."

"Nothing. But I can find out for you."

"OK. Do that."

"For you, my dear, I'd do anything."

She was, at one and the same time, glad and nauseated to hear that.

The drive home from Roxbury to Eastham took several hours. Darcy's phone was ringing as she walked into the house.

It was Will Webster. "I got the information on that turbojet."

"Really?" In the aftermath of finding her father, she'd forgotten all about the mysterious plane.

"Aeroflights Limited #107. It was supposed to pick up someone named Walter Brinkley."

Walter Brinkley. Of course. What other name would an old newsman invent? "Where was he headed?"

"St. John's in Newfoundland. From there to the Azores."

"The Azores?"

"Right. Islands in the middle of the Atlantic, or damn near there. The manifest specifies Corvu, the smallest of the islands. Population 300. Landing strip the size of a lean piece of bacon."

"Sounds like a good place to get lost," Darcy said.

"Almost as good as Vermont."

She was about to hang up when she thought of another project for him. "Hey, would you..."

"What?"

She thought for a moment. "Never mind. Thanks for your help, Will."

She'd been about to ask him to dig up Paul Menard's service records for her. But Will had had enough problems with the government in the past. She didn't want to drag anyone she liked into this.

23

It was a different Darcy Cameron who appeared in Ned Epstein's doorway the next morning. The amiable smile was gone, along with the breezy attitude.

"I need your help," she said.

The atmosphere in the office was a hectic clatter of keyboards, telephones and copy machines as the staff approached the afternoon deadline. Ned reached for his jacket. "Let's find a place to talk."

She shook her head. "This is fine."

"Yeah? It's pretty noisy."

"I know."

Ned shrugged. Apparently she liked it noisy. Go figure. "Have a seat."

Darcy lowered herself into a chair. "Let's begin by getting something straight. I know what you're all about. You're after a story."

He started to interrupt, but she said, "Let me do the talking, OK? You're after a story. And I'm..." She hesitated, working her jaw. "I'm looking for information."

"Sounds fair."

She slid a piece of paper toward him. "I need to find this man's military service record."

He glanced at the paper. "OK. Shouldn't be that hard to do." In fact, he had no idea how to go about locating service records. But Granny probably would.

"Good," Darcy said. "I have a feeling this is going to

turn into a big story. Maybe the story of a lifetime. But there's one condition. You can't write about it till I tell you."

"Sure." He wasn't sure what she was talking about, but he was already imagining a Pulitzer prizewinning story, a book deal, Ned Epstein on national television. "It's a deal."

"No, I want you to think about it. Because Ned?" She leaned closer. "If you write about this before I tell you to, the secretary will not just disavow any knowledge of your actions. The secretary will have you castrated."

He nodded. This was definitely not the same woman who had come looking for help a few days ago. This was a woman who could do it.

He rang Granny. "Come here for a minute."

The office was uncomfortably quiet as they waited for Granny to arrive. "So your father's a fisherman," Ned said.

She frowned slightly. "Who told you that?"

He began to realize it wasn't smart to make small talk with a lawyer, at least not one with Darcy Cameron's instincts. "Oh, we were just chatting and—"

"You were what?"

Now he was in trouble and he knew it. The last thing he wanted was a repeat of the little brother debacle. They'd reestablished a relationship—tenuous as it was— and he didn't want to blow it.

"OK," he said. She would probably find out sooner or later anyway. "I took him out to lunch. Just for background. I'd like to do a bio piece on him some time."

She nodded. "What did he tell you?"

"He talked about working for the network. Shop talk, that kind of thing. But he told me I'd have to talk to his old boss if I wanted more background. That's when he mentioned fishing."

"I see."

"He asked me to tell Keene they should go fishing sometime."

"Keene?"

"Arthur Keene. Ran the international desk at the network from the 60s to the 80s." He said this as if it was common knowledge among the fraternity of broadcasters.

Granny walked in wearing a look of mild annoyance, which evaporated when he saw Darcy.

"You remember Darcy Cameron," Ned said.

"Sure." Granny was unlikely to ever forget Darcy Cameron.

"We're looking for some information," Ned said, handing Granny the paper. "Can you find this guy's service records?"

"Doubtful. I don't think they keep service records on-line. But I'll try."

He took a seat at Ned's computer and began roaming the web, scouring search engines, checking and eliminating sites, moving so quickly that they could barely follow his progress.

After several minutes he said, "OK, I've found his unit number. ODA 785. But there's nothing about what he did."

"OD-what?" Darcy asked.

"ODA. Operational Detachment Alpha. That's a Special Forces A-team. Twelve soldiers, including a captain. You'd know that if you played video games."

Ned shook his head but refrained from saying that Darcy Cameron probably didn't play video games because she had a life. "So now what?"

Granny stared at the wall for a moment. "Well, if we can't find this guy's individual records, maybe we can find out what his unit was up to. Hang on."

He went back to tapping at the keyboard. A minute

later he said, "This looks like the right place."

The web site on the screen claimed to have the historical records of every army unit from the Revolutionary War to the present. A disclaimer explained that the records of any unit's operations were classified for a period of time, then declassified based on security.

"When did this guy serve?" Granny asked.

"Early eighties," Darcy said.

"I'll give it a shot." He entered a search for ODA 785.

Information classified.

He tried a different approach, but the response was the same.

Information classified.

He tried several more times, using different approaches. Each time the system responded "Information classified" or "No records found."

"Very strange," Granny said.

"What?" Darcy asked.

"It's been over twenty years. That should be plenty of time for any dirty laundry to air out. But the records for that unit are still locked tight. If you didn't know what you were looking for, you'd never even know the unit existed."

Darcy left Epstein's office a short time later, having reminded him about their agreement and the consequences of his failure to comply with it. Two thoughts weighed on her mind. First, somebody didn't want her to know what happened to ODA 785; she had done enough tracking to know when someone was sweeping the trail behind them. If she was ever going to find out about Paul Menard's unit, she'd have to pry it out of Menard himself.

The second thought was this: Her father was no fisherman. She had once encouraged him to go on a deep-sea fishing expedition organized by The Village's recreation director. He informed her that he'd never gone fishing in his life and wasn't about to start now. The very idea of fishing was repugnant to him.

So what had he really been trying to tell Arthur Keene?

The Central Intelligence Agency had four main branches: the Directorate of Operations, which conducted clandestine activities; the Directorate of Science and Technology, which supplied agents with the gadgets that helped them do their work; the Directorate of Intelligence, responsible for analyzing the mountains of data gathered by human and electronic surveillance; and the Directorate of Administration, which ran the day-to-day operations of the agency. This branch was responsible for the agency's finances, buildings and equipment, everything from spy satellites to pencil sharpeners. It also included the Office of Security, charged with protecting the agency from infiltration by foreign intelligence services.

Each of the directorates considered itself the most important. The Operations branch did the "real" spy work. Science and Technology provided the tools to get that job done. The Intelligence folks were certain that without them, the information gathered would be so much gibberish. But Administration wrote the paychecks, and its members often felt unappreciated. There was no love lost between the Operations and Administration branches of the CIA.

Howard Chase drummed his fingers. He had been on hold for five minutes—after being passed from department to department—waiting to speak to someone about Marshall Cameron.

Finally, a male voice said, "Office of Security."

"Yes, this is Chase in Operations. I've had a call from one of our alumni. He's worried about one of his old colleagues. Marshall Cameron? I guess you folks were involved in finding him?"

"More or less."

"Well—this is probably nothing—but he relayed a message to his old handler and used his exfiltration code."

"He what?"

"I know, crazy right? I mean, if I was in the Sunnyview Rest Home surrounded by old ladies playing canasta, I'd probably want out too."

"Did he say why he wanted to be pulled out?"

"I don't think so. I just told my man I'd have someone check on Cameron to make sure he's OK."

"I'll take care of it."

"Great. I mean, I'm sure you folks are busy there—"

"Thanks for your call," the agent said curtly.

"I'm sorry, I didn't get your name," Chase said.

"Fredericks," he said, and hung up the phone.

Once again, Fredericks pondered the case of Marshall Cameron. For the past few days he had been quietly digging into the Cameron's records: the official account of his overseas activities, reports from the field, memos. He had also been asking around—quietly, so as not to alert or annoy Devlin.

From what Fredericks had been able to piece together, Marshall Cameron had once been a valuable asset to the company. Then came the Al Biqa incident, which he had botched royally. After that came his hasty departure and elevation into the public eye—a move that had all the marks of a shell game, a diversion to prevent embarrassment. But embarrassment to whom?

Raymond Devlin scanned the transcript of Darcy Cameron's activities for the previous day. From New York, she had gone to Newport, where the agent in charge had lost track of her. Later that day, upon returning to her office, she had used her computer to search for web sites that contained the phrases "SERVICE RECORDS" and "MILITARY RECORDS."

She had not gotten far, which didn't surprise Devlin. The records of individual servicemen were not kept on-line. The last thing the government needed was for terrorists to know that Lieutenant John Doe, who had a wife and two kids, had once spent time roaming around the Middle East.

Devlin flipped the page and his eyes narrowed. Stymied in her search for general information on service records, Darcy Cameron had changed tactics. After "Enter search term," she had typed

Paul Menard

The search had returned a number of hits, none of them related to the Paul Menard that Devlin knew she was looking for. But it was only a matter of time. Darcy Cameron was a lawyer and—according to the dossier Fredericks had compiled on her—an excellent researcher.

A faint alarm sounded on the computer next to his desk. As a rule, Devlin didn't like using computers. It was easier to make an assistant find records or write memos. But he had instructed Fredericks to set the system up for a special purpose: monitoring the activity of web sites with the records of army units and their operations. The system would alert him whenever anyone searched those sites for a list of specific words and phrases that Devlin had loaded into it. It was, essentially, an electronic tripwire.

He hit the enter key.

Activity noted: http://www.milhist.gov/search

He hit the enter key again.

Nothing happened.

He tried several other keys without luck, then grabbed the phone and punched an extension. "How the hell does this thing work?"

"I'll be right there," Fredericks said.

He arrived a minute later and took a seat at Devlin's computer. "You have to click on the entry."

He did, and a record of the search began scrolling down the screen.

Search: ODA 785
Information classified.

Search: Operational Detachment Alpha 785
Information classified.

Search: Special Forces 785
No records found.

Search: Delta Force 785
No records found.

"Who is it?" Devlin said.

At the bottom of the screen was a button labeled "Trace." Fredericks clicked the button and a new window opened. It contained a program called HoundDog, developed by the CIA for its own use. HoundDog could follow an Internet user's electronic footprints through a tangled maze of routers, access points and ISPs, right back to the user's front door.

It took HoundDog thirty-two seconds to do the trace.

"It's Ned Epstein," Fredericks said. "He's logging in through a site called wofb.com in Rutland, Vermont."

"Who?"

"The broadcaster who had lunch with Cameron the other day."

Devlin slammed a fist on his desk. "Son of a bitch."

"Did you need me for anything else?"

Devlin waved him away without speaking and considered his next move. Darcy Cameron had made the connection to Paul Menard. Unable to find his service records on her own, she'd apparently gone to Ned Epstein for help, or else Epstein had stumbled onto Menard by himself. Either way, one of them would eventually find those records. And that was something Devlin could not allow.

He picked up his clear line. This call would be outside of official channels. No one else would ever know about it.

A woman answered. "Yes?"

"This is Mr. Grisham." It was a code name Devlin had chosen, one that amused him. "I have a few deliveries I'd like you to make." He gave her the details.

"Certainly. When did you want those deliveries made?"

"Soonest possible."

"You understand there will be a rush charge?"

"Of course."

Devlin hung up, then made a call on his regular office line.

"Fredericks."

"Yes," Devlin said. "You can discontinue the surveillance of Darcy Cameron."

Fredericks hung up the phone, wondering what the hell was going on. For days, Devlin had been vitally interested in everything about Marshall Cameron, his daughter, and anyone who had anything to do with them. Meanwhile, Cameron was sending coded messages to old friends to ask for help. Reporters were digging into military records. And now the surveillance of Darcy Cameron was being discontinued.

Fredericks had intended to tell Devlin about the message Cameron passed to his old contact. But then the computer problem interrupted. Now he decided that it could wait. There was something he wanted to check first.

He went to the departmental library and pulled out the staff directory. He could have found the same information using the computer on his own desk, but that would have left a trail.

He flipped through the directory and found the entry he was after.

Lieutenant Colonel Raymond Devlin b. Arlington, MA March 31, 1948. Graduated Arlington H.S. 1965. US Army OSC 1967, Second Lieutenant. Army Intelligence School, Holabird, MD, 1969. 5th Cavalry Division, Vietnam, 1969-71. 320th Special Forces Detachment, 1971-1976. Special Forces Officers Course, 1976. A-Detachment Commander, 1978-1982. B-Detachment Commander, 1981-1983.

Fredericks studied the last line. A Special Forces company consisted of six A-teams and one B-team. The B-team was the headquarters unit for the whole company. As commander of a B-detachment, Devlin would have had several A-teams reporting to him.

Fredericks was willing to bet that one of those teams was ODA 785, a unit Devlin didn't want anyone asking too many questions about. Somehow, that unit was connected to Marshall Cameron, a deluded man who had engineered his own disappearance, who believed his life was in danger. A man who, Fredericks was beginning to suspect, wasn't as crazy as they'd thought.

Patricia Hayes hung up the phone and called to her cleaning woman Ruth, who also did house-sitting for her. "Ruth, I know this is last moment, but can you house-sit for a week?"

Ruth stopped dusting and said, "I think so. I was going to visit my sister in Fort Myers, but I can change that. We were going to go to the flower show there, but it runs for two weeks so we can do it the next week. They do such a nice job there." She took a breath and said, "Is everything all right?"

"It's my friend Alice. Her emphysema's acting up again."

"Oh, I'm sorry to hear that. And she'd been doing so well. That's such a terrible disease. My Herb had it. He smoked three packs a day and always said, 'Well, something's got to kill you,' and in the end it was the cigarettes. But that's too bad about your friend. It seems like she hasn't had an episode in...what, a few months now?"

"Right." It wasn't hard lying to Ruth. Her specialty was talking, not paying attention. She never noticed that Hayes never called her mysterious friend, only received calls from her. Nor did Ruth notice the absence of birthday cards, Christmas cards, or any other form of written communication from the friend.

"Anyway," Hayes said, "I told her I'd come give her a hand again."

"Oh, you're an angel. I hope when I get older I have a friend like you to take an interest in me. It's a shame the way folks are so separated these days. People just don't have the support they used to."

She was still babbling when Hayes excused herself to weed the tomatoes, the task she'd been about to begin when Raymond Devlin called. There was just enough light to finish before she would need to pack.

Weeds were the bane of Hayes' existence. No matter what she did, they came back. She could cultivate, mulch, cover, and pluck them, but they kept coming back.

In a way, the weeds were symbolic. A perfect climate —like that of Sanibel Island, Florida where Hayes lived— would grow anything: flowers, vegetables, fruit trees. And of course, weeds.

Democracy was like that. A free society provided fertile ground for great ideas and institutions, as well as undesirable elements. For the most part, the system took care of those problems. And if justice didn't always prevail, at least it kept order.

Occasionally, however, justice was subverted. Murderers got off on technicalities. Traitors escaped public exposure. Known enemies masqueraded as curious visitors. At times like that, the garden of democracy needed weeding. That was where Patricia Hayes came in.

Hayes had been trained as an assassin by the CIA. But she had never fit in well with the company's structure— the hierarchy, the bureaucratic ass-kissing, the subservience to politicians who didn't have the balls to do what needed to be done. So she had quit and gone into business for herself.

She didn't need to work often. Her departure from the CIA had been amicable, and she had been given severance and retirement packages that, along with occasional freelance assignments, allowed her to live comfortably in her island bungalow, tending the gardens that surrounded it. At the going rate, one or two jobs a year were enough to support her. The assignments came from a short list of clients, people who knew her skills and trusted her discretion, people who moved at the highest levels of government. Hayes never questioned their judgment in these matters. If they determined that a weed needed to be eliminated, that was enough for her.

Of course, there were different types of weeds, and different methods for removing them. Hayes plucked the tiny shoots of pigweed and Bermuda grass from between the rows of her tomatoes and considered the methods she would use to exterminate the particular weeds that Raymond Devlin had identified.

24

Darcy's Aunt Eleanor lived in a faded brownstone on West Brookline Street in Boston, a broad, tree-lined thoroughfare that provided several places from which an observer could see what was happening without being noticed. But the back door to the brownstone opened onto an alley, one that was hidden from view unless you were in a helicopter passing directly overhead.

She called her aunt shortly before arriving—she wanted her watchers to know where she was going, but not to have enough time to bug the place. Upon her arrival, she visited with her aunt briefly, then warned her that if anyone came looking for her, she was to tell them Darcy wasn't feeling well and had gone upstairs to lie down.

With that, she slipped out the back door, glancing up at the strip of sky above the alley; she would not, in fact, have been surprised to see a helicopter there. The alley emptied onto Tremont Street, where she caught a cross-town bus to Roxbury.

This time, she went straight to the Sportsman's Lounge. But Menard's stool was empty.

"Paul Menard?" she asked the bartender.

"Haven't seen him in a coupla' days."

"Any idea where he is?"

"Nope."

She went to Menard's boarding house, where his

landlady was every bit as helpful as before.

"I don't know where he is. If you find him, tell him his rent's due." She stood in the door, blocking it.

"Do you mind if I go up to his apartment?"

"Fine with me." She stepped aside. "But you better hold your breath. It stinks up there."

It did stink, like meat that had gone bad. She knocked on the door. "Mr. Menard? It's Darcy Cameron. I need to talk to you."

There was no answer, no sound at all from within.

"Look, I don't care if you believe me. I don't care what happened over there. But I need to talk to you."

She listened for a moment, heard nothing, and pulled out a set of master keys. As a search and rescue worker, she was permitted to carry them. But this wasn't a search, and if anyone found out she was using them to break into Menard's apartment, she'd be up disbarment creek without a paddle.

The third key she tried opened the door. She stepped in and closed it behind her.

The stench hit her instantly, a nauseating reek of spoiled meat. She glimpsed a filthy kitchen and decided to avoid it. She headed for the bedroom but got no further than the bathroom in the hall, where the body of Paul Menard sat on the toilet, several empty pill bottles on the floor around him. The body had already begun to decompose, swelling and straining against the confines of his clothes as if they had shrunk around him.

Swallowing hard, choking back the urge to vomit, she forced herself to stay and assess the situation. It looked as if Menard had killed himself with a cocktail of prescription medications. No one else knew about it yet, and she didn't want to be the one to bring it to their attention.

She left, closing the apartment door quietly and

retreating from the building without alerting the landlady. Her hands shook as she stepped outside. She jammed them into her pockets, unable to stop the shaking or clear the image of Paul Menard's decomposing body from her mind.

She headed back to her aunt's house, grappling with the death of Paul Menard. Apparently, whatever happened on the Golan Heights had tormented him until he couldn't live with it any longer.

So why was she in such a hurry to find out what it was?

Patricia Hayes stepped from the closet in Paul Menard's bedroom, where she had hidden when the knock came at the door. She covered her mouth and nose as she passed the bathroom and stepped to the living room window, peering around the edge.

Darcy Cameron strode away from the front door—Hayes recognized her from the law school photograph she had obtained. If she had known it was Cameron, she could have killed two birds with one stone.

Or one bird. Paul Menard had already been dead when she arrived. At first, she'd been annoyed at him for committing suicide—she couldn't very well charge Devlin for killing a man who was already dead when she got there.

Or could she? How would Devlin know that she hadn't killed him? The suicide was a perfect cover, just what an accomplished operative would invent to conceal an assassination.

She headed for the door and passed the bathroom again. She did not notice the dark-tipped feather that lay on the floor beside Menard's body.

Jack O'Brien stood in the doorway to Ned Epstein's

office, his face red, hands clutched, the veins in his neck pulsing as if they were about to explode. "What the hell have you been doing?"

"About what?" Whenever O'Brien erupted, Ned played it cool. If nothing else, it seemed to annoy the Jackass even more.

"You know goddamn well. Didn't I tell you to lay off the Cameron story?"

Ned shrugged. "Sure." He actually hadn't thought much about Marshall Cameron for the past couple of days, other than to make some random searches for Al Beaker and Special Forces unit 785. So why was O'Brien bent out of shape?

"Then why the hell are you still nosing around?" he asked.

"Who told you that?"

"Someone who warned me that my taxes were about to be audited with an ultra-fine titanium-toothed comb if you didn't lay off."

"What?"

"That's right." O'Brien planted a fat forefinger in the middle of Ned's desk. "I don't know what the hell is up with Cameron, but apparently someone doesn't want him to be bothered, and they know how to pull strings so he isn't."

Ned found it hard to believe that whoever was strong-arming Jack O'Brien had Cameron's best interests at heart. And he still didn't know what the connection between Cameron, Al Beaker, and ODA 785 was. But if the little bit of digging he had done was enough to rattle the powers that be, there had to be some awfully big skeletons buried somewhere.

"Now listen, and listen good," O'Brien barked. "I better not hear any more about this, or you're history. Have you got that?"

It was perhaps the lowest moment of Ned's life. He was being threatened with termination from a second-rate job at a third-rate TV station, a job he detested but couldn't afford to lose.

"OK," he said. "I got it."

Jane Chandler met Ernie Kessler at Madam's Organ, another Adam's Morgan hot spot. This time the venue was Kessler's choice, a brash, party-hearty dance club where every night was Mardi Gras—loud music, fluorescent lights, and stuffed animals posed in obscene positions on the wall. The place made Chandler feel old.

Over the blare of techno-cacophony Kessler said, "Raymond Devlin was Junior's company commander." There was a note of triumph in his voice; he loved knowing something she should have known.

"That can't be right," Chandler said. "Wagner was the commander of his unit."

"Right, he was the *unit* commander—the guy who actually goes out on missions with an A-team. But A-teams always report to a B-team, the command and control side of things. The head of the B-team is the company commander, and he's in charge of the whole shebang. That was Devlin."

Chandler scowled. It was the kind of information she should have had at her fingertips.

"Here's the really interesting part," Kessler said. "Devlin is an old friend of the Wagner family. They've got connections going back to Harvard."

"Devlin is Ivy League?"

"No. But his father was. He and President Wagner senior were in the same house at Harvard, the same one Junior ended up in later. Apparently Devlin didn't have the grades for Harvard, and his old man was unable—or unwilling—to play the alumni card to get him in. So

Devlin went to Vietnam instead. He was an MP for a couple of years, then went to OCS and came out—"

She held up a hand. "Slow down. He went to what?"

"OCS. Officer Candidate School. He came out of that as a second lieutenant. Later, he did his Special Forces training and eventually became a B-detachment commander, with six A-teams reporting to him."

"And one of those teams was Wagner's."

"Bingo. You have to wonder if Junior's old man pulled some strings to get him assigned to a detachment led by a family friend. It almost looks as if the old man told Devlin to keep an eye out for him."

It did indeed. And now Wagner was watching out for Devlin. In itself, that wasn't unusual. It could simply have been good old-fashioned patronage, except for one thing.

They had been looking for a body. And apparently they had found it.

25

For two days, Darcy did nothing outside of her usual routine. She ate, slept, walked Pepper, and tried to forget the image of Paul Menard's putrefying body that had burned itself into her memory.

Her father was still not speaking to her. When she called on the phone, the nurses answered, but they could not convince him to talk to her. She stopped by to visit, but he simply stared out the window, refusing to respond to her. Worse, she couldn't be sure if he was still punishing her for betraying him or if he simply didn't recognize her any longer.

The nurses—a procession of women and men from some agency The Village had enlisted—were young, efficient, and endlessly patient with her father. She was grateful for them, the only real link she had with him these days.

On the third day after Paul Menard's death, Darcy climbed the stairs to her office and saw an express package lying outside the door. The label indicated it had come from an attorney in Boston. She didn't recognize the name.

Inside the package was a manila envelope with Darcy's business card attached, along with a cover letter.

Dear Ms. Cameron,
I am an attorney with the Legal Aid Foundation in

Boston, providing pro bono services to low-income residents of the metro-Boston area.

On May 24, Paul Menard came to me seeking advice. Mr. Menard seemed distressed and indicated that he might not have long to live, though he declined to elaborate on his reasons for believing that.

She read the date again. May 24. The day after she talked to Menard.

Mr. Menard's main concern was that, in the event of his death, the enclosed sealed envelope be delivered to you. I agreed to act as custodian of this material and to forward it to you should I ever receive notification of his death.

Unfortunately, I must report that on May 26, Mr. Menard passed away, apparently by his own hand. In accordance with his instructions, I have not examined the contents of this envelope, nor alerted anyone else of its existence. Mr. Menard left no instructions as to what you were to do with this, indicating that its disposition was up to you.

She opened the manila envelope. Inside was a single sheet of lined paper.

Darcy Cameron,

If you get this, it means I'm dead. Which means you were telling the truth. If they think I told you anything, or might tell you anything, it's all over for me.

Don't blame yourself. It was bound to happen sooner or later. Someone else would have found me if you hadn't. It was only a matter of time.

Be careful what you do with this. If they killed me, your life isn't worth shit. Whatever they did to me, they'll do to you.

Paul Menard

Fear and anger slurred together in her chest. Paul Menard had not killed himself. She stared at the letter: *Be careful what you do with this.*

She shook out the envelope. Another, smaller envelope slid out, the size of a credit card. It was marked "Bank of Boston" and had a downtown Boston address. Inside was a safety deposit key.

That afternoon, Darcy made another visit to her aunt in Boston, skipping out once again through the back door. She took side streets and caught a taxi that brought her to the address on the bank envelope.

Anticipating trouble at the bank, she had brought a forged power of attorney—another act that would get her disbarred if it were ever discovered—but she didn't even need it. Menard had forged her name on the signature card. The guy had obviously been thinking ahead.

A middle-aged woman removed the box for her and led her to a private room to view its contents. It was a small box, containing a single manila envelope. She opened it and removed several handwritten pages and a faded color photograph of soldiers standing around a jeep.

I, Paul Menard, do solemnly swear that this is a true story.

In 1983, I served with the 11th Special Forces Group as a member of Operational Detachment Alpha 785.

We were stationed in the Golan Heights, training Israeli forces and running sweeps into Lebanon to clean out nests of Hezbollah and other militants. Needless to say, this was a covert operation.

When we heard about the missionaries being taken

hostage, we wondered if we'd be called on to rescue them. But it didn't happen. So we sat around waiting for the army or the U.N. to get off their butts and do something.

We were the best-trained soldiers in the world, which made us pretty cocky. We figured we could do anything. And the captain in charge of our detachment was the cockiest of all. He decided we were going to rescue those missionaries.

This has to be clear: We undertook the mission without orders or authorization from anyone. Our company commander probably knew what was up, but he didn't say anything. I guess he figured if we succeeded, it would be a feather in his cap, and if we didn't, he could deny knowing anything about it.

We had intel reports that the hostages were being held at a farm outside of Jubb Jannin in the southern end of the Bekka valley. The CIA had a source who told them the various militias were all getting together for a powwow at a different location that night and only a small force would be guarding the hostages.

The Bekka valley wasn't a friendly place at the time. It was crawling with Hezbollah, Abu Nidal, and a half-dozen other militant groups. The Syrians had some bad-ass air defense on the eastern side of the valley, and the militants had shoulder-fired rockets courtesy of the Iranians, for anyone who was stupid enough to try flying over the valley. Needless to say, this wasn't a mission any of us was too anxious to go on.

We flew in after sunset, two H-60 Blackhawks coming in low over the hills. I mean low, like at twenty-five or fifty feet. The Blackhawks had barely enough room for our unit plus the missionaries we planned to recover. We split up, six men to a chopper, in case one of them went down—which seemed like a pretty good possibility.

The farm was located right up against the mountains. We came in hugging the mountains and landed five miles away, then made our way to the farm. That took three hours—we were moving slow because we didn't want to draw a lot of attention to ourselves. We figured we had enough time to get there, snag the captives, get back to the choppers and get out of there before dawn. The plan was to set fire to one of the outbuildings and snag the hostages while the guards were putting out the fire.

The mission was a disaster. The militants were all there and they knew we were coming. Someone had set us up, probably the CIA's own informant. We lost one of our guys right away, and then another one. It was pretty hot for about an hour, but we had more firepower than they did and we were able to finish them off. That's when we found out that all the missionaries had been killed. Some of them probably died in the crossfire, and some of them had been executed by the militants.

We called in the helicopters and got our buddies out of there. The captain told us to leave the civilians. There was nothing we could do for them.

When we got back to base, the captain met with our company commander. He and Devlin...

The name stopped her. Raymond Devlin. Devlin, who had appeared on broadcast television lamenting the loss of three young soldiers in a training accident.

Devlin and the captain came out a half-hour later and gave us the official story—the missionaries had been killed by a rival militia group. Our own guys had been killed by a land mine.

Mark Herriman was furious. He couldn't stand the captain—said he was a rich bastard who was just looking to make a name for himself. Mark told me he was going to report the captain, since the whole thing was his fault. Mark must have told someone else, too, because the next thing I know, he was assigned the job of "laundering" the bodies of our two buddies. The plan was to put the bodies in a jeep with a timer and enough C4 explosive underneath to make very small pieces out of it. Mark was supposed to start the timer, ditch the jeep, and then get the hell out of there.

But something went wrong. The explosive went off when Mark started the timer. And instead of two accidental deaths, we had three. But there's something you need to know. Mark was an Engineer Sergeant, a demolitions expert. He knew everything there was to know about explosives. What happened to Mark in that jeep wasn't an accident.

So the rest of us kept our mouths shut after that. If anyone higher up suspected anything, they kept it to themselves. They were just grateful to have a cover story. Our captain came from money and he had a lot of connections, the main one being his father, who was a senator at the time and chairman of the committee that controls army appropriations. No one in the army wanted to piss him off.

But the whole thing stank, especially about the three guys we lost. They were good men, and it was only because the captain wanted to cover himself with glory that we lost them—not to mention the civilians.

For a long time, I figured the truth would come out— some reporter would stumble onto the pieces, put it all together, and justice would be done. But it didn't happen, which shouldn't have surprised me, I guess. There are two kinds of justice in the world—a kind for ordinary people, and a kind for the rich and powerful, like John Wagner.

A cold wave of panic passed over Darcy. She studied the photograph of the soldiers. Paul Menard stood in the middle of the group, grinning and unmaimed. To one side, slightly apart from the group, was their captain, arms crossed over his chest, radiating confidence. The face was younger and thinner. But there was no mistaking the pointed chin, the dark eyebrows, the eyes like warm lasers. It was John Wagner, future senator from New York. Future presidential candidate.

She slid the papers back into the envelope as carefully as if they were a bomb that could explode at any moment. Which they were. The only question was, who would they kill when they blew up?

26

An icon flashed on the computer screen. Fredericks clicked it, initiating a program called Watson. Watson was a news retrieval program, far more powerful than anything run by Google, Yahoo or Microsoft. If you were tracking a word or phrase and it appeared in print anywhere on the planet, Watson would find it and report back to you. Often, that meant hundreds of hits. This time, there was only one.

Paul Menard

Fredericks clicked the entry.

Boston Herald - Obituaries
Menard, Paul J.
Paul J. Menard died at his home on Tuesday. A 1977 graduate of Danvers High School, Menard served in the U.S. Army from 1977 to 1983, achieving the rank of Staff Sergeant. He received a medical discharge in 1983 as the result of wounds received during operations in Lebanon.

The obituary did not list the cause of death. Nor did it mention any friends or family. Fredericks wasn't surprised to hear that Menard had none.

He thought for a moment, then walked to the office of

Sarah DiPrima, a young researcher whom he suspected had a crush on him.

"I've got a little project I could use some help with," he told her. "Interested?"

Sarah's freckled face opened like a sunflower. "Sure."

"Strictly under the counter, right? No records, plausible deniability."

She straightened her shoulders and erased all but a trace of her smile. "Yes, sir."

"I never spoke to you about this."

"I never saw you."

Fredericks pulled out a paper with the words "US Army Special Forces, ODA 785" written on it. He held it up just long enough for her to memorize. "Got that?"

"Got it."

He tucked the paper back in his pocket. Later, he would destroy it. "I'd like to know the current status of every employee of that company."

"Okey-doke," Sarah said.

Halfway up Mount Connell, Darcy stopped at an outlook and gazed at the rolling green hills below. Even here, a quarter mile from the peak, one could see hundreds of miles in all directions.

She took a deep breath, the air as sharp and crisp as a ripe McIntosh apple. Pepper nosed around, marking bushes and chasing bugs. She too relished the chance to get out of the office and romp. It had been too long for both of them.

Darcy took a long pull from her water bottle and looked back at the highway that ran past the Eastham Airport. There was no traffic on it. In fact, she hadn't seen a single vehicle since she'd pulled into the trailhead parking area across from the airport. A realization came to her then, not through reasoning, but instinctively. She felt it in her gut: They had stopped following her.

She had no idea when they had stopped. But now, recalling her movements for the past few days, she felt certain it was true. Oddly, the realization was not reassuring. Experienced storm watchers know that when a storm is brewing, there is often a period of calm just before all hell breaks loose.

She shook off the feeling and called Pepper. "Come on, girl."

They continued climbing on the old Higgins Peak trail, a little-used, winding path that skirted the mountain in a northeasterly direction. Halfway up, the trail came within a short bushwhack of the East Ridge trail. That trail passed, at one point, through the woods directly behind The Village.

Darcy gazed in the direction of The Village. From where she stood, it was hidden by a ridge of tall evergreens, but she knew exactly where it was.

"It might work," she said aloud. Pepper looked up at her, wondering. Darcy dropped a hand to scratch the dog's head, still staring absent-mindedly at the horizon.

It had to work. If there was a storm brewing, she didn't have much time.

On the way home, Darcy stopped at a pay phone—probably the last working pay phone in Vermont, well away from her office—and made several calls. Although she didn't think she was being followed now, she wasn't taking any chances.

Her final phone call was to Janis.

"Hey, what's up?" Janis said.

"I'm ready to get back to work."

"Really? What did you have in mind?"

Darcy told her exactly what she had in mind.

"Do you want me to call Jackie?" Janis asked.

"No, I'll do it. I've got some special instructions for her, too."

Sarah DiPrima knocked on Fredericks' door, a look of curiosity and dismay on her face. "I've got that information you asked for."

Fredericks read the look. "Come on in."

She closed the door behind her and handed him a handwritten list of names.

Detachment Commander - John Wagner
Detachment Technician - Kevin McKenna - ?
Team Sergeant - Robert LeJeune - retired
Operations Sergeant - Gary Gardner - retired
Weapons Sergeant - Jesus Rodriquez - retired
Asst. Weapons Sergeant - Jason Reilly - ?
Engineer Sergeant - Mark Herriman - retired
Asst. Engineer Sergeant - Douglas Baskett - ?
Medical Sergeant - Tyrone Whitcomb - retired
Asst. Medical Sergeant - Michael Lincoln - retired
Communications Sergeant - Paul Menard - retired
Asst. Communications Sergeant - Michael Hodge - retired

"I couldn't find all of them," she said, indicating the question marks. The look on her face said she didn't think anyone was going to find them any time soon. "The rest are all retired, starting with these three." She pointed to LeJeune, Rodriquez and Herriman.

"The company seems to have a pretty high retirement rate," he said.

"That's what I thought." She scratched notes next to the names of the retirees. The first three had died in a training accident. Next to the others she wrote: murdered, suicide, car accident, apparent heart attack, died in prison.

"Dangerous business," Fredericks said.

"Especially lately." She put check marks next to the names of Gary Gardner, Michael Lincoln and Paul Menard.

"Makes you wonder what's going on."

"It sure does." She pointed to the first name on the list. "The only one still active is the president of the company."

"The president," Fredericks said with a slight nod.

"Right." The irony was not lost on her either.

Ned Epstein's phone rang. The voice that spoke had an edge of military authority to it. "Ned Epstein?"

"Yes?"

"I have some information you've been looking for."

"What information is that?" He glanced at the caller ID. It showed an unfamiliar number with a 202 area code.

"Regarding ODA 785."

Ned sat up quickly. "What is it?"

"You might want to look into the service records of Senator John Wagner."

Ned's heart thumped like a drum roll across his chest. This was it. This was what Woodword and Bernstein must have felt the first time they spoke to Deep Throat. Suddenly, the mystery of Marshall Cameron had become a Very Big Story.

On the other hand, it could also be his last story. Somebody had put the squeeze on Jack O'Brien to make him lay off the Marshall Cameron story. At the very least, if O'Brien found out Ned was still working on the story, he could be looking for his next job from the sidewalk. Or worse—and he didn't want to think about what "worse" might mean.

He decided to play it cautious. "What else can you tell me?"

"Not a damn thing," the voice said. "You're the

reporter. Act like one."

The line went dead.

Ned punched a button on the phone to bring up the caller ID from memory. He scribbled the number on a pad and called Granny. "If I give you a phone number, can you tell me where it came from?"

"Probably."

Granny called back in less than a minute. "It's unlisted, but it came from Langley, Virginia."

"Langley," Ned said. "Isn't that where..."

"It sure is."

Ned's mind raced, trying to make the pieces fit: Marshall Cameron. National Rescue Services. Seconics. Al Beaker. Paul Menard. ODA 785. And now Senator John Wagner and the CIA.

The CIA.

That piece stopped him. The CIA knew what he was up to, and someone there was tipping him off.

That was either the best or the worst news Ned Epstein had ever heard.

Fredericks returned to his office, still not sure why he had phoned Ned Epstein. Call it civil disobedience. The members of ODA 785 were all dead except for John Wagner, and Raymond Devlin didn't want anyone looking at the unit's records. Fredericks didn't know what that added up to, but he'd decided someone else needed to wonder about it besides him.

Sarah DiPrima appeared in the doorway. "You wanted more information about the people in that company?"

He waved her in. "What did you find?"

She handed him a manila folder. "A few stories about their...retirement parties."

If she hadn't been too young for him, he would have kissed her. "You are wonderful."

She blushed, spun on her heels and left.

Most of the articles were sketchy: brief notices of soldiers passing away in training accidents or—after their discharge—from car wrecks. A tabloid featured a grisly photo of a body draped over a toilet, bloated almost beyond recognition. Another story detailed the murder of a small-town police chief. A detail from that article jumped out at him: *Police are investigating whether an eagle feather found beside the body was related to the murder.*

He flipped back to the article about the death of Paul Menard. The photographer had focused on the gruesome image of Menard's corpse. But one corner of the photograph showed the bathroom floor, and lying on it, a feather: long, light-colored, with a black tip.

Fredericks placed the two stories side by side and knew it was no coincidence. An eagle feather beside a body on a highway in Maine was a curiosity. An eagle feather next to a body inside a Boston apartment was a signature.

27

Granny appeared in Ned Epstein's door. "OK, here's the deal on Wagner."

Ned waved his hands. "Quiet, for god's sake." He motioned Granny into the room and shut the door behind him. "O'Brien finds out about this and my ass is grass."

Granny fell into a chair. "I started with Wagner's web site. Nothing special there, just the usual God and glory PR fluff. Senator Wagner served his country with distinction, blah, blah, blah. No details."

"OK."

"Then I did a more open-ended search on the web. Lots of gossip and rumors, but not much in the way of hard facts. Wagner did his undergraduate and law degrees at Harvard. From there he went into the army with a direct commission."

"What does that mean?"

"It means he didn't have to go through ROTC, or Officer Candidate School, or any of the other ways you become an officer. They made him a 2nd lieutenant right out of law school."

"Is that unusual?"

"Apparently not, if you went to Harvard, have more money than the Saudi royal family, and your daddy is a U.S. senator who's poised to become president."

"Membership has its privileges."

"Exactly. The thing is, direct commissions tend to piss

off the rank and file, the folks who come up through the ranks. Also, most people who get direct commissions enter the army in their own field—medicine, engineering, whatever."

"But not Wagner?"

"Nope. Coming out of law school, he should have gone into the Judge Advocate General corps—basically, the army's private law firm. Instead, he went into the Infantry. That probably took more string pulling."

"But there's nothing illegal about all this? Nothing that would cause a scandal if people found out?"

Granny shrugged. "Rich people get all the breaks. What's new about that?"

Ned leaned back, shaking his head. "So what's the connection to ODA 785?"

"Good question. Everyone knows Wagner was in the Special Forces—"

"Which sounds more glamorous than being an army lawyer and prosecuting grunts who fall asleep at the guard post."

"Also handy if you're planning to run for president someday. But as to where he served, what unit he served with, where they were stationed? Good luck finding that out."

"Suspicious."

"We're talking the Green Berets, remember? They don't exactly publicize their exploits. And even if the records were declassified, Wagner would be the only one with the authority to release them."

"How convenient."

"It's perfect, from a political standpoint. You get all the glory for having been in Special Ops, but no one can ever find out exactly what you did."

Ned stared at the wall for a moment, as if outlining his next move. Then he picked up the phone.

"Now what?" Granny asked.

"What the hell," Ned said. "Let's go to the source."

Jane Chandler's phone rang for the millionth time that day. "Yes?"

"Someone from a TV station in Vermont?" her assistant said. "He says it's important?"

Chandler sighed. She had spoken to her assistant more than once about upspeak, explaining how it put her in a subservient position and lessened her authority. For some reason, the girl just didn't get it. "Take his number."

Chandler hung up. These days, she was fielding calls from CNN, Fox, the New York Times and Comedy Central. Broadcast outlets in Vermont were not on her A-list. The Cow-Town Chronicles would have to wait.

Darcy arrived at The Village just before dinner. She had told the nurses she planned to take her father out to eat—after the Epstein affair, they had asked to be alerted about such outings so they could plan his medications—but the advance notice served other purposes. If the CIA was listening in on her father's phone conversations, it would let them know as well.

It also gave the nurses time to cajole Cameron into going out with his daughter. She knew her father had no desire to spend time with her, but she hoped he would go along just to escape their relentlessly cheerful nagging.

It worked. By the time Darcy arrived, Cameron would have gone to dinner with Joseph Stalin if it meant escaping the clutches of Julie, a petite redhead whose conversation was a necklace of clichés strung on a thread of talk-show philosophy.

"Now you take care," she said, seeing them to the door. "And have a wonderful time. It's such a gorgeous day. We don't get enough of these."

Cameron glared at her and Darcy had to suppress a smile. For a man of his intellectual capacities—even diminished by Alzheimer's—Julie's endless chatter would be worse than the Chinese water torture.

She drove to the Eastham Inn and parked in a tree-shaded lot beside the building. As they stepped onto the Inn's front porch, Darcy noticed a blue Taurus with Massachusetts plates pull up and park across the street. The driver made no move to get out of the car.

The front door of the inn was an enormous dark oak affair that opened into a foyer of even darker mahogany. The ceiling was antique pressed tin, and there were wooden sconces on the wall. The maître d' greeted Darcy and her father with a patrician Yankee air. "Good evening, Mr. Cameron. Nice to have you with us again."

Cameron nodded, not deigning to respond. So far, Darcy thought, the Alzheimer's hadn't affected her father's personality greatly. He continued to carry himself like a wealthy man—not monetarily, though his years at TimeLine had certainly left him well off. His was a wealth of deference, an invisible barrier that insulated him from the concerns that troubled ordinary people: anxiety about the opinions of others, self-doubt, fear of violating social rules. He was immune to these, as if they were viruses from which his fame protected him.

The maître d' led them to a corner table in the formal dining room, but Darcy hesitated. "Could we sit in the front room? It's so much brighter there."

"Of course."

He seated them by a tall window that looked out onto the front porch. Peering past the curtain, Darcy saw the Taurus, still parked. The driver—a woman in sunglasses, dark hair pulled back tightly from her face—sat studying a map.

A waiter appeared with menus and asked for their

drink orders.

"Scotch. Rocks," Cameron said, staring at the menu.

Darcy glanced at the waiter and shook her head. "Ginger ale, please." Her father's medications ruled out alcohol. "Iced tea for me."

"Very good."

She studied the menu. "Try the lobster pie today?"

Cameron glanced at her over the top of the menu as if she were a stranger who had accosted him on the street.

"Or not," she said.

The waiter returned. Darcy ordered a Caesar salad. Her father ordered by pointing to the menu. When their meals arrived, she tried again to engage him in conversation, to no avail. She gave up and they ate the rest of their meal in silence.

As they left the Inn, the Taurus was still parked across the street, the driver studying the map. She had been doing that for forty minutes. With sunglasses on.

On impulse, Darcy called to her. "Do you need help finding anything?"

The woman looked up, smiling. "Oh, no, I'm fine, thank you. Just trying to decide the best way to get to my friend's house."

Darcy nodded. *I'll bet you are.*

She drove back to The Village, glancing periodically in the mirror. When they were almost out of sight of the Inn, the Taurus pulled out, headed in their direction.

Darcy felt an odd sense of satisfaction. The trial run had confirmed her suspicions: They might not be following her, but it was clear they were still watching her father. And this time she knew about it.

Ned Epstein was putting the finishing touches on his lead story—another big box store being developed despite local resistance against it—when Granny knocked on his door.

"Can I borrow your car?"

"When?"

"Tonight." He glanced up and down the hall. "I've got a date with Kim. We're going out for a drink after work."

Kim was WOFB's receptionist, a woman with long brown hair and excellent posture—which was surprising, given the weight the poor girl carried on her chest. Granny had been hounding her for a date for months and it looked as if she'd finally given in.

As a matter of principle, Ned wanted to support Granny's attempt to scale Mount Kim. But this was his Beemer they were talking about—a six speed 535i, one of the few remnants of his once-prosperous life. "I don't know—"

"C'mon. You know I can't take her out in the truck."

That was true. Granny's truck looked as if a homeless person lived in it. Maybe several homeless people.

Ned shook his head. "What are you going to do if you get a second date?" Given Granny's social skills, that seemed highly unlikely, but he was giving him the benefit of the doubt. "You can't keep fooling her by using my car."

Granny shrugged. "After the first date, she'll be in love with me and she won't care."

"Right." He pulled the keys from his pocket and tossed them to Granny. "Just don't wreck it, OK?"

Granny dropped the keys to his truck on Ned's desk. "You're the best."

"Don't I know it."

At the end of the day Granny stopped by the front desk, where Kim was gathering her belongings. "All set?"

"I sure am. What a day." As they walked to the car she told him a long story about the office manager, who was insisting she work this weekend even though she had worked the previous weekend and she was supposed to have this one off and it wasn't fair because...

Granny tried to pay attention but found it difficult, distracted as he was by the bright pink stretch top Kim was wearing. He was also thinking about the effect her appearance would have on the regulars at the Rusty Gate Grill, and enjoying that nearly as much.

He guided her to the BMW, which looked as if it had just been washed and waxed. God bless Ned.

"Nice car," Kim said.

Granny flushed. "Thanks."

The Rusty Gate Grill sat just outside of town at the bottom of a long, slow descent. As the car crested the hill, Granny noticed that the brakes seemed a little mushy. He pumped them, but they were still soft.

The next moment, the brakes were gone. The brake pedal went to the floor and the car gathered speed even though his foot wasn't on the gas.

"Oh, man," Granny said.

Kim braced herself. "Shouldn't you slow down?"

"Yeah. I'm working on that." He pumped the brakes. Nothing.

60 mph. 70. They were racing toward the bottom of the hill, where the road veered to the left. He knew of only two ways to stop the car, neither one of which was guaranteed to work.

He pulled the emergency break up slowly, hoping it would slow them without flipping the car.

That worked a little, but not enough. He knew one other trick. If it didn't work, they'd probably crash and be killed. If it did work, Ned would kill him anyway.

He downshifted into fourth and let out the clutch. It ground, but slowed the car a little. He progressed through third, second, and first, each time slowing the car marginally and leaving little pieces of its transmission on the highway.

At the bottom of the hill Granny yelled, "Hang on."

He took the turn and the car went into a skid, sliding off the road and into a ditch. The car slammed into a phone pole, crumpling the front end and deploying the air bags.

28

Darcy was at the Eastham post office first thing in the morning. She watched as the postmaster slapped an express mail sticker on the package. "You're sure this will arrive today?"

He glanced up at the wall clock. "Pickup's at 10 am." He checked the zip code again. "This close, it should be there in a few hours."

"Great."

She drove to The Village and showed up at her father's apartment, unannounced this time. Pepper was with her. "I thought we'd go for a walk," she told the nurse.

Her father sat frowning with disapproval at a program on the History Channel. He looked up as Pepper bounded past Julie and placed her head in his lap. Cameron gazed into Pepper's eyes intently, saying nothing but scrubbing her forehead with his knuckles.

"A walk?" Julie said. "Well, that's a surprise. But I'm sure he could use some fresh air." She called to Cameron. "Doesn't a walk sound nice?"

Cameron's eyes didn't leave Pepper. "It's too damn cold to walk."

"No, it's not," Darcy said. "It's beautiful out. Just a bit cool."

He shot her an annoyed look. "No thank you."

Once again, Julie came to the rescue. "Well, it's up to

you. If you'd rather stay in and watch Days of Our Lives with me..."

Cameron sighed heavily. "I'll walk."

"Let's take your jacket," Darcy said. "Just in case."

Julie saw them to the door. "Have a wonderful time, now."

"Thanks," Darcy said. *We'll damn sure try.*

As they walked through the lobby, they passed Wakefield's office. Wakefield stood by his secretary's desk, gazing down the front of her blouse. He looked up, saw them and called cheerfully, "Mr. Cameron—going for a constitutional?"

"No," Cameron mumbled without stopping. "I'm going to Istanbul."

"Right. Excellent."

Darcy couldn't help but grin. Even in his confused condition, her father did not suffer fools.

As they stepped out the front door, Darcy zipped up her dark blue windbreaker. "Let's go this way," she said, choosing a path that wound around the back of the property.

Pepper ran ahead of them, nosing around the flowering trees, reading the messages left by previous canines. Darcy waved to her father's neighbors as they tended their tiny gardens or practiced putting on miniature greens. Cameron stared straight ahead and ignored everyone.

They came to a place where the path curved out of sight of the buildings, up against the woods that formed the rear boundary of the grounds.

Darcy glanced around and nodded into the woods. "Let's go for a walk in there."

Cameron eyed her. "Why?"

"No reason. It's just a nice day for a walk in the woods."

He continued staring at her but said nothing. Darcy called Pepper and took a few steps into the woods. Pepper, realizing where they were going, bounded past her.

Her father hesitated for a moment and then, to Darcy's immense relief, stepped through the low underbrush in the direction of the East Ridge trail.

Ned showed up at the garage and the mechanic walked him to the Beemer, which sat forlornly at the back of the lot. "You got any enemies?"

"What do you mean?"

The mechanic nodded in the direction of the car. The hood had been peeled back like a crumpled piece of aluminum foil. "Your friend's lucky he wasn't going down a steeper hill. See this?"

He bent over the engine and pointed to the brake lines running from the master cylinder. "See how those lines are crunched? Looks like someone took a set of pliers to them. Soon as there was any pressure on the system, brake fluid would've been squirting out of the leaks. Wouldn't take long to bleed the cylinder dry."

"You think someone did that on purpose?"

The mechanic shrugged. "Could'a happened in the accident, I guess. But check this out." He lifted a set of wires whose ends had been neatly cut. "These are the wires that go to your brake warning light. Without these, you'd have no idea you were losing the brakes."

"Someone cut them?"

The mechanic raised his eyebrows. "You tell me."

Ned stared at the damage but was picturing the road just before his house. It was even steeper than the hill before the Rusty Gate and turned sharply at the bottom where it ran along the Gilbertville Gorge. If a person came down that hill too fast and missed the turn, he'd end up in the gorge, a fifty foot drop onto granite boulders.

"Like I say, your friend was lucky," the mechanic said.

Ned nodded, his mouth dry. "Yeah."

It took Darcy and her father only a few minutes to reach the East Ridge trail. From there, they headed north, climbing now. An eighth of a mile farther, they arrived at a bare outcropping swept by gusting winds. Pepper ran ahead, peering over the edge.

"Careful, girl," Darcy called. The trail was treacherous there, skirting a ravine that descended precipitously into scrub and bracken. At the edge, a single misstep could easily send a person crashing downward. It was not a fall one would be likely to survive.

Darcy stood gazing into the ravine, the wind whipping the jacket around her. Cameron had stopped on the trail behind her, staring to one side. "Someone's been bushwhacking here."

Darcy looked to where he pointed. The signs were subtle—a tussock of bent grass, dried leaves that had been crunched underfoot. And one intentionally broken and twisted branch.

She stared at him for a moment, amazed that his powers of observation were still sharp despite the disease.

"You're right," she said and whistled for Pepper, who had run ahead on the trail. As Pepper ran back, Darcy nodded at the break in the path that her father had found. "We're going this way."

He glared at her. "Why should I go anywhere with you?"

If he meant to hurt her with that, he had succeeded. But she didn't have time to wallow in that now. It was time to tell him. She swallowed the ache and pressed on. "Because we're going fishing."

She knew from the look on his face that she'd been right. That seemingly innocent expression was a code of some kind.

He studied her face. "Who are you?"

The question felt like a slap in the face, but she could tell he was not being facetious. He did not know her. She steadied herself. "Dad, it's me, Darcy. Your daughter."

A look of disgust came over his face. "No, you're not."

She waved a hand. "It doesn't matter. I just have to get you out of here."

"I'm not going anywhere until you explain yourself."

Her mind raced, searching for a way to gain his cooperation. Bullying wouldn't work, and her father wasn't the kind of person you could wheedle into doing what you wanted. She was not a good liar, and she had never thought of herself as an actress. But desperate times called for desperate measures.

"I'm your exit contact," she said. "I've made arrangements to get you out of here. But we don't have much time."

He appraised this for a moment, then shook his head. "It won't work. They're watching too closely."

"We have to try. It's not safe for you here."

"Why should I trust you?"

She was improvising now. "Because I know what's going on. I know about Al Biqa. I know about the massacre, and Wagner, and Devlin. And I know they're not going to leave you alive if it messes up their plans."

He stood still, blinking, trying to digest all this.

"Mr. Cameron," she said. "Trust me. I know I screwed up once. But I'm trying to make it right now. Please, trust me."

A gust of wind whipped around them, kicking up sand off the rocks. In the distance, a hawk screeched.

"All right," Cameron said finally. He sat on a log and began untying his shoe.

"What are you doing?"

"I've got something in my shoe."

She grabbed his arm. "We don't have time for that. They're going to be after us."

"That's why I have to get rid of this," he said, shrugging off her grasp with a strength that surprised her. He pulled off the shoe and pointed to a tiny slit in the sole. "Tracking device. Why do you think they weren't worried about letting me go with you?"

Darcy stared at the shoe, uncertain whether this was real or dementia-induced paranoia.

"Give me your car keys," he said. She hesitated and he held out a hand. "Just give me the damn keys."

She handed them over and he dug into the slit with the point of a key. A small cylinder, like an automotive fuse, popped out.

He put his shoe back on and stood. Beyond the outcropping, the land descended into the ravine and past that, a thickly wooded hollow. He threw the transmitter on a high arc that descended into the trees and disappeared from sight. "Track that, you bastards."

Julie McMillan finished her notes on Marshall Cameron and closed the chart. In the short time she had been caring for him, she'd seen a marked diminution of his abilities. Although he was generally lucid, his periods of delusion seemed more frequent now, as well as his mood swings. In mere moments, he could go from rational to confused, from complacent to agitated. It seemed unlikely that he would be able to live on his own much longer, even with assistance. But then, you never knew. Maybe Devlin was right, and Cameron was just faking it.

She pulled a tablet computer from her purse and

entered the latest information on Cameron. The data was instantly encrypted and uploaded via wireless link to a central computer at Langley.

This assignment was Agent McMillan's first since completing her training. She had thrown herself into the part of the ditsy nurse as if her very life depended on her acting skills. Someday, in a less congenial setting, it just might.

Meanwhile, here in the upscale comfort of The Village, McMillan was restless. She hadn't gone through the rigors of training just to baby-sit a retired agent, even if he was a celebrity.

She clicked on the TV, found the most obnoxious soap opera she could, and pressed the memory button. Then she switched to a cable channel showing a police drama. As soon as she heard Cameron at the door, she would hit the memory recall button.

Her cell phone rang. The display told her the call was from headquarters. "Yes?"

"Where is he?" The voice belonged to one of the anonymous operators who manned the tracking desk.

"Out for a walk with his daughter. Why?"

"Something happened to the transmitter. We got odd signals—very rapid movement, then no movement at all."

"Give me the coordinates," McMillan said.

She pulled out her computer and entered the coordinates. A topo map showed the current location of the transmitter, a half-mile into the woods north of The Village.

What were they doing there? She considered the possibilities: Cameron had bolted and his daughter hadn't been able to stop him. Or they had foolishly gone for a hike and he'd fallen off the trail.

Or the third possibility: They were on the run.

She ran a series of scenarios in her mind and knew she

would need help. "I'm calling backup," she told the operator.

She hung up and called the agent with whom she shared responsibility for Cameron. "We've got a possible fugitive."

"I'll be right there."

Moments later, she was running from the building, and almost ran into Leonard Wakefield as he stepped from his office.

"What's going on?" Wakefield demanded.

The nurse ignored him and ran out the front door. Wakefield jogged to Cameron's apartment and saw the open door, the empty apartment. "Oh, damn. Not again."

Harvey Warren pushed the chair back from his desk and hit the wall just a couple feet away. Cursing, he eased his way out from behind the desk and stepped over the snoring German shepherd. He strode to the reception area, looking for a place to pace or a window to stare out of.

It was a futile search. The Eastham police department sat in a few cramped basement rooms in the back of the town hall, the same rooms it had been in since the building was put up over a century ago. In that time, the number of residents, police officers, and arrests had increased exponentially, making the current quarters a joke. Other towns, even those much smaller than Eastham, had brand-new municipal buildings with spacious, modern facilities for their police departments.

But not here. At town meeting every year the subject of new headquarters for the police came up. Every year Warren made an impassioned speech about their need for better offices, and every year the skinflint Yankees voted it down. It was like a play that had a disastrous one-night stand every year, with Harvey Warren playing the lead.

The phone rang at the front desk. The receptionist

answered and called to Warren, "It's for you."

Warren returned to his desk and picked up the phone. "Warren here."

"Hello, it's Leonard Wakefield, at The Village."

Wakefield reminded the chief of one of those nervous little dogs, the kind rich people owned. "What can I do for you?"

"It's Mr. Cameron. I think he's wandered off again."

"You think."

"Well, his room is empty, and the nurse ran out of here just a moment ago. She seemed quite upset."

Warren remembered the nurse, a little redhead with muscular arms and legs that didn't seem to go with her bubbly personality. She would probably be energetic in the sack.

"I don't want to alarm the other residents again," Wakefield said. "And I'd hate to raise a big fuss about this —"

"I understand," Warren said. He understood that Wakefield was more worried about saving face than about what happened to The Village's residents. Still, this was his chance to show Wakefield—not to mention the state police, and that perky redhead—that Eastham's police could handle this kind of thing on their own.

"I'll take a ride out and see what I can do," Warren said.

"Would you? That would be wonderful. And I don't think there's any need to tell—"

"I'll be there in a few minutes," Warren said, and hung up. He whistled for the dog. "Come on, you bum. Time to earn your keep."

29

Devlin swore and slammed a fist on his desk, rattling the pens and coffee cup on top of it. "How long ago?"

"Just a few minutes," Fredericks said.

"And the daughter is with him?"

"It looks that way."

Devlin shook his head. "I knew it. She was probably part of it all along."

Fredericks said nothing. In a moment, Devlin would have Darcy Cameron graduating from an Al Qaeda training camp. He considered reminding Devlin that it was the daughter who turned Cameron over to them the first time, but decided against it. "Do you want search and rescue again?"

"No, not this time. We've got too much exposure on this situation as it is. The agents who are there can handle it."

Fredericks didn't know what to make of that. At this point, Marshall Cameron was looking more like a fugitive than a missing person, yet Devlin didn't seem interested in chasing him.

"But we should have someone there when they find him," Devlin added. "How quickly could you get there?"

"A couple of hours, at best."

"All right. Do it."

Fredericks left, pondering the fate of Marshall

Cameron. By the time he got to Vermont, Marshal Cameron and his daughter could probably be long gone, one way or another. That meant he wasn't being sent to take charge of the situation. He was being sent to pick up the pieces—and sweep them quietly under the rug.

Cruising along Rt. 100 near Eastham, Jackie Bradley heard the call on the local police band.

"Unit 2, we've got a possible missing person at The Village on Madison Lane. Unit 1 is en route with the K9 unit."

A moment later, her cell phone rang. She smiled, knowing who it was before she looked at the caller ID. "Bradley here."

"This is Chief Warren in Eastham. We've got another situation with Marshall Cameron."

"Now what?"

Warren gave her the details in a perfunctory manner. "I'm heading over there with my dog, but I thought I'd let you folks know what was up."

Right, Bradley thought. You thought you'd cover your ass since you made such a hash of things the last time. "All right," she said. "Thanks for keeping us informed. But this sounds like a fugitive situation—right up your alley." She knew that would give Warren a Dragnet hard-on that he couldn't resist. "Besides, your dog is trained for this kind of thing, and it's your jurisdiction."

"Right," Warren said.

Bradley could almost hear his chest expanding; Harvey Warren was playing with the big boys now. They had finally realized that he was the right person to take care of these problems.

Which was exactly what she wanted him to think.

Harvey Warren peeled into The Village parking lot,

blue lights flashing. As he pulled up in front of the Village Square he saw a crowd of people milling around outside the entrance. They were dressed for hiking, some sporting radios and binoculars.

Warren stepped from the squad car and one of the group—a local realtor that Warren recognized—approached him.

"What's going on?" Warren asked.

"We heard about Mr. Cameron," the realtor said. "What can we do to help?"

Shit, Warren thought. That was just what he needed. People tromping around, destroying any scent trail his K-9 might pick up, making it even harder to find Cameron. How had they found out about this so quickly?

He didn't have time to worry about that now. He would deal with these idiots after he spoke to Wakefield. "Wait here," he said.

Warren strode into the Village Square and encountered a man and a women dressed in SWAT attire. The man stood punching buttons on a GPS unit. The woman saw Warren, shook her head and said, "It's all right. We've got everything under control here."

Warren stared her down. "Who the hell..." Then he recognized her. It was Cameron's nurse.

She flipped a badge open. "Agents McMillan and DiOrsi. Central Intelligence Agency."

"Central..." Warren blinked. "The CIA?"

"Are you by yourself?" McMillan asked.

Warren nodded. "I didn't think this called for—"

"Good." She glanced out the window toward the cruiser. "Is that a search dog?"

"Yes. He's been trained to—"

"Is he ready to work?"

"Yeah, sure."

"All right," McMillan said. "We can use your help."

"You can use—" Warren was about to bite her head off but checked himself. This was the CIA. They probably had jurisdiction here. "OK."

Agent DiOrsi approached with the GPS unit. "I've got a signal on the tracker."

"All right," McMillan said, and nodded to Warren. "Let's go."

As they stepped out the front door, McMillan saw the crowd. "Who are all these *people?*"

"No idea. I didn't call them," Warren said.

"Who did?"

"I don't know."

She frowned and nodded toward the squad car. "Get the dog."

Warren jerked a thumb towards the crowd. "What about them?"

"Never mind them. Just get the dog."

He retrieved the German shepherd while DiOrsi consulted the GPS and pointed them in the general direction that Marshall Cameron had traveled. Once the shepherd found the place where Cameron had left the walking path, they didn't need the GPS. The dog was off, bounding into the woods, barely slowing to sweep the ground with his highly-sensitive nose. The agents trotted behind him and Harvey Warren struggled to keep up.

Ten minutes later they came to the East Ridge trail, and followed that to an outcropping that overlooked a ravine. DiOrsi consulted the GPS. "We're close."

The shepherd seemed distracted, running to the edge, sniffing along the trail again, then returning to peer down into the ravine, whining.

"What's he doing?" McMillan asked.

"He wants to go down there," Warren said. "But he doesn't know how."

He followed the dog's line of sight and saw the body.

It was a woman, her body crumpled from the fall, blonde hair pulled back in a ponytail. She wore blue jeans and a dark blue windbreaker.

"That's her," Warren said. "She must have fallen."

"Where's Mr. Cameron?" McMillan asked.

"How should I know? He's got Alzheimer's, right? He could be in Canada by now."

McMillan instructed DiOrsi to climb down the ravine and see if there was anything to be done for Darcy Cameron. "We'll wait up here."

DiOrsi began the long climb down. Loose soil, scant footholds and dense ground cover slowed his progress. As he descended, he saw that a lower trail connected with the ravine, one that was hidden from the trail above. Ironically, Darcy Cameron's body had landed in a place she could easily have walked to.

He touched ground and unhooked his line. From behind him came a soft pattering. He snapped around.

A golden retriever raced up the trail toward him. DiOrsi crouched into a defensive posture, but the dog charged past him as if he were a tree stump. It wasn't interested in him. It was headed for the body.

Then came footsteps. A woman in outdoor gear ran up the trail, her jacket emblazoned with search and rescue badges.

DiOrsi stepped in front of her. "What are you doing here? You people weren't supposed to—"

The dog barked, and the woman pushed DiOrsi aside. "Excuse me, I've got to attend to my dog."

She knelt, massaging the dog's neck. "Good job, Scooter." She pulled out a rubber ball and tossed it up the trail. The dog took off after it.

McMillan called down through the brush, "What's going on down there?"

"I don't know," DiOrsi yelled. He approached the

woman. "What the hell are you—"

He stopped. Behind her, Darcy Cameron was sitting up. DiOrsi stared, his mouth open, as she pushed back a sleeve and glanced at her watch. "Good work," she said to the other woman. "Twenty-two minutes."

She stood, dusting leaves off her pants, and now DiOrsi saw that it was not Darcy Cameron. It was a woman who looked, especially from a distance, very much like her, a woman who wore the same clothes that Darcy Cameron had been wearing when last seen. But it wasn't her.

"What the hell's going on here?" he asked.

"Training session." The searcher held out a hand to DiOrsi. "Janis Levine, Vermont K-9 Search and Rescue."

DiOrsi ignored the hand and looked at the other woman, who nodded and said, "Ellen Westheimer."

He looked from one to the other, then back up the precipice he had just descended. Maybe this was all just coincidence—the volunteers that no one called for, the training session that just happened to be held on this day at this time, the woman who looked just like Darcy Cameron. But something told him they had been snookered. Darcy Cameron was still very much alive, and still on the run.

Darcy had worried that her father wouldn't be able to keep up with her. She needn't have. Regardless of his mental capacity, he was as physically fit as a forty year old.

Still, they would need time. The route she'd planned would take even the hardiest hiker an hour to cover. She just hoped her plan would provide the time they needed.

Pepper ranged ahead of them, following the path they had laid out before. At this point, the problem was to keep her father moving. When he stopped, he seemed to forget what they were doing. That was typical of Alzheimer's victims, so she kept his mind occupied by talking about things he could remember—the past.

"Tell me what happened at Al Biqa," she said as they bushwhacked their way to the Higgins Peak trail.

He hesitated, as if he were assembling the pieces for a report. "I was at Rashaya. Non-official cover. I was supposed to be covering the kidnapping for the networks. But I was really there to set up negotiations with the kidnappers."

"And something went wrong."

"Yes. I had a contact," he said, ducking under a branch. "He told me most of the kidnappers would be away at a summit meeting with the other militias." He shook his head at the memory. "I passed the information up the line, but I told them it was suspect. Hashem's loyalty was only as good as the last payment we'd given him. I didn't trust him."

He stopped, looking around as if suddenly wondering where they were and what they were doing there.

"So you passed along the information about the summit meeting," Darcy said quickly. "Then what happened?"

He began moving again. "Then Wagner decided to play cowboy. His unit went in, the hostages were killed, they lost some men, and the Army of Allah was wiped out. It was a bloodbath."

"How did you find out about it?"

Cameron stopped and looked at her as if it was a stupid question. "I was there."

Darcy stared at him. "You were there? At Al Biqa?"

By now they had broken through the underbrush and emerged onto the Higgins Peak trail. As they headed west Cameron said, "Wagner asked me if I wanted to go along for the ride. That's the kind of ego the man had. He wanted me there so I could write a first-hand account of the triumphant rescue." He shook his head. "The man was already planning his political future. Nothing like a dramatic hostage rescue to spice up the bio."

"Except it went bad."

"Extremely bad. International fiasco, body-bag bad."

"And you were blamed."

"Of course. Golden Boy Wagner wasn't going to take the fall. Uncle Ray Devlin was covering his ass with a Teflon-plated shit deflector."

"So Devlin and Wagner came up with the story about the dueling militia groups?"

"Right. Who was going to contradict them? Everyone who had been there from the Army of Allah was dead. The missionaries were all dead. The only ones left who knew the truth were the soldiers under Devlin's command."

"And you."

Then came a pause, like a musical beat—the momentary rest before the orchestra plays the climactic chord, the phrase that sums up the entire piece.

"And me," Cameron said. "They did have to deal with me. That's when I decided it was time for a career change and applied for the TimeLine position."

"You applied for that? I thought..." She shifted, trying to maintain the fiction of being his exit contact. "I heard the agency arranged that."

Cameron snorted. "That's what a lot of people thought. No one knew what happened at Al Biqa, but they figured the TimeLine job was a payoff for keeping my mouth shut."

Of course, Darcy thought. It would certainly look that way to an outsider.

"I didn't even want the damn job," Cameron said. "But I didn't have a choice."

"Why not?"

"Given what I knew about Al Biqa, my long-term prospects were not good. I needed more visibility. A roving journalist who accidentally gets killed by a sniper in the field wouldn't attract much attention. But a celebrity would."

She saw it now. Her father had purposely taken a job he didn't want so that every eye would be on him. At least then, if anything happened to him, someone might get suspicious.

"As long as Devlin thought I was loyal, he didn't have to worry," Cameron said.

Darcy understood the implication: When Devlin learned of Cameron's disease, he must have begun to worry. A man who couldn't control his own mind, who sometimes didn't know what he was talking about, was a ticking time bomb. And her father had known that sooner or later, Devlin would decide to defuse that bomb.

"But that wasn't the main reason I took the TimeLine job," Cameron said. "I also had my family to think about."

Darcy hesitated. His family? Exactly what family was he talking about? Given the secrets she had uncovered in the past few days, nothing seemed implausible, and for a moment, her old fears resurfaced: Her father had a secret family somewhere, the one he had hidden all these years, the children on whom he had lavished the attention she never got.

"What family?" she asked, not really wanting the answer.

He frowned, as if this were information she should know. "My daughter. Darcy."

She kept walking but nearly stumbled, heart racing, eyes filling. He had been so lucid, had remembered the events of the past so clearly, that she had almost forgotten about his disease. She coughed, rubbed a sleeve across her eyes, and walked on.

"I never wanted them to be able to use her against me," Cameron said. "So I pretended she didn't exist. That was the hardest part of the whole damn thing."

The tears came too fast now, faster than she could blink them away or rub them on her sleeve. She simply kept moving, facing forward on the trail, hoping he would not see the wet lines on her face or hear the gulping breaths as she swallowed back thirty years of pain, anger, and loss.

30

Ned Epstein sat pondering the fate of his beloved BMW and of his career. At this point, both were wrecks.

A few days ago, he had imagined himself on the trail of the Really Big Story, saw himself writing a book about his exploits, appearing on talk shows. Instead, he had come to a dead end. He had left eight messages with Senator Wagner's campaign staff, none of which had been returned. He'd had no luck uncovering more about Wagner's service record, and he still had no idea what that had to do with Marshall Cameron or his disappearance, let alone the CIA. Now his car was wrecked and there was a very good chance it was because someone wanted him dead.

He had reached the end of the line. And there, at the very end, was the annual zucchini festival in Bennington, an event that rated a 9.9 on the cornball scale, complete with zucchini recipes, zucchinis races, and an idiot in a giant zucchini costume.

"Get over there and grab some footage," O'Brien had insisted. "We've got a hole in the 6 o'clock."

The zucchini festival, Ned thought. It had come to this.

He called Granny—who was still able to work despite the neck brace the doctor insisted he wear—and was about to head out when one of the mailroom kids stuck his head in the door. "Express package for you," he said and handed over an envelope.

There was no name on it other than his, no return address.

Ned zipped the package open and pulled out a sheaf of photocopied pages, along with a note.

Here's your story. Do what you can with this. Broadest distribution possible. If anything happens to me, there's a story there as well. D.C.

He wondered at the initials for only a moment: D.C. Darcy Cameron.

He scanned the pages and adrenaline shot through him like an extra-large triple espresso. This was what he'd been looking for. It was all there—Al Biqa, not Al Beaker —along with Paul Menard, ODA 785, and at the heart of it, John Wagner.

The phone rang. It was O'Brien. "Why haven't you left yet?"

A slow smile spread across Ned Epstein's face as he determined the most creative, satisfying and memorable way of telling Jack O'Brien just where he could stick the annual zucchini festival.

Darcy, Cameron and Pepper emerged from the woods onto the highway directly across from the airport. Cameron hesitated as they crossed—Darcy wasn't sure if he remembered the accident, but his instincts were clearly telling him to be careful. "It's OK," she said, taking his arm.

Outside the hangar, a Cessna 182 equipped with floats stood idling. As they jogged to it, the mechanic strolled out of the shed.

"Are we ready to roll?" Darcy shouted.

He nodded. "Ready when you are."

Cameron checked out the ponytailed mechanic and

frowned. "Where are we going?"

"I told you," Darcy said. "We're getting out of here. But we've got a little side-trip to take first, and Roy here is going to take us."

"Where?"

"I'll explain on the way. Let's go."

Roy helped the two passengers and the dog aboard and closed the door. They took off, circling back over the runway as they climbed. Darcy gazed down at the trailhead on the other side of the road as a German shepherd, a person in a SWAT uniform, and one angry police chief emerged from the woods and stared up at them.

Devlin stared at the tracking report his assistant had handed him. "What does all this crap mean?"

The assistant swallowed. "Given the plane's altitude, we can make a rough approximation—"

"Just tell me where the hell they're going."

"They're headed southeasterly," the assistant said. "Towards Boston."

"Boston?"

"Yes, sir. There's something else. The plane had floats on it."

"Floats?"

"For a water landing."

"A water landing? Why would they—" And then he realized.

He dismissed the assistant and placed a private call to Patricia Hayes. "They're headed to Boston. Get there. Now."

In 1764, an enterprising merchant named John Rowe purchased a spit of land on Boston harbor, the site where the original settlers had placed cannon to defend the city.

There, Rowe built a wharf and a warehouse to store the goods his ships brought to the new world from exotic ports of call: silk, oranges, and a historic load of tea that never made it to dry land.

Two hundred years later, Rowes Wharf had become a derelict, the result of a declining shipping industry. Its rotting piers were lined with tumble-down fish shacks and coated with a slick glaze of sea slime and algae. Then, in the 1980s, a new infusion of merchant cash and urban renewal transformed the pier. The shacks were replaced by an upscale complex of shops, offices, exclusive apartments and the Boston Harbor Hotel. Narrow side streets became pedestrian walkways. The aging ferry service to Georges Island was transformed into a world-class marina. And the formerly rundown dock area became one of Boston's toniest neighborhoods.

In the master bedroom of the hotel's Presidential Suite, Senator Wagner stood by a picture window that provided a stunning view of the marina and the harbor, its blue-black surface dotted with million-dollar yachts. In the distance, a steady parade of planes arrived and departed from Logan airport.

Wagner's cell phone rang, disturbing his reverie. "Yes?"

"Cameron is on the run," Devlin said. "And his daughter is with him this time."

"What? I thought you—"

"There's more. I think they're headed your way."

"Oh, for the love of—"

"I've got someone headed there right now. Of course, simply detaining them won't resolve the matter. Given Cameron's condition, there's no telling how or when he might complicate matters. And now with his daughter's involvement..." His voice trailed off.

"What are you saying?"

"We need to fix this. Permanently."

Wagner considered this for a moment. He'd come too far to have his plans ruined by a senile newsman and his interfering daughter. He took a deep breath. "All right. Do what you have to do."

Devlin hung up the phone and clicked off the recorder attached to the line. It would never have occurred to Wagner that Devlin recorded all their conversations. For a Harvard graduate, the man was an idiot.

Of course, it hadn't been brains that got Wagner into Harvard in the first place, it was his family connections, connections that hadn't been good enough for Devlin. So while Wagner was getting drunk with coeds in Cambridge, Devlin had been dodging rounds from a Chinese-made assault rifle in Khesanh.

That was how it had always been. Devlin worked his tail off to become an officer. Wagner became an officer with a signature on a piece of paper. Devlin fought for every promotion he received. Wagner got promotions he didn't even ask for. Pay raises, transfers, and choice assignments had all come easily to Wagner. When he decided to join Special Forces—a decision that infuriated his father but which he could not be talked out of—the Senator arranged for him to be assigned to Devlin's command. The old bastard had even had the balls to ask Devlin to keep an eye on him.

Which Devlin had done. He'd watched as Wagner alienated the men under his command, endangered their welfare, and eventually got three of them killed because of his recklessness.

Or two of them. To be fair, the third man wasn't entirely Wagner's fault. Herriman had been an unavoidable casualty of the need to cover Wagner's ass. Just as Paul Menard had been. And as Marshall Cameron and his daughter would soon be.

All this because John Wagner was poised to become president of the United States. Ray Devlin would do whatever was necessary to make that happen. Because come inauguration day, Wagner would be sitting at the big desk in the Oval Office, and Ray Devlin would be right behind him pulling the strings.

And if Wagner ever had any doubts on that score, Devlin had the recordings to remind him of his place.

In the parlor of the Presidential Suite, Jane Chandler looked over her checklist once more. The press luncheon would begin in a half hour. After lunch, select members of the press—the big guns—would receive private face time with the Senator. Then came late-afternoon photo ops: a children's choir at Faneuil Hall, veterans at the USS Constitution. Then back to the hotel for dinner with key supporters, followed by a very-very-VIP reception in the Presidential Suite.

All told, this event was costing the campaign very big bucks, but it would be worth it. A major policy announcement called for a top-notch location to reinforce its importance. And the Presidential Suite had been the obvious place to set up their headquarters, a suite of rooms that had hosted dignitaries and celebrities from Jimmy Carter to the Saudi royal family, from Liza Minnelli to Survivor winners. As far as Chandler was concerned, John Wagner was all these rolled into one: statesman, royalty, celebrity and pop icon.

Wagner wandered from the master bedroom into the parlor, his eyebrows furrowed and a tie half knotted around his neck. "Have you got a list of the approved press for this shindig?"

"Sure." She sifted through the papers on the desk, knowing exactly where the list was but not wanting to find it too quickly. "What's up?"

He shook his head, a brief, dismissive jerk. "I just don't want any surprises."

Neither did Chandler. She found the list, handed it to him and studied his face as he scanned it. Just minutes before, he had been his cheerful, arrogant self. Now he seemed distracted, focused on some point inside his skull.

She didn't like it. This was the biggest event of the campaign and they couldn't afford to blow it. So what was going on?

He handed the list back to her, with no sign that he'd seen anything untoward, but without looking at all relieved. "I don't want anyone at the luncheon who isn't on that list."

That was a problem, Chandler thought. There were always a few last-minute additions and she didn't want to leave a reporter from the New York Times standing out in the foyer just because they'd neglected to RSVP. "What about—"

"Nobody," he said. "I don't care who it is."

"Right," she said, and watched his back as he retreated into the master bedroom.

She turned and stared out the picture window as a small plane came in from the north, circled and descended towards the harbor. That seemed unusual. Given Logan Airport's location—right on the water's edge—first-timers flying into Boston often felt as if they were going to land in the water, but she'd never seen a plane actually put down in the harbor. Some VIP must have made special arrangements for that.

She shook off the distraction and turned back to her checklist. But in the back of her mind, she continued pondering Wagner's anxiety about the press list and hoping to God that didn't have anything to do with Raymond Devlin.

31

The flight to Boston had taken less than an hour. Cameron dozed as Darcy stared out the window and overheard the clipped phrases of air traffic control guiding them in.

"Eastham one zero niner, this is Logan Tower. You are cleared for descent to Boston Harbor."

The plane came in low with Faneuil Hall and Quincy Market to their right. They touched down and motored to within a few hundred yards of the hotel marina.

"Now what?" Cameron asked, gazing out at the hotel's grand arch and the gold-domed ferry pavilion.

"Curbside service," Darcy said, a smile playing at the corners of her mouth. "For very special guests only."

Moments later, a launch put out from the hotel's private wharf. It pulled up next to the plane and the pilot extended the stairs to its deck.

Darcy stroked Pepper's head. "I'll be back, OK? You behave yourself."

Pepper whined, understanding that she was not going with them. Roy clicked his tongue at Pepper, who turned to him as he massaged her head and ears, staring into her eyes.

Darcy shook her head. The man wasn't much on human communication, but he knew dogs.

"We'll be back in an hour or so," she told him. "Whatever you do, don't let anyone else take Pepper."

"OK."

Darcy and Cameron stepped aboard the launch, where a young woman in a brilliant white blouse and matching teeth greeted them. "Mr. Cameron," she said. "Welcome to Boston."

Cameron patted her shoulder. "Thank you."

He took a seat and Darcy sat behind him. "Big day in Beantown," she said, gazing at the yachts that lined the wharf.

"Yes, it is," the hostess said. "It seems as if everyone's in town today for the press conference."

At the dock, a young man in an equally immaculate white shirt and silk tie met them. "Mr. Cameron, welcome to the Boston Harbor Hotel. It's a pleasure to have you with us."

"The pleasure is mine," Cameron said with a majestic nod. Darcy marveled that, despite his periodic mental lapses, he so quickly fell back into his role as the beloved newscaster emeritus, like a comfortable suit he simply hadn't worn in awhile.

"If you'll come with me," the young man said, "I'll take you to your room where you can freshen up before the luncheon."

Phil Tierney, head of security for the Rowes Wharf complex, watched from his sixth-floor office window as Marshall Cameron strolled from the dock to the hotel. The unorthodox arrival of Cameron had been another headache for Tierney, one more thing to deal with on a day when the hotel was already swarming with VIPs, the media and curious onlookers—not to mention the usual guests, all of whom expected to receive world-class treatment.

Tierney had been surprised to receive the request from Cameron's secretary; he hadn't even known Marshall

Cameron was still alive, let alone working. And the water landing was unusual, not a courtesy they would offer to just anyone. But the hotel had a reputation: For the right people, anything could be made to happen, and Marshall Cameron was in that select group.

Cameron's arrival had required a few adjustments to the wharf's security routine—the hotel complex was a nexus of human commerce, from the ferry that brought guests from Logan airport right to the hotel entrance, to an endless stream of taxis depositing guests at the cityside entrance, to the wharf's parking garage connected to the hotel by a pedestrian walkway.

Surrounding the entire area—and complicating Tierney's job—was a public promenade, open to anyone who felt like strolling the red brick walkways. On a warm, sunny day like today, the promenade would be busy, even without the appearance of Senator Wagner. But Tierney was confident his team, coordinating with the Senator's own people, could handle the situation. At least he didn't have to deal with the Secret Service. By law, the feds didn't start protecting presidential candidates until 120 days before the election. That meant they wouldn't start until after the Fourth of July, and that meant Tierney didn't have all the headaches that came with working with the Secret Service—special clearances, checks and rechecks of all locations, endless paperwork.

Still, he wasn't taking any chances. Wagner was a highly visible candidate and any one of the people passing on the promenade below could be a threat to him or another of the hotel's guests.

On the promenade six stories below, Jamal bin Taimur Hashem—or Jacob Stein as the hotel knew him; Americans could never tell the difference between an Israeli and an Arab—strolled past the Wharf Room, the largest of the Harbor Hotel's function rooms. The Wharf

Room sat on John Rowe's original wharf and provided harbor views on three sides. It was the perfect setting for an important occasion.

Through the tall windows Hashem saw that the room had been set up for a luncheon, with white tablecloths, crystal and flowers on the tables. In the center of the head table was a podium flanked by the American flag and that of the state of Massachusetts. It didn't take a genius to figure out where the press luncheon would be held.

The room was empty now, except for the white-shirted waitstaff straightening chairs and laying out silverware. In a short while, the room would be filled with the journalists who had begged, wheedled and sweet-talked their way into invitations, along with invited guests who would kill for a chance to speak with Wagner—and one uninvited guest who planned to kill him.

This was the last of Hashem's assignments, an operation that was far more complex than the others he had undertaken. Killing the other members of Wagner's unit had been easy. There had been no bodyguards, no security details, and no warning.

That was why he'd left the killing of the unit's captain for last. Wagner would have no warning either. It would only be afterwards, when they put the clues together, that they would realize what had happened, and who had done this.

He knew Wagner would have security, a great deal of it, but that did not concern him. He was sure he could get around it. He also knew that he would undoubtedly be killed in the process. But that did not matter. What mattered was the honor of the house of Hashem, an ancient family that dated back to the time of the Prophet himself.

That honor had been affronted at Al Biqa, when the American forces had killed six members of Hashem's family, including two of his brothers. The fact that his brothers had planned to ambush the Americans was beside the point, and the death of the infidel missionaries was of no importance. They deserved to die anyway, before their pernicious teachings could spread any further.

But the deaths of Hashem's brothers had to be avenged. It had taken Hashem a great deal of time and money to track down and kill the members of the unit responsible for their deaths, but he had done it. Now there was only one left.

It was pure chance that the captain of the unit was also the leading candidate to become the Americans' next president. Or was it? Perhaps Allah had allowed this to come about to send a message to the Americans. The death of their favorite son would prove to them that their power was gone. They were weak and their day was over. And Jamal bin Taimur Hashem would deliver Allah's message to them.

The host opened the door and gestured for Darcy and Cameron to enter. Despite its small size, the room still smelled like money: antique furnishings, floor length drapes, flowers, exquisite harbor view.

"Are you sure this room will be sufficient?" the young man said. "Perhaps one of our suites—"

"No, no, this will be fine," Darcy said. "As I said, we won't be staying, we just need a place for Mr. Cameron to change before the meeting."

"Very good." He opened the closet, where a plastic garment bag hung from the rack. "I had the suit you ordered sent up. If there's anything else I can do for you —"

"I think we'll be all set," Darcy said. "And again, we'd prefer that as few people as possible know about Mr. Cameron being here."

"I understand. Your privacy is our utmost concern."

He left and Darcy pulled the garment bag from the closet. "I had to order this over the phone. I hope it fits."

Cameron studied the suit, shirt and tie, then glanced at his shoes. "They don't go together."

She pulled a shoe box from the closet. "I thought of that, too." She pressed him into the bathroom. "Now get changed. We don't have much time."

Back in his room, Hashem checked the setup one more time. His attire was a perfect copy of that worn by the hotel's waitstaff. The service cart bore the remains of the room service breakfast he had ordered, with one change: the sterling water carafe had been washed and dried, its contents replaced with a Ruger 345 semi-automatic pistol.

It was a matter of timing. He would leave the room, taking the cart to the kitchen via the service elevator. Outside the kitchen, he would ditch the cart but keep the carafe and make his way to the Wharf Room. He would proceed quickly to the head table, ostensibly to refill the water glasses. Then he would shoot Senator John Wagner.

32

Darcy answered the knock on the door. A tall, dark-haired woman in a business suit said, "Hello. I'm Elizabeth Patterson, hotel security." She looked familiar and Darcy assumed she'd seen her as they passed through the lobby. "I'm here to escort Mr. Cameron to the press conference."

Darcy shook her head. "We didn't ask for—"

"I know, and I apologize for the confusion. This has all happened quite suddenly. We've received warnings about Senator Wagner's security and we've been placed on alert. We don't want to alarm anyone, but we're providing extra security for our most important guests."

Darcy glanced at her watch. The reception would begin in ten minutes. She didn't want to arrive too early. "All right. We'll be right with you."

She closed the door and gave her father final instructions. "Remember, I'm your secretary. Let me do the talking. When the time for questions comes, you ask him about Al Biqa. Afterwards, a lot of people will want to talk to you. Let me handle that part, all right?"

Cameron frowned. "I did press conferences for forty years. I think I can handle it."

You didn't have Alzheimer's then, Darcy thought. "All right, let's go."

They stepped into the hallway. Cameron saw Patterson and raised his eyebrows.

"Security," Darcy said, taking him by the arm.

Cameron studied the willowy brunette. "Things are looking up," he said. "Security used to mean ex-football players with no necks."

Patterson smiled and took his other arm. "Shall we?"

They walked to the elevator, passing another guest room just as the door opened. A waiter emerged, pulling a service cart. He glanced at the trio as they passed, nodding politely. His eyes lingered a moment on Cameron's face and Darcy saw a spark of recognition. That guy would have a story to tell his family tonight: Guess who I saw at the hotel today?

Cameron gazed back at the waiter, meeting his eyes. Each looked away and the waiter pushed the cart toward the opposite end of the hall.

At the elevator, Patterson pressed the button to open the doors and stepped aside, holding the door for Darcy and Cameron.

Cameron hesitated, drawing Darcy to one side. "That was him," he whispered.

"Who?"

"Hashem. My contact with the Arab militia. The one who set us up at Al Biqa."

Darcy glanced down the hall as the waiter pushed the cart into a service elevator. "The room service guy?"

"Yes."

She studied his eyes for a moment, wondering if he was lucid or delusional again. There were thousands of Middle Eastern people in Boston, but for some reason her father had fixated on this one. He had never been xenophobic—he had hobnobbed with too many intellectuals and urbanites for that—but maybe his disease had made everyone with olive skin, dark eyes and curly hair into an Islamic terrorist.

She glanced at her watch. The press conference would

begin in five minutes. She didn't have time to deal with this now. "We'll talk about that later," she said, and steered him into the elevator.

Hashem stepped into the service elevator, holding it open until he heard the other elevator doors close, then looked out.

He had been recognized. He was sure of that. There was no mistaking the face of Marshall Cameron. And Cameron had recognized him as well, even after all these years.

He pressed the switch to turn the elevator off and considered what do to. He had not expected Cameron to be here and had never planned on killing him—though Cameron had been at Al Biqa, he had only been an onlooker and not responsible for the crimes committed there. But he was here now, and if he recognized Hashem, he would surely raise an alarm.

So Cameron would have to be killed. But doing that would attract attention, which Hashem could not afford until he had killed Wagner.

In seconds, Hashem had changed his plans. He ran back to his room, tore off the white vest that was the trademark of the hotel's wait staff and grabbed his suit jacket. He stepped back into the hallway and studied the numbers above the guest elevator, watching to see where it went. Since Marshall Cameron had ruined his first plan, Marshall Cameron would become his backup plan.

Patterson pressed the button for the hotel's lowest level. "We'll take the lower level connector to the Wharf Room rather than the promenade," she said. "It's safer that way."

As the car descended, Patterson stared at the elevator buttons. Darcy glanced at her profile, and in that instant she remembered. It was the same profile she'd seen in the car across from the Eastham Inn that day she'd taken her father to lunch.

Darcy turned, facing the elevator door, willing herself to be calm. She knew now: They had followed her, had known where she would go. And there was no way they were going to let her or her father get anywhere near Senator Wagner.

She reached for the control panel. "You know, I just realized I need something at the gift shop—"

Patterson's hand snapped up and grabbed Darcy's wrist before she could reach the buttons. "No, you don't."

She stared into Darcy's eyes and Darcy knew she'd been right. And this person knew that she knew.

Patterson released her grip and pushed Darcy against the wall of the elevator. She pushed aside her jacket to reveal a holstered pistol. "Don't try anything heroic," she said. "It will be the last thing you do."

The elevator arrived at the lower level and opened onto a hallway with painted concrete walls. Patterson gestured for Darcy and Cameron to step out. "This way."

Their heels clicked on the hard floors, Patterson following closely behind. They passed the service elevator, whose doors stood open, and saw the waiter again. He stood at the back of the car, wearing a suit coat now, with one hand held inside it. "Mr. Cameron," he said. "You will step in here, please."

Shit, Darcy thought. *Dad was right.*

Cameron hesitated and Patterson reached across her chest into her suit jacket.

Hashem pulled a pistol from his waistband and shot her twice in the chest. As she fell, Darcy grabbed Cameron by the arm to pull him away, but Hashem turned the gun on them.

"No." He motioned to Patterson's body with the gun.

"Bring her in here."

Darcy dragged Patterson into the elevator. She was still alive, but barely.

Hashem closed the elevator doors and clicked it off. "We are going to the reception," he told them. "You will be my ticket."

Now Darcy realized. This was not about her father. This was about Wagner. She turned to Cameron and said, "I'm sorry."

"It's all right," Cameron said. "I'm not going to help him."

Hashem raised the pistol and held it to Darcy's chest. "Yes, you are."

Cameron stared at him hard. "All right."

Hashem nodded toward Patterson's body. "Put her in the corner."

They propped the body back against the corner of the elevator. "Now take the tablecloth off the cart and cover her with it."

When they were done, Hashem pushed the cart in front of the body. It would not take long for someone to find her, Darcy thought. But perhaps he didn't need much time.

Hashem flicked the elevator switch on and opened the doors. "We go now," he said to Cameron. "I am your assistant and you don't go anywhere without me." He looked at Darcy. "And you are..."

"His secretary," she said quickly. "He really doesn't go anywhere without me. People would notice."

"All right. Go."

33

The check-in area for the luncheon was a long, linen-covered table manned by two of Chandler's people. Journalists stood in rows before them, announcing their affiliations—newspapers, magazines, broadcast and online outlets—each receiving a packet of information as the assistants checked their names off the list. A few dropped their cards on the table, disdaining to identify themselves aloud, while others simply stood there, expecting to be acknowledged by their mere presence.

The hubbub around the table hushed and the attendees turned to see the crowd part, like the sea around Moses, as Marshall Cameron and his entourage approached. Younger journalists reached out to shake his hand as if he were Ben Franklin stepping out of the pages of a history book. The old-timers greeted him by name as if to demonstrate to the others that they were close personal friends, though Darcy wondered if Cameron had any idea who they were.

She approached the sign-in table, her mind racing, all too aware of the gun hidden in Hashem's waistband as he followed close behind. She had wanted to confront John Wagner; she hadn't wanted to kill him. Now his life was in danger and there was nothing she could do about it without sacrificing her own life or that of her father. That wasn't a tradeoff she was ready to make, not for a man who had senselessly wasted the lives of dozens of people to further his own ambitions. But to do nothing went against the fiber of her being.

A young man at the table looked up at them. "Marshall Cameron," Darcy said quietly. "And his assistants."

The young man studied the list with a worried expression. "I'm sorry, but I don't see..."

Of course you don't, Darcy thought. We were just planning to bluff our way in. She glanced at her father, who seemed completely at ease. She wondered if he even remembered that they were hostages now or if he was simply reliving a pleasant dream in which everyone paid him homage as the wise old man of broadcasting.

The campaign staffer continued flipping pages as if that would make Cameron's name magically appear. Hashem nudged Darcy, pressing her to take action.

"Look," she said finally. "This is ridiculous. This is Marshall Cameron. He doesn't have time to—"

"Just a moment," the staffer said. He called to his supervisor, a woman whose nametag identified her as Jane Chandler. They stood to one side and held a whispered conference.

Chandler nodded, took the list and studied it as if she didn't already know it by heart, and that Marshall Cameron was not on it. She hadn't even known Cameron was still working. But she wasn't going to cause a scene by refusing admission to someone of his stature, no matter what Wagner had said. If Cameron was on their side, the senior citizen vote of the entire country would be safely in their pocket.

She fixed a welcoming smile on her face. "Right this way, Mr. Cameron," she said, leading his party past the check-in table and into the Wharf Room. "We'll find a place for you near the front."

A jazz combo filled the room with light, up-tempo versions of patriotic songs. Sunlight streamed in through tall windows, illuminating the red, white and blue bunting that hung from the ceiling.

Cameron entered the room as if he were royalty, nodding to the attendees who were already seated, shaking more hands. Chandler guided them to a table near the head table where Wagner would speak. Darcy followed, feeling like Marina Oswald, about to go down in history as a not-exactly innocent bystander to a heinous act. Hashem followed like a shadow attached to her back, and she knew she wouldn't get far if she tried to do anything unexpected.

Cameron sat and Darcy placed herself on his right. Hashem took the seat on his left, the three of them facing the head table. The room filled quickly, the atmosphere that of a noisy victory celebration before the fact; at this point, Wagner's victory in the upcoming election was a foregone conclusion and the attendees were giddy with the knowledge that they were taking part in a historic moment.

When all the guests were seated, the band played a fanfare. They stood cheering as Wagner entered the room, like a football hero walking onto the playing field. He shook hands and slapped backs as he progressed to the head table, then did a double-take when he saw Marshall Cameron—a theatrical gesture that Darcy suspected was meant to cover his very real surprise at seeing her father there.

He strode toward them, hand extended. "Marshall, good to see you again. How are things in Vermont?"

He's good, Darcy thought. The personal touch, the exuberant welcome to an uninvited guest. You'd never know that Marshall Cameron was the last person on the planet Wagner hoped to see there.

Cameron stepped in front of Hashem to shake Wagner's hand. If Hashem had meant to shoot Wagner at that moment, her father's unconscious gesture prevented it. "Senator," he said. "How are things in Pound Ridge?"

That was a gibe, Darcy knew. Pound Ridge was the Westchester town where Wagner had purchased a million dollar home to establish his residency before running for New York's open senatorial seat. It was a home that, according to rumor, he rarely visited.

Wagner's smile dimmed only a fraction. "Great, just great." He slapped Cameron's back and winked at Darcy, "Take care of him, now."

Darcy knew what that meant as well: Don't let him do anything stupid.

They took their seats and Darcy scanned the room, assessing the security situation. Outside, on the balcony overlooking the harbor, heavily armed security guards scanned the waterfront. Inside, state troopers were stationed at each corner. A pair of muscular young men in suits stood on either side of Wagner.

And that was it. She had no idea what kind of security presidential candidates received, but she had imagined more, especially since the days of Robert Kennedy's assassination in a Los Angeles hotel.

The mayor of Boston, a Wagner supporter, stood to introduce him. As he spoke, Darcy glanced at Hashem. If he were going to act, it would probably be soon.

The mayor spoke briefly, warming up the crowd and providing the usual accolades for the guest of honor. "And now, ladies and gentlemen, I give you the next president of the United States, Senator John Wagner."

The crowd stood again, cheering as Wagner stepped to the podium. Darcy glanced at Hashem and knew this was it. He would have no better opportunity. Her mind raced, calculating what to do, unable to come up with anything.

Her father began to rise, wavering unsteadily. He put one hand on the table to steady himself and the other hand gripped his chest. A groan escaped from his lips.

Oh God, Darcy thought. Not now. He was having a heart attack. The strain of all this was too much for him. She helped him sit, glancing over his shoulder at Hashem, who had stepped back slightly. Now, all eyes in the immediate vicinity were on Cameron, which only improved Hashem's situation.

Hashem reached into his jacket, pulled out the pistol and raised it. As he did, Cameron's hand closed around a fork. He spun quickly and jabbed the fork into Hashem's thigh.

Hashem cried out and the pistol fired wildly at the ceiling, ripping through the bunting. In seconds, security guards turned on Hashem, took aim and fired. He fell, crashing into the table behind him. As he did, a long, black-tipped feather fluttered from his jacket to the floor.

The room erupted into shouts and screams as Wagner's aides rushed him out. Guards ran past the guests as they stumbled away from the blood-spotted body of Hashem. Darcy helped her father to his feet, assessing the situation. Wagner was gone; there was no way they were going to confront him today. Worse, the police would have questions for them about Hashem.

"Are you OK?" she asked him.

He frowned. "Of course." His voice was strong and steady, and in that moment, she realized the heart attack had been a ploy.

"All right," she said. "We've got to get out of here."

As they strode toward the exit she said, "That was slick."

Cameron dismissed it. "I'm afraid I used the wrong fork. It's been so long since I've stabbed someone at a formal dinner."

The main doors had been closed to prevent anyone from leaving the room. "This way," Darcy said, pointing them toward the kitchen.

In the kitchen, harried chefs were only now realizing that something had happened in the ballroom. Darcy conducted her father past the food prep stations and put on the tone of a marketing person. "As you can see, the kitchen is state of the art, nothing but the best." They headed for a side door. "Now I'll show you the dock area."

Outside, a crowd had gathered, their attention directed toward the chaos inside the Wharf Room. As Darcy and Cameron made their way through the crowd, a few pointed and whispered, but Darcy pushed through before anyone could speak to them or ask for an autograph.

Scanning the wharf area, she found the young hostess who had greeted them upon arrival. "I'm afraid my father isn't feeling well and we need to get back to our plane quickly."

"Certainly. We'll have the tender take you right out."

They boarded the boat and Cameron nodded back toward the confusion at the Wharf Room. "That was amusing," he said. "Now what?"

"Plan B," Darcy said. "Escape from The Village."

34

In the Presidential Suite, Senator Wagner was being checked out by a doctor in the master bedroom. Jane Chandler paced the parlor, deciding how to play this. The trick would be to encourage shock and outrage on the part of the media while projecting a calm, in-control attitude on the part of the candidate. She would have to appear concerned at all times, and not display what she really felt: elation. Surviving an assassination attempt was the best thing that could possibly happen at this point. Public sympathy would be on their side. From here on out, no other candidate would be able to get a word in edge-wise.

Her assistant approached, holding a cell phone. "Call for you? Ned Epstein?"

"Who?"

"That newscaster from Vermont. The one who's been trying to get in touch with you?"

"Tell him I'll get back—"

"He said it was important. He wants to ask you about Senator Wagner's military service? Something about a massacre?"

An alarm rang in Chandler's mind, like the blare of a hurricane warning signal.

She grabbed the phone. "Jane Chandler."

"This is Ned Epstein. I'm here in Boston on special assignment for Fox."

"Yes?"

"I wonder if you'd care to comment on allegations of Senator Wagner's responsibility for the deaths of civilians in the Al Biqa massacre in 1983?"

The color drained from Chandler's face. "Excuse me?"

"A former member of Wagner's unit has blamed him for the massacre at Al Biqa, claiming there was a cover-up. Do you have a comment?"

She covered the phone, took two deep breaths to steady herself, then said, "I'll have to get back to you on that."

"But you have no comment for now."

"No, I'm not saying 'no comment.' I'll have to get back to you."

"Fine. But we're going with this story at noon. So I thought you'd want to comment."

Chandler glanced at her watch. It was an old reporter's trick—call the campaign so late that they would have no chance to respond.

It didn't matter. He could have given her all day and she still wouldn't know what to say. She had no idea what had happened at Al Biqa. She had been in high school at the time and barely remembered the incident.

But she knew instinctively that John Wagner had been there. Raymond Devlin had been there. And other people had been there, people who had been quiet up till now. People who were starting to talk. And once they talked, everyone would be talking.

She handed the phone back to her assistant and did a quick calculation. Retreating to her own room, she closed the door and made a call on her cell phone.

"I'd like to speak to Congresswoman Reinhardt," she said. "This is Jane Chandler."

A half hour later, John Wagner shook off the doctor

and strode out of his room, calling over his shoulder. "I'm fine, for God's sake."

He surveyed the parlor, where the aides all seemed very busy doing nothing. "Where's Jane?"

No one answered.

"Where the hell is Chandler? We've still got a campaign to run here."

He stormed into her room. "Chandler?"

The room was empty, her luggage gone, the bed a heap of expensive linens.

"Jane?"

A single sheet of paper sat on the desk, a piece of hotel stationary. Even from a distance, he recognized her signature at the bottom of a brief message. And despite the carefully designed and soundproofed walls of the Presidential Suite, John Wagner heard a door slam somewhere.

The Cessna landed smoothly at Eastham airport and taxied to the hangar, where a Mitsubishi turboprop sat idling.

Cameron stared out the window at the tail of the turboprop, noting its Canadian license tag. "Did you have to give them another deposit?"

"No," Darcy said. She had guaranteed the flight, using the same credit card number her father had used—a number Will Webster had tracked down for her. "Apparently the deposit Mr. Brinkley gave them before was enough."

Cameron snorted. "It certainly was."

As they stepped from the Cessna, the pilot of the Mitsubishi—dressed in a starched white, short-sleeved shirt and dark tie—greeted them and pulled down the steps to the cabin. "Mr. Brinkley," he said. "Welcome aboard. Traveling alone today?"

Cameron glanced at Darcy. For the first time that day, a look of uncertainly drifted over his face. He had been fearless while running from dogs and guns, conning his way into the campaign event, wrestling with an assassin. But now, facing a trip by himself, he seemed worried.

Darcy hesitated. She had made all the arrangements. The people meeting him at his destination would take him to a private home where he would be cared for, protected, and where no one would bother him. It would only be for a short while, until things settled down here and she was able to find a new place for him, a place the CIA did not own.

But he would still be two thousand miles away. And any chance she had of getting to know him would continue to slip away.

She turned to the pilot, "Have you got room for another person and a dog in there?"

"Sure. But you're going to need papers for the dog."

She reached into a pocket, pulled out a roll of bills and peeled off several large ones. "Will that cover it?"

He tucked the bills into his pocket. "We'll figure something out."

As they climbed aboard, a noise came from somewhere to the southeast. They looked up, recognizing the rhythmic pulse of helicopter blades.

The pilot of the Westland Super Lynx gazed from the window. "That's it," he said, pointing to the Eastham Airport as it appeared beyond the line of pines.

Fredericks took in the landing strip, the hangar, and the turboprop that idled in front of it. Even at a distance, he recognized Darcy Cameron stepping onto the plane. "Don't let them take off."

"No problem." The Lynx was more than capable of outmaneuvering the turbo. If need be, it was capable of shooting it down.

On the ground, Darcy saw the helicopter and knew it wasn't carrying sightseers.

"Can you outrun that?" she asked the pilot.

"The helicopter? Yes. The guns on the helicopter, no."

The helicopter landed directly in front of them and two agents hopped out. Darcy recognized one of them as Fredericks.

The agents planted themselves on either side of the plane, guns drawn. "Hands in the air," Fredericks yelled. "Come out slowly."

They did as they were told. Fredericks spoke as the other agent patted them down. "Did you have a nice time in Boston?"

Neither Darcy nor Cameron said a word.

The second agent pulled an envelope from Darcy's jacket and handed it to Fredericks. Fredericks opened the envelope and studied its contents. His eyes narrowed as he read and a vein in his jaw pulsed. Darcy had studied witnesses on the stand, people who were trying to hide their feelings but whose demeanor gave them away. She could tell Fredericks was angry.

"It won't do you any good to destroy those," she said. "I've made copies. In a little while the story will be plastered everywhere."

Fredericks glanced at her, then back at the papers. "That's going to make some people very unhappy." It didn't sound like a threat, simply an assessment of the situation.

He stared across the street and Darcy followed his gaze toward the bare trees covering the foot of Mt. Connell, steel gray with a reddish haze. The buds on those trees would soon blossom into lush green foliage. It was odd how quickly things could change, even in nature.

Fredericks seemed to come to a decision. He turned to

the other agent, "Don't let them go anywhere." He called to the airport attendant, Roy. "Is there an office around here?"

Roy led him to a glass-walled cubicle just inside the hangar. The others watched as Fredericks went in, closed the door and spread the papers he'd taken from Darcy on a desk. He pulled a device from his pocket, no larger than a cigarette lighter, and held it over each of the papers.

The process took several minutes. Fredericks returned and handed the envelope to Darcy. Then he turned to Cameron. "I understand that you just saved Senator Wagner's life."

Cameron studied him. "The quality of mercy is not strained."

A corner of Frederick's mouth rose, almost a smile. "If the information in that envelope is true, you would have had good reason not to interfere."

Cameron shook his head. "Wagner is a bastard, a thug, and a fool. I'd rather see a baboon as president than him. But that's not the way we do things in this country."

Darcy saw a softening of Fredericks' face. "No sir," he said. "It's not."

Fredericks stared at her father for a moment longer. He pointed into the hangar. "I'm going back in there to file a report," he said. "It's a report that will have repercussions in high places. I strongly suggest that you do not take this opportunity to leave."

He nodded to the other agent and the two of them disappeared into the office, where Fredericks stood with his back to them.

Darcy looked at the others. "Is he kidding?"

Cameron said nothing, gazing steadily at the agents in the office.

The pilot touched Darcy's arm. "Ma'am? I think we're supposed to leave."

Darcy considered this for a moment. He was right. Fredericks was letting them go. Apparently there were some good guys left in the world after all. "Then let's get out of here."

Inside the office, Fredericks heard the roar of the turboprop starting up. The other agent moved toward the door but Fredericks put a hand on his arm and shook his head. "We're almost finished here."

Uploading the images of Darcy Cameron's papers from the digital camera to his laptop had taken only a few seconds. Finishing his report and composing the letter to the Director of Central Intelligence had taken a bit longer. The report carried the designation "CRITIC," indicating a message of the utmost urgency.

Fredericks hit the Send key with a sense of satisfaction. Technology was a wonderful thing. There was more than one way to shoot down an object that was on a dangerous trajectory.

The body of Patricia Hayes was found twenty minutes after the attempt on the life of Senator Wagner. She was identified as a former employee of the Central Intelligence Agency. The information reached Fredericks shortly before he arrived back at headquarters.

He opened Devlin's door without knocking. No one ever opened Devlin's door without knocking.

Devlin looked up, saw him, and exploded. "God damn it, I thought I told you not to let them—"

He stopped. Behind Fredericks stood another man and a woman. "Who the hell—"

They held up badges. "Federal marshals Juster and Conseco," the woman said. "Raymond Devlin?"

"Yes?"

"We'll need you to come with us."

"Now? I'm afraid that's not—"

"Right now, sir."

Devlin glared at Fredericks. "What's this about?"

Fredericks glared back. It was about obstruction of justice, abuse of power and murder. But he would let others explain that. "It's about thirty years late."

Epilogue

The island of Corvo is the smallest of the Azorean islands located off the coast of Portugal. It is inhabited by fewer than three hundred people, people who know each other intimately and are related by ties of blood and faith, commerce and tradition. They are people who know a stranger when they see one. And most important, they know how to keep a secret.

Graciela Baltazar, a stout woman with tight gray-brown curls framing a round face, stood outside the tiny building that served as Corvo's terminal, hangar, and ticket office. "Welcome to our little island," she called.

Darcy whispered to Cameron as they stepped off the plane. "Deep cover here. As far as they know, you are an American businessman on extended vacation."

Cameron nodded curtly and bowed to Graciela. "It is a pleasure to meet you."

The matron giggled girlishly, clearly taken with him. "I take you to your lodgings."

"There's been a slight change," Darcy said. "Do you have room for me and my dog for a short time?"

"Of course, of course. There is guest room in apartment. We can make up bed."

Pepper sniffed the ocean air, tail thumping madly on the tarmac. Darcy knelt to her. "What do you think, girl? Want to stay for a little vacation?"

Pepper barked, her mouth hanging open in the semblance of a grin.

"I'll take that as a yes."

Cameron held the door as Pepper hopped into the van, then gestured to Darcy. "After you."

Graciela piloted the van along winding roads that led up the hillside to her home. Darcy sat with her head against the headrest, eyes closed, until she realized that Cameron was staring at her.

She turned to face him. "What is it?"

A worried look clouded his face. "Do I know you?"

She took his hand. "Not yet." She rested her head back and closed her eyes again, still holding his hand. "Not yet."

THE END

Acknowledgments

We are grateful to Gene Cole and Dr. Bradley White for technical and military details. Many thanks to our early readers: Amanda Clawson, Sara Dowse, Bill and Eileen Elliot, Pat Fairchild, Dot Grim, Bobbie Nylander, Tom Pisaturo, Michelle Sheldon and Barbara Strawbridge. A special note of thanks to members of the Molasses Pond Writers Group for support and encouragement.

Cover design by David Nelson.
dnelsondesign@gmail.com

About the Author

Michael Manley is the pen name of authors Ken Sheldon and Stan Miastkowski. Ken Sheldon has been a freelance writer and editor for over 30 years. He was formerly the West Coast bureau chief for *Byte Magazine*. Stan Miastkowski was a broadcast and print journalist for nearly 35 years. He was also a search and rescue worker who participated in dozens of rescue and recovery operations, including operations following the September 11 attacks in New York. He passed away in 2009.

Connect with Michael Manley online at

http://michaelmanleybooks.com

Facebook:
https://www.facebook.com/michaelmanleybooks

Email:
michaelmanleybooks@gmail.com

Continue reading for a preview of Michael Manley's THE FAMILY.

THE FAMILY

MICHAEL MANLEY

Prologue

1990 - The dawn of the social media era.

They were parked on Mallorca Boulevard, two men in a black van with smoked glass windows. The driver, a tall man with white-blonde hair swept back over his head, looked into the rear-view mirror as a pewter-colored Mazda 626 came around the corner. "Heads up."

The other man, stocky, balding, glanced into the side mirror and spoke into a microphone headset. "Unit two, engage."

On the other side of the street, a tan Lexus pulled out of a parking spot near a small Victorian apartment building.

Normally, Peter Jacobson had to circle the Marina twice before finding a parking space anywhere near his apartment. Tonight, on the first pass, a car pulled out of a spot just steps away from his apartment. In San Francisco, this borders on a supernatural event.

He eased into the spot, still listening to the cassette in the deck. He pulled a hand-held computer from a briefcase on the seat next to him and began to scribble notes across its opaque surface. The tape ended, and he hit the rewind button.

He glanced up at the apartment's windows. They were empty. Allison hadn't arrived yet. He picked up the cell phone and dialed a number.

"Thank you for calling the Peabody Herald. Our normal business hours are..."

Jacobson punched an extension number, left a message, and hung up.

1

Randall McLagan walked out of the Peabody News Shop, stuffing change into his wallet, the latest copy of PC Monthly tucked under his arm. He wasn't watching where he was going and almost walked into a young man who stood just outside the door.

"Excuse me, sir?"

Randall looked up and eyed him warily. The kid wore dark pants, a white shirt and a plain, pencil-thin tie. He looked like a contestant on a high school quiz show. Amway, Randall thought. Maybe Mormon. But he remembered that Mormons generally come in pairs, and he didn't think Amway sold on the street. He lowered an eyebrow. "Yes?"

The kid held out a colorful package. "Would you like to try out a new online service? It's free."

Randall snickered. Over the years, people on street corners had tried to sell him everything from television sets to "solid gold" watches. Nobody had ever tried to sell him software, especially not in Peabody, New Hampshire. Times were definitely changing. All right, he'd play along. "What's it called?"

"The Family, sir?" he said, his voice rising slightly as if he weren't sure himself.

"The Family." It had the sound of something a bunch

of teenagers had cooked up in their garage. Randall took the package from the kid and looked it over. It was a bright, colorful design, emblazoned with promises of free access to the Internet, e-mail, and a host of other services. "What's the catch?"

"No catch, sir. We're just trying to introduce people to our service."

"How much?"

"It's free, sir. The introductory disk comes with all the software you need to connect to the Family. Even the phone call is free."

"You're kidding. How do you make any money at that rate?"

The boy shrugged. "You can make a donation if you'd like."

Randall nodded and pulled a dollar from his wallet, remembering P.T. Barnum's comment about the birth rate of suckers. "OK, I'll give it a shot."

As he handed the bill to the kid, the door to the news shop flew open. The owner, an old man with thinning white hair, emerged like an angry bear from a cave, waving his arms and yelling at the kid. "I thought I tol' you to get the hell outta here."

The kid mumbled a quick thanks to Randall and headed off down the street. The shop owner dismissed him with a wave of a liver-spotted hand. "Bunch a' nuts. Hanging around, bothering my customers."

"What's the problem?" Randall asked. "He was just..."

A telephone rang in the shop. The old man cast a suspicious eye at him and disappeared back inside.

Randall turned, shaking his head. Apparently, that kid "wasn't from around here," as the old joke went. In

Peabody, you weren't considered a local until you had lived in town for twenty years. Randall had lived in the area for four years. It only felt like twenty years.

He had come to Peabody straight out of college, taking an entry-level job with the Peabody Herald—not the type of job a Dartmouth graduate dreamed about, but it was a job. He had planned to spend a couple of years at the Herald before moving up to a larger, daily paper like the Boston Globe or the Chicago Sun.

Four years later, Randall was still at the Herald, still writing about controversies over school budgets, the disturbing problem of teen loitering at the town park, and an endless stream of births, deaths, and basketball games.

Recently, the monotony had been broken somewhat by a new assignment, a weekly column of local news and gossip called "Around Town." He had been asked to write the column when its previous author passed away at the age of eighty-five.

"Dear God," Randall whispered as he leaned against the huge wooden door of the Peabody Herald building. "Don't let me be here till I'm eighty-five."

The door creaked open into a wooden-floored lobby where a chunky woman with hair like a blonde Brillo pad looked up from the reception desk. "Good morning, Randall."

"Morning, Linda."

As he passed the desk, the switchboard buzzed and the receptionist punched a button. "Good morning, Peabody Herald." She paused, punched another button and called after him. "Randall?"

"Yes?"

"It's Mrs. Torelli," she said, clearly sorry to be the bearer of bad tidings.

He winced. Just what he needed first thing on a Monday morning.

Rita Torelli owned a piece of property that the old grange building sat on and was trying to sell the property to the Medi-Aid drugstore chain. She was the scourge of town fathers, zoning boards, and anyone else who dared criticize her plans, which Randall had done in his last column.

He lowered an eyebrow in Linda's direction. "Technically, I'm not in my office yet, am I?"

"That's right, you're not." She punched a button. "I'm sorry, Mrs. Torelli…"

Randall retreated to his office, a converted storage closet with a single small window. He opened the window, which faced the newspaper's parking lot, allowing a faint breath of fresh air to flow into the office. He would have to close it before the end of the day, or the exhaust fumes from the cars leaving the lot would asphyxiate him.

The message light on his phone blinked insistently. He tossed his jacket over a chair and punched the button to retrieve his messages.

"You have eight messages," the system informed him. The first message had arrived at 5:10 PM on Friday afternoon.

"Mr. McLagan?" it began. "This is Rita Torelli. I just read your column and I'm…"

Rita hadn't wasted any time. The paper didn't even hit the stands until five o'clock. He jumped ahead to the next message.

"It's Rita Torelli again. I'd like you to call me as soon…"

He sighed and skipped ahead.

"Mr. McLagan, how is an honest woman supposed to..."

And the next message.

"Yes, I've already called several times..."

He hung up the phone. Knowing Rita Torelli, all eight messages were from her. She was a firm believer in the squeaky wheel theory, and would never rest until she had given him a piece of her mind. Maybe several pieces.

Right now, Randall had a more pressing problem than Rita Torelli. His column was due, and he hadn't started it yet. In fact, he didn't even know what he was going to write about. He had already covered all the latest controversies, and the old chestnuts—New Hampshire's arcane tax structure, problems with schools, the lack of parking in downtown Peabody—had all been done to death.

It wasn't exactly what he'd had in mind while studying journalism at Dartmouth. He had pictured a career at a large city newspaper or a national magazine, where he would expose government corruption, ferret out the truth about corporate scandals, and write poignant commentaries about modern society. Instead, his days were filled with annual budgets, track meets, and Rita Torelli.

He turned to his computer and flipped it on. If not for the computer, he was sure he'd have gone insane long ago. The computer was his link to the world outside Peabody, a world where real issues were debated, real work was done. He turned it on each day with the expectant desperation of a man on a desert island scanning the horizon for a rescue ship.

As the computer booted, his eye fell on the disk from the kid outside the news shop, and he a thought. Maybe that was his column: the computer revolution was everywhere these days, even on the sidewalk outside the Peabody news shop.

He zipped open the package and stuck the disk in the computer. He knew his editor wouldn't like this. Harold Dodge, the crusty owner and editor of the Peabody Herald, already thought Randall spent too much time on the computer.

A peaceful, classical theme emanated from the computer and an icon appeared on the screen: a spinning globe, superimposed with the image of a large Colonial house. He clicked on the icon and the image enlarged to fill the screen.

"Welcome to the Family," a silken female voice said. "You are about to enter a world of entertainment, activity, and friendship. You are about to enter the Family."

The door to the house swung open, revealing a large foyer.

"Here in the Family, you'll find free access to the Internet, free e-mail, and a teleconferencing system with ongoing discussions on hundreds of topics, from Art to the Zodiac." Graphic images representing the topic areas drifted across the screen.

"You'll also have access to the world's largest collection of free software, as well as an incredible library of online sources for personal and business growth." Well-known magazines, journals, and references appeared, glinting as if illuminated by a spotlight, then faded.

"Health, personal finance, travel...it's all available in the Family. And it's all absolutely free."

So far, Randall had heard the word "free" three or four times. He was beginning to pick up a theme. So what far as he could tell, there were no advertisements anywhere.

Randall noticed a Member's Area and asked Carolyn about it.

That's an area containing special features available only to members. If you'd like to join the Family, I can sign you up today, Randall.

What kind of special features?

I'd be happy to tell you about all the member benefits once you sign up. Would you like to do that today, Randall? There's no cost to join.

She hadn't answered the question. But before he could repeat it, she broke in.

Are there any other questions I can answer for you, Randall?

Just one. If this is all free, how do you pay for it? Where does the money come from?

The Family is a non-profit organization, Randall. We receive support from our members and from a variety of private institutions.

That sounded like a canned answer if he'd ever heard one.

Would you like to sign up today, Randall?

He was tempted, but he was also skeptical. The Family sounded too good to be true, and if Dodge found out he had signed up for something that cost money, he'd never hear the end of it.

Thanks. I'll need to think about it for a bit.

There's no obligation, Randall, and no fee. If you like, I can sign you up for a free membership right now.

This lady sure knew the hard sell.

Let me think about it. I'll get back to you.

OK. It was great to meet you, Randall. Come back

soon!

He leaned back in his chair. He had plenty of material for a column, but he needed a local angle, something more than meeting the kid outside the news shop. Then it came to him: the town grange, once home to a vibrant social structure, now stood empty, facing destruction and replacement by a discount drugstore. Where had the people gone who once frequented that building? These days, they were meeting electronically, via computer.

He began writing, and the words flowed. In half an hour, he had a good chunk of the column done. But he still had a few questions. How did the Family give away so much for free? Was there some catch?

He glanced at his watch. There wasn't time to do a lot of research on this. If he was going to get this column in on time, he needed the inside scoop, and needed it fast.

Then he remembered. Of course: Peter. If anyone would know about the Family, it would be Peter.

Peter Jacobson had been his best friend in college. After graduation, Peter had landed a job with PC Monthly magazine, a West Coast startup that had since become one of the most successful publications in the business.

Randall reached for the phone, then hesitated.

He hadn't spoken to Peter in months. They had drifted apart in recent months. After the move to San Francisco, Peter's career had soared while Randall's floundered. It seemed San Francisco and Peabody were far apart in more ways than just geography.

He had visited Peter once, but they argued most of the time, Peter trying to convince him to move to the West Coast. Randall had found himself defending a job he hated, his pride keeping him from admitting that Peter had chosen the better path.

His ego bruised, he had only spoken to Peter a few times after that. The last time he'd called, Peter had been with a woman—Angie, or Andrea, a new girlfriend apparently—and he seemed distracted. He said he'd call back, but never did. Randall had meant to call again, but hadn't gotten around to it.

He hesitated a moment longer, then decided it had been long enough. If nothing else, this was a good excuse to reconnect. He needed some information on the Family, and Peter was the person to supply it.

He pulled a phone list out of the desk, found Peter's work number, and dialed.

A receptionist answered. "PC Monthly magazine. How may I direct your call?"

"I'd like to speak to Peter Jacobson."

The receptionist hesitated. "Just a moment, please."

Canned music drifted over on the line for a few seconds, then a woman's voice spoke. "Human resources. Can I help you?"

Human resources? Why couldn't companies hire receptionists who knew what they were doing? "There's been a mistake," Randall said. "I'm trying to get through to Peter Jacobson."

"Can I ask who's calling, please?"

"My name is Randall McLagan," he said, beginning to be irritated.

"And your company, Mr. McLagan?"

What was this? Was Peter so important now that he had everybody in the company screening his calls for him?

"I'm a personal friend."

She hesitated. "Mr. McLagan, my name is Joanne Reed." Her tone had changed slightly. It was softer now, less guarded. "I'm the director of human resources for PC Monthly."

Nice to meet you, Randall thought. Now put me through to Peter.

"This is very difficult...I guess you haven't heard yet."

"Heard what?"

"It's...I'm afraid I have some difficult news for you."

He felt something sink inside. Her tone, her manner told him this was not good. "What?"

"Peter...died this weekend."

"What?"

"I'm sorry. It came as a shock to all of us here, too."

His mind raced. "What happened?"

"We don't have all the details yet. Apparently he...fell from the Golden Gate Bridge."

A chill passed through him, dragging a hundred questions behind it. Fell? How did he fall? What was he doing? Wasn't there anyone with him? Don't they have guardrails on the bridge?

He wanted to ask if she was sure but stopped himself. Of course she was sure. His mind seized, not knowing what to say next.

She spoke into his silence. "The funeral service is tomorrow. I can fax you the information if there's any possibility you can attend."

The words landed in his ear like stones skipped over dark water...a funeral...for Peter...Could he go?...Of course he would go...but could he get the time off...for a funeral...for Peter...

She spoke again. "Would you like me to fax that to you?"

The words penetrated the fog that had settled around him. "Yes, yes, please."

She waited. "If you'll just give me your fax number."

"Sure." He tried to recall the office fax number, a number he normally knew by heart. He stared blankly at the telephone list. A moment later, he remembered that he was looking for the fax number. When he found the number, it didn't seem right somehow. Nothing seemed right now. He had not seen Peter in months. He'd been meaning to call, but hadn't gotten around to it. Now it was too late. He was angry, frustrated.

How could Peter die before he'd a chance to talk to him?

At the front desk of the Peabody Herald, Linda put a caller through to the advertising department and went back to daydreaming about Randall McLagan. Like most of the single women in Peabody—and more than a few of the married ones—she lusted after Randall. He looked like a young Paul McCartney, his eyes dark brown, his hair thick and worn a bit longer than most of the guys in Peabody. It was the kind of hair a woman wanted to stick her fingers in and mess up—a fantasy she entertained herself with periodically.

A door opened in the hallway behind her and she glanced over her shoulder. Randall appeared in the doorway to Harold Dodge's office.

"All right," came Dodge's gravelly voice. "I'll run a repeat or something. Just make sure you're back here by Wednesday. We can't afford to be late to the printer again."

Randall nodded, as if he'd barely heard the words. "OK."

He closed the door but remained standing outside it for a moment, staring blankly down the hall as if he was having a hard time deciding what to do. He looked like a child playing a game for the first time, not knowing what the rules called for next.

He went to his office, and minutes later walked to the front desk, pulling on his jacket. "Linda, I have to go away for a couple of days. Would you go through my voice mail and take care of whatever's on there?"

"Sure, Randall. Have a good trip."

He said nothing, and left. She pulled out a message pad and punched in the access code to retrieve his voice mail. There were eight messages, seven from Mrs. Torelli, and one that seemed to be personal. She thought about calling Randall at home to pass that one along, but decided not to. He didn't look as if he needed to be bothered right now. Besides, he'd be back in a couple of days. She would leave the message on the system and he could return the call when he came back.

"Randall," the message began. "This is Peter."

###

Continue reading The Family at your local independent bookstore or ebook retailer.